The Works of Leonard Merrick

THE ACTOR-MANAGER

The Works of

LEONARD MERRICK

CONRAD IN QUEST OF HIS YOUTH. With an Introduction by Sir J. M. Barrie.

WHEN LOVE FLIES OUT O' THE WINDOW. With an Introduction by Sir William Robertson Nicoll.

THE QUAINT COMPANIONS. With an Introduction by H. G. Wells.

THE POSITION OF PEGGY HARPER. With an Introduction by Sir Arthur Pinero.

THE MAN WHO UNDERSTOOD WOMEN and other Stories. With an Introduction by W. J. Locke.

THE WORLDLINGS. With an Introduction by Neil Munro.

THE ACTOR-MANAGER. With an Introduction by W. D. Howells.

CYNTHIA. With an Introduction by Maurice Hewlett.

ONE MAN'S VIEW. With an Introduction by Granville Barker.

THE MAN WHO WAS GOOD. With an Introduction by J. K. Prothero.

A CHAIR ON THE BOULEVARD. With an Introduction by A. Neil Lyons.

THE HOUSE OF LYNCH. With an Introduction by G. K. Chesterton.

WHILE PARIS LAUGHED: Being Pranks and Passions of the Poet Tricotrin.

NEW YORK
E. P. DUTTON & COMPANY

THE
ACTOR-MANAGER

By LEONARD MERRICK

WITH AN INTRODUCTION BY
WILLIAM DEAN HOWELLS

NEW YORK
E. P. DUTTON AND COMPANY
681 FIFTH AVENUE

INTRODUCTION

ANGLO-SAXON fiction, either in its English or
in its American condition, is not so rich in form
that one who feels its penury can pass any exception by, and not dread coming to actual want.
A keen, perhaps a quivering, sense of this, was
what made me, in my first acquaintance with the
novels of Mr. Leonard Merrick, resolve to share
with the public my pleasure in their singular
shapeliness. No doubt, a great many of our
short stories have form; but here it is a question
of novels, and not of short stories. In short
stories, it is rather difficult not to have form; in
novels, it is so difficult that I can think of no
recent fictionist of his race or nation who can
quite match with Mr. Merrick in that excellence.
This will seem great praise, possibly too great,
to the few who have a sense of such excellence;
but it will probably be without real meaning to
most, though our public might very well enjoy
form if it could once be made to imagine it. In
order to this end, we should have first to define
what form was, but form is one of those elusive
things which you can feel much better than you
can say; to define it would be like defining charm

in a woman, or poetry in a verse. Possibly, in
order to enforce my point, I should have to bid
the reader take almost any novel of Mr. Merrick's and read it; for then he would know what
form was. Possibly, this is the conclusion to
which I must come now, but I do not deny that
this would be what is called "begging the question."

As to the world which this excellent form
embodies, it may be said, first, that every writer
of fiction creates the world where his characters
live. Of course, if he is an artist, it is vital to
him to believe he is representing the world where
he lives himself; and in a certain measure he is
doing so, but he is always giving their habitat
stricter limits than his own. One of the con-
ditions of every art is that its created world
must be a microcosm; even if it is not avowedly
a fragment, the portrait it paints of life is a
miniature where everything but the essentials are
left out. If its effects are wisely meditated, it
will sometimes show that the essentials are the
little things and not the large things. The scene
does not matter; the quality or station of the
actors in it does not count; nothing matters or
counts but the effect of reality. It is a very
narrow world Mr. Merrick deals with, and of
events so few that it is wonderful how con-

tinually he provokes the reader's curiosity and holds his interest, though for the young and kind, or for the old and wise, it is a world which will always have a glamour, will be misted in an illusion such as wraps the persons whom its people are engaged in representing, either in the novel or in the drama. In other terms, and I hope simpler terms, his story is commonly the story of obscure talent struggling to the light in those very uncertain avenues to distinction and prosperity; and he contrives to vary it only by the different phases of their failure or success, which is always the same sort of failure and success. I do not know why the events should be of more appreciable human concern than comparable events in the lives of rising or falling painters, sculptors and architects, who should equally appeal in their like quality of artists. But it is certain that we somehow feel an enchantment in the career of the artists who create characters in fiction, or represent them in the theatre, which we do not feel in the careers of those other artists. It may be that this is because we live longer with their creations or representations, and therefore are better acquaintance or closer friends with the creators. You cannot linger two or three days on the details of a picture or a statue or a building, as you can on

those of a novel, or even three hours, as you can
on those of a play; and you cannot know them so
well that you long to know the author or actor,
and attribute to him all sorts of personal interest,
which perhaps experience would not realize in
him. In any case, it is certain that, since fiction
ceased to concern itself solely with kings and
princes, or even with the nobility and gentry, it
has found nothing of such sovereign effect with
the reader as the aspirations and adventures of
people, the younger the people the better, trying
to get past the publisher or the manager into the
light of the public square. These at present
share the sort of "pull" which the pirate and the
robber, the seducer and the seduced, the pick-
pocket and the pauper, the bankrupt, the rightful
heir, the good and the bad trades-unionist, the
muscular Christian, the burglar and the detec-
tive, all once enjoyed in turn, and now enjoy no
longer, at least with the polite reader; and it
ought to be fortunate for Mr. Merrick that his
novels are mainly concerned with them in the
hour of their surpassing attractiveness. I have,
of course, no belief that he chose them because
of their pull; it is much more probable that, in
the strange way these things come about, he was
chosen by them because of his personal intimacy
with their experiences. It is scarcely pertinent

to conjecture that the material of his fiction, out
of which he has shaped its persons and events,
is employed at first hand. A much more important fact is that he is always and instinctively
artist enough to employ it for the stuff it is, and
that he has not attempted, so far as I can make
out, to pass off any clay image of his fabrication
for a statue of pure gold, or even of gilded
bronze. No squalor of that world of his is
blinked, and we learn to trust him, not perhaps
quite implicitly, for a faithful report of the world
he knows so well, but implicitly enough, because
he seems to have no question as to his function
in regard to it. He is quite as honest as a Latin
or a Slav would be in his place, and never as
dishonest as some other Anglo-Saxon might be.

He is not so much in the bonds of superstition
concerning passion as most novelists, and therefore he is not of the inferior novelists; he ranks
himself with the great ones in that. He has the
courage to own that certain veritable passions
die long before those who have known them are
dead. Apparently, he has seen this happen in
the world among real men and women, and he
portrays the fact as he has seen it happen. His
fidelity cannot recommend him to the "world that
loves a lover" so much that it will not allow that
he can ever cease to be a lover; but it ought to

make him friends with the few who love truth better even than lovers. At any rate, it is the event in several of his books, in perhaps the best of them, though sometimes he sacrifices to the false god also, and has lovers go on loving with a constancy which ought to have made him a wider public than I am afraid he has.

Of the two arch-enemies of love, prosperity and adversity, he makes the oftener study of adversity. There is a great deal of grim adversity in his books, which sometimes remains adversity to the end, but also sometimes puts off its frown. It is the more depressing when it becomes or remains the atmosphere of that ambition which seeks fruition in the successes of the theatre. If we are to believe him, and somehow Mr. Merrick mostly makes you believe him, the poor creatures, usually poor women creatures, who are trying to get upon the stage, are almost without number, and certainly outnumber the struggling journalists and authors a hundred to one. The spectacles of their humility and humiliation, of their meek endeavours and cruel defeats, are of such frequent recurrence in his novels and tales that, after a little knowledge of them, one approaches the scene with an expectation of heartache through which nothing short of the mastery dealing with them would support one. In the

monotony of the event, it is very remarkable
how he distinguishes and characterizes the different children of adversity, especially the daugh-
ters. They are commonly alike in their adversity,
but they are individual in their way of experienc-
ing it. In fact, in an age of intensely feminized
fiction, he is one of the first of those who know
how to catch the likenesses, to the last fleeting
expression, of women; and especially women of
the theatre. Probably, these are not essentially
different from other women, but they have an
evolution through their environment which no
one else seems to have studied so well. Sometimes they are good women and sometimes they
are bad, but they are so from a temperament
differently affected by their errant and public
life, their starved or surfeited vanity, their craze
for change and variety, and they keep a sim-
plicity, a singleness, in their selfishness and
depravity, such as differences them from women
bred amidst the artificialities of the world on the
other side of the footlights. It would be easy
to name a score of them from his pages, but it is
sufficient to name Blanche Ellerton in *The
Actor-Manager* as a supreme type; Nature
meant her for the theatre only.

There is no perceptible mechanism in the story
of *The Actor-Manager*, in every way the best of

Mr. Merrick's stories so far as I know them. At all moments of it you feel that it happened, and that the people in it are alive, with a life of human probabilities beyond it. I can recall no English novel in which the study of temperament and character is carried farther or deeper, allowing for what the people are, and I do not remember a false or mistaken line or colour in it. For anything to equal it, we must go to the Slavs, in such triumphs of their naturalness as Tourguénieff's *Smoke,* or the society passages of Tolstoy's *War and Peace.* The French stories are conventional in their naturalism beside it; perhaps a Spaniard like Galdós has done work of equal fineness. It is not alone in Royce Oliphant, with the stress of his hereditary conscience, or in Blanche Ellerton, depraved both by her artistry and by her ambition, that the author convinces; Otho Fairbairn, who becomes the "scoundrel" that Blanche not less deliberately than hysterically makes him for his money, and Alma King, who is as good an artist as Blanche and yet a good woman, and Blanche's mother whose sentimental novelettes support her contemptuous husband in the production of his real but unmerchantable masterpieces, and Blanche's plain sister with her famine for a little love, a little admiration from men, are all in their several ways entirely lifelike. The theatre itself, which began as a theatre of art, and ended as a theatre of profit, has almost a human appeal in its tragedy, as if it were a sentient organism, with a heart to be broken and a soul to be lost. Nobody who is not inevitably bad is very bad; in the book the world is the world we live in.

Why, then, is not this masterly novelist a master universally recognized and accepted? That is something I have asked myself more than once, especially in reading the criticisms of his several books, not one of which has lacked the praise of some critic qualified to carry conviction of its merit. Perhaps the secret is that the stories are almost always very unhappy. There is no consolation in their tragedy; they do not even "raise a noble terror," such as was once the supposed business of tragedy. Upon the whole, they leave you feeling mean, feeling retroactively capable of the shabby things which have been done in them. Another secret may be that, when the poverty which haunts them is relieved in this case or that, you are left with a sense of the vast poverty still remaining in the world; if a struggler is given a chance to get his breath, the great struggle of life goes on. Still another secret may be that there is no fine world, no great world, in the books; we scarcely recall a person of title in any of them, and people who like to associate with the rich or great, when they are "taken out of themselves," have not the company of so much as one high-born villain, one corrupt *grande dame*. Socially it is not "good company" we find ourselves in, and morally it is not even the "best company" as Jane Austen calls it; and yet it is somehow consoling, somehow encouraging to have known such a good and clever man as Royce Oliphant, such a good yet gifted woman as Alma King, even such a kind wrong-doing soul as Otho Fairbairn, or such a gentle, modest, unselfish creature as the mother of Blanche Ellerton, earning her husband's bread by writing the popular novelettes which enable him to write his unpopular novels and despise her trash on a full stomach. Very likely Mr. Merrick may have had his moments of consciously contriving the story in *The Actor-Manager* and of actuating his characters in conformity with a preconceived plan, but he does not suffer his readers to share these humiliating moments. For all they know, the things happened from the nature of the characters in the given circumstances with no apparent agency of his.

W. D. Howells.

THE ACTOR-MANAGER

THE ACTOR-MANAGER

CHAPTER I

THERE used to be, in the neighbourhood of the
Museum, an eating-house, of which the feature
was a three-course dinner for sixpence. On a
board in the doorway was inscribed "First-class
Room Upstairs," and this was well worth visiting. Its true attraction, however, did not lie in
its steaming soup, its colonial meat, nor its im-
pregnable pastry, but in the study of its patrons.
Eschewing the ground-floor, where, to the casual
observer, the dirt of the diners obscured their
interest, one found oneself among pale-faced
girls in sage-green frocks of eccentric pattern,
among young men with bilious bows and abun-
dant hair. These were "art-students"—to use
the comprehensive term by which the students
of painting describe themselves—the fact was
evident at a glance, before scrutiny discovered
the mark of the Roman Gallery in charcoal on
their fingers. A greasy coat, white at the left
elbow, and frayed under the right cuff, confirmed

1

the impression that its wearer was a hack from the Reading Room. Sometimes a reporter and his note-book might be recognised; more frequent was the sight of a violin-case, or a roll of songs. Occasionally a denizen of the foreign quarter behind Tottenham Court Road stumbled upon the establishment—to sigh for the forbidden cigarette, and renew his allegiance to the restaurants of Charlotte Street; now and again a stray shop-girl out of employment, or an excursionist up for the day, gaped at the costumes of the company—approving the cuisine and disdaining the clientèle. A little woman with spectacles and close-cropped hair suggested mathematics; and a Pole, whose unkempt locks swept the grime on his velvet collar, left one in doubt whether to attribute to him operas or infernal machines.

On a certain winter afternoon, the room, usually so full, was deserted save by two persons. One was a man of about thirty; the other was a girl, five or six years younger. Though they had often noticed each other there, they were not acquaintances, and to-day each was at once interested and a shade embarrassed by the other's presence. When the waitress reappeared with pudding, the silence between them had not been broken, but the man, stealing another glance, saw that the girl was crying.

They were seated close together; the room contained three long tables, but two of them were bare, and the cloth extended but half-way down the third. The preparations for custom had been slight to-day at the eating-house, and of all its struggling frequenters, of all its hopeful and its hopeless band, only these two apparently had had nowhere else to go. The attendant, who had returned to her chair behind the counter, contemplated them with an air of compassionate protest. The date was December the twenty-fifth.

He looked quickly away, out at the dreary street. He understood the tears that stood in his companion's eyes—if he had been a woman, his mood would have required the same relief. That, though, was not his thought; the thought of which he was suddenly conscious was that he wished the girl and he knew each other. He was alone, and loneliness had never ached more strongly in him. In fancy he had been reliving his life, lingering at the milestones, and scenting afresh the fragrance of mornings passed away. He remembered Christmas at the Vicarage—had seen himself a child again in his father's church. The old man's face and white hair above the pulpit, and the laurel and crimson berries round the font, flashed close—seemed close enough for him to clasp them. He remembered his scholarship, his joy, the moment when his father's lips had trembled at the news; reviewed his boyhood at Harrow, and his confidence at Oxford. It was to be the Church then for him, too. He recalled the first touch of indecision; the time when the cry of art within him became insistent; the night when he announced the change in his intentions. Under the snow in the cemetery his father lay now, beyond the reach of disappointments. Thank God the bond between them had never weakened! The long battle which was still unwon had been mentally refought since his meagre breakfast; and the sense of solitariness, the longing for sympathy was acute as he stared through the window at the empty street.

He spoke a second later:

"We're spared the outrage of a Christmas pudding made fashionable in a mould here. If a Christmas plum-pudding's not as round as a cannon-ball, it isn't a Christmas plum-pudding."

"No," she said. She sought for a continuation. "And it ought to be very big," she added.

"With a sprig of holly and blue flames."

Momentarily he saw the Vicarage again. If Christmas were good for nothing else, it would serve to remind us we were once innocent and happy, and didn't know it; for everyone associ-

ates Christmas more vividly with his own childhood than with Christ's. The girl did not reply
further; she looked down at her plate. The man
looked wistfully at the girl; and the attendant,
with a smothered yawn, looked at the clock.

"I think I've seen you here before," said
Oliphant. "I wonder they're open to-day. I
was half afraid I shouldn't get any dinner."

"It was the same with me—I'm only in lodgings, and——" She shivered, and pinned her
jacket more closely across her chest.

"Are you cold?"

"The fire isn't very Christmassy, is it? Do
you know what I'm going to do when I get up?
I'm going to walk round the Squares and look
into all the dining-rooms where hateful rich
people are having port and walnuts, and toasting
themselves before the most expensive coal. I
shall loathe them violently."

"And then?" said Oliphant, smiling.

"I shall go home."

"And then?"

"I shall howl."

Though he had not failed to notice her previ-
ously, he was surprised that he had not noticed
her more. He regarded her with rising interest,
even with gratitude. Her face, though lacking
in colour, had a beauty which was accentuated

by the style in which the dark hair was worn—parted in the centre, and waving loosely over her brow and ears. Her eyes at first sight had looked black, but he saw now that they were grey.

"My programme 'll be as lively as yours," he said.

"You've nowhere to go either?"

"Oh, I've a large selection of thoroughfares; and *I* can go home too. There's no place like home, and it's often very fortunate."

"What do you do?" she asked.

"I'm an actor."

"Are you? I shouldn't have guessed it. I'm an actress."

"I wondered if you were; I was sure you acted or sang. Are you playing anywhere?"

"I was in the Independent Theatre last month—did you go? I haven't done anything since then; it's such a bad time of the year. I was very fortunate to be in the Independent; I was playing at Ealing, and the Margetsons saw me and offered me the engagement. I understudied Mrs. Margetson. If I could have played Hilda!"

"Oh, Ibsen attracts you?"

"Well, I should like to play Hilda Wangel in *The Master Builder.* I should like to play Hilda; and I long to play Juliet, and—oh, I who am nobody, how I should love to create Lucy Feverel on the stage!"

"You read Meredith?"

"Because I'm an obscure actress can't I read? Oh, I know, I'm not surprised you stared! But *I* might have stared at *you* for knowing it was Meredith. Lucy! She's the nineteenth-century Juliet, isn't she? Are you one of the enemies of the Independent, or one of the people who care nothing about it?"

"Neither," he said. "The greatest work will never appeal to the greatest number. How should it?"

"That's discouraging!" She rested her elbows on the cloth—her fingers interlaced, and supporting her chin—her eyes lifted to him attentively.

"I mean the greatest creative work. Does an actor or an actress create? You used the word, but I'm afraid we don't. The best of us interpret —like Paderewski, Sarasate; Wagner creates. Shakespeare created Hamlet; the actor who plays the part tries to interpret his intention. Need he be any the less an artist because the nature of his art demands collaboration?"

"His collaborators aren't all Shakespeares," she said; "nor Ibsens."

"Oh, there may be more brains in the actor

than in the part! What banalities are considered seriously because he gives them life!"

"But good work is knocking at the stage doors!" she cried; "why isn't it admitted? Why does the actor put the banalities on? When he is his own manager, why not produce things that are worthy of him?"

"Because the best only appeals to the minority, as I say. If you want a proof of it, remember that England claims the greatest dramatic poet the world has known, and then look down the list of the travelling companies—see how many are playing his work! You know!—it's appalling. Managers wouldn't pay fees for trash, instead of taking poetry for nothing, if the poetry drew as well; you can be quite sure of that; for their ambition is to make money."

"Is it yours?" she asked impatiently. "If *you* were an actor-manager, what would *you* produce?"

The attendant folded her novelette, rose, and came round to the table.

"It's shuttin' up time, please," she said; "we're only open to four o'clock to-day." She tore out two vouchers, and picked up the coins.

"I wish I had spoken to you over the soup," said Oliphant, watching the girl put on her gloves.

She smiled. "I was praying you wouldn't speak at all—I felt so miserable. But I am glad you did. Good-bye."

"Good-bye," he said; and she preceded him down the stairs. "I won't wish you 'a merry Christmas,'" he added, as they reached the foot, "but I hope it won't be too wretched. Are you going to take that walk and 'loathe them violently'?"

"I think so—it'll be something to do."

She seemed undecided whether to extend her hand; then made as if to offer it.

"You wouldn't let me come with you?" he said hesitatingly; "I——"

"I think not," she said; "thanks."

They stood on the desolate pavement, looking away from each other. The daylight was slowly fading, and on the pallor a yellow gas-lamp leapt into the perspective.

"You don't mind my having asked you? I—I meant no harm."

"No, I understand," she said; "but——"

"It would lessen the awfulness for half an hour," pleaded Oliphant. "I've no one to talk to, I've nothing to read, and it'd be a charity. Can't you imagine we've been introduced? Do let me! . . . Will you?"

She wavered for an instant. "For half an hour then," she responded. "Come!"

"Thank you very much. Which way do we go?"

"Oh, the loneliness of London!" exclaimed the girl as they crossed the road; "the loneliness of it!" She glanced at him and sighed. "This is very improbable," she remarked.

"Probabilities aren't pleasing," said Oliphant. "The greatest probability is that 'the part is already cast'!"

"It's a hard profession if one has no influence. Have you been in town?"

"I've just got my first engagement here. We open in about a fortnight. The Queen's. I speak twelve lines. On tour I've been playing good parts.

"How dreadful! What you must feel!"

"I do. But I couldn't endure the provinces for ever. I want to get on; I ought to get on— I've worked so hard, and hoped so long; it's time I did something. If I'm playing in London, a chance may be easier to find—in the companies on tour one is buried. Don't you think so?"

"I've played several small parts in London," she said, "but they have led to no better chance for *me*. Oh, I'm discouraged! I haven't struggled so long as you, I daresay; but a girl's weaker, and I'm discouraged."

"Are you quite alone?"

She nodded. "I lost my mother last year; she was all I had. When she died, it——" Her voice quivered, and they strolled on in silence. "I think it made it crueller," she continued softly, "to know that she thought I'd get on better without her, because—because it was my joy to help her as much as I could while she lived."

"I envy you!" said Oliphant; "all *I* did was to cause my father pain."

"Didn't he want you to be an actor; is that what you mean? Did you quarrel?"

"He didn't quarrel with me, but he was disappointed. And he was the best father a man ever had."

"I like you for saying that," she answered. "What did he want you to be?"

"What he was himself—a clergyman."

"Really?" she said with surprise; "and you felt you couldn't?"

"I wanted to, once. It was as I grew older that my views changed. I don't mean religious views or anything like that—I simply felt that my temperament forbade it and that the stage was the only career possible for me. You asked me in there what I'd do if I were an actor-manager. I went into the profession because I loved it; because it seemed to me the stage might teach as high a lesson as the pulpit—that it might be the loudest, greatest voice in all the world. More powerful than the Church, because the Church is precept and the stage is action; more intimate than the sister-arts, because it speaks in a simpler tongue. And it should *be* art; but art —art is revelation! Shall I tell you what my dream is?"

"Yes," said the girl earnestly, "do; tell me your dream!"

Instinctively they had paused. They were by the pillar-box at the gates of the British Museum. In the immense quietude theirs were the only human figures; the London that gorged, and the London that starved, were both out of view.

"I see," he said, "a small theatre, and at this theatre the one literary medium for the drama isn't held to be the baldest prose; poetry is neither divorced from this stage, nor limited to Shakespeare—it's thought possible to test the work of a poet who has *not* had centuries of advertising! But the realist is as welcome as the poet; I should think he *was* welcome! Only the plays are literature, and they are real plays. The men and women live! They aren't puppets pulled by inexorable strings through four acts to a

conventional end. Reward for virtue and pun-
ishment for vice are shown to exist in the soul
and not in material success and failure. To
depict the world as a school, where virtue wins
the prize, and vice gets a flogging, is immoral.
The parts around me aren't written down to
bring *my* part into greater prominence. The
dramatist who comes to me is free—free to be
true to his convictions and his art; free to choose
his characters where he will, and to trace their
legitimate development; free to make the 'lost'
woman noble, and the 'godly' woman vile—for
such things *are!*—and the love within him for
all humanity would point the moral when it
needed pointing. The real playwright is your
real optimist—your real Christ-follower—for he
shows that sin doesn't mean damnation, and that
there is redemption for the pure in heart. The
one command laid upon him is to see things
nobly—that his deeper vision shall help the
crowd. Where shall I find such writers? There
are dramatists not known, and well-known
writers who could write much better. By degrees
I gather round me a band of—of the *âmes bien
nées,* the—how shall I say it?—the———"

"The elect!" she put in rapidly; "yes, I understand French. It would be a good name for the
house—The Elect!"

"I produce men who don't work for the stage now, or whose manuscripts are considered hopeless because they don't appeal to the largest public. With a small theatre I could afford to depend upon the educated minority. There is a Press waiting for such an endeavour, and, though at first the notices are bigger than the returns, they gradually win for me the recognition of all the public that I'm addressing. Believe me that public is large enough to keep my house open all the year round. Miss——er—my companion in misfortune, my theatre becomes a force in intellectual London; I'm famous, happy, I have fulfilled my ambition, I'm the manager of the—the Theatre Royal Day-dream. . . . I've been keeping you standing still in the cold; forgive me!"

She caught her breath. "You're an artist," she said, "I believe you'll succeed. This is one of the moments when I think that to be an artist and fail, is something."

"We are both artists," he said; "The Two Bohemians!"

"I haven't told you my name. It's Alma King."

"I'm so glad we met, Miss King. Mine's Royce Oliphant. You see the benefit of giving a thing a trial—we couldn't know each other better if the formal introduction had taken place. Now could we?"

"Look!" she murmured, halting again in two or three minutes.

He glanced at the window that she indicated. "Ah, the opportunity for the violent loathing!"

"No, only for the imagination after all. How torpid they look after their dinner! But it's cosy in the firelight, isn't it? I wonder what they do—one can't see their features? Trade, of course. Trade in saddlebag armchairs digests the turkey, and art in the streets builds castles in the air. Observe the adipose children!"

"Their figures aren't distinguishable."

"I feel they're adipose—I told you this was an exercise of the imagination. Oh, the servant has come to pull the blinds down! The entertainment is over. I don't think we'll look in anywhere else—other people's comfort is very saddening."

They waited there, by the area railings, in Bedford Square, nevertheless, till the last of the blinds was lowered. Illuminated, the interior had a fascination—the group on the hearth, and the gleam of decanters under the crimson shade above the damask; the glinting picture-frames, and the splendour of a Christmas-tree. Meanwhile on "The Two Bohemians" a little snow began to fall.

"You must go home," said Oliphant regretfully. "Do you live far away?"

"No, close," she said; "in Alfred Place. And you?"

"In Burton Crescent."

"Oh, how wet you'll get! You'd better leave me here; it's coming down more heavily."

"Nonsense! I'll see you to your door. We go through Store Street, don't we?"

They hastened their steps, but both were sorry that the end had come; to each of them the prospect of the evening looked unutterably dismal.

"I suppose I may see you at dinner again?" asked Oliphant, as they turned by the little post-office at the corner. "Have you any regular time?"

"About two, as a rule."

"Shall you be there to-morrow?"

"I don't know," she said, stopping; "perhaps. This is the house."

"Good-bye, then," said Oliphant, "and thank you again. I won't keep you standing in a snow-storm to listen to pretty speeches, but I'm grateful to you. I should like to think we're going to be friends."

She drew out a latch-key, and faced him for a

moment with steadfast eyes. Then quite simply she said:

"I want you to come in, Mr. Oliphant, please; and we'll have some tea."

She opened the door; and, delighted, he followed her along the dark passage, into a room to which she led the way. The fire was low, and it was not until she had lighted the lamp that Oliphant perceived that she was compelled to make shift with one room only. The asperities of bed and washhand-stand, however, were mollified by a shabby screen. He chose a seat where they would be behind him, and noted the resemblance between the broken vases on her mantelpiece and those on his own. A framed photograph was among the vases, and the girl took it up and showed it to him.

"This was a likeness of my mother, Mr. Oliphant," she said.

The dignity of the action thrilled him with pleasure and respect; he felt that she could not have done anything more beautiful.

She removed her jacket and gloves, and, kneeling on the hearth, coaxed the fire into a blaze.

"Are you very wet?" she said. "As soon as the kettle boils, things 'll be more cheerful. I wait on myself very much here—I find it better."

"Have you been here long?"

"No; only since the Independent perform-
ances—nearly two months. It isn't very comfortable, but . . . I shall move when I get another engagement. In the meanwhile I have to
put up with it." She pulled the pin from her
hat, and passed her slim hands over her hair.

"You are looking at my 'library'! It's modest,
isn't it?"

"I can only see the titles of two-thirds of the
library," he said; "*The Works of Shakespeare,*
and Archer's *Masks or Faces*—you know your
Masks or Faces, do you! What is the little
one?"

"The little one is ninepennyworth of Brown-
ing. I'm studying *Any Wife to Any Husband*—
because I shall never in my life be given an
opportunity to recite it."

"Recite it now," said Oliphant.

"No, thank you. But what a recitation it
would make! I don't know why no woman ever
does it. Ah, it's lovely—isn't it divine! Do you
read much? But of course you do. I wonder
if you've ever tried to write?"

"What makes you ask that?"

"Have you?"

"Once."

"A play?" she exclaimed.

"Oh, yes; a play, of course."

"It hasn't been produced, I suppose?—Oh, how rude that sounds!"

"The assumption's correct. It has been accepted three times, but has *not* been produced. It's in an agent's hands now; and I suppose it will stay there—unless he loses it. It's a drama."

"Good?" she inquired, settling the kettle afresh.

"*I* thought it was very good. So did everybody else who read it—only nobody puts it on. Your kettle won't sing! Isn't that what you call it—'singing'? Shall I draw up the fire for you with that newspaper?"

"The water was cold," she said; "it'll be all right in a minute. I'll ring for a second cup and saucer. Tell me about your drama."

"The idea—the foundation-stone at least—is a shade melodramatic, perhaps; but the theme doesn't make a play melodrama if there's no bombast in the treatment?"

"I don't know," she said; "but even if it does, mightn't a melodrama without bombast be as much art as anything else? 'The great future for the stage lies in perfect freedom: freedom to try every kind of experiment—to be realistic or idealistic, prosaic or fantastic, "well made" or plotless; freedom to go anywhere, like the British Army, and do anything.' Have I a quick study?—I've only read the book once. What *is* the foundation-stone?"

"It was suggested by the Tichborne Case. Life, of course! But so many phases of life become melodrama when they're transferred to the stage."

The bell drew from the basement a seven-year-old child with wooden eyes, and fat unhealthy cheeks. Jam and mince-pie clung to his chin, and he snored.

"Will you ask your mother to let me have another cup and saucer, Norman?" said the lodger deprecatingly. "Say I've a friend here. . . . We shall have it directly," she continued, as the child shuffled out, "and then you must tell me the plot."

They sat opposite each other on the narrow hearth. Momentarily the dramatist was as strong as the actor in Oliphant, and the play for which he had hoped so much three years ago moved him to confidence again. The girl, her hands clasped loosely round her knee, leant forward, stirred by visions in which a mighty theatre hung upon her voice and the conquest of London was achieved. Both turned at a peremptory knock, and started as the door was thrown open.

The demeanour of the woman who stood on the threshold was as excited as her method of

announcing herself. Her face was white, and
when she began to speak she trembled.

"This is pretty goings-on," she said; "this
won't do 'ere! I don't 'ave it, and that's all about
it." She turned to Oliphant. "I'll trouble you
to leave the 'ouse. Now then!"

"Mrs. Imms!" stammered the girl, as white
as she.

"My good woman," exclaimed Oliphant horribly distressed, "what do you mean? I assure
you—— There isn't the slightest reason for
you to be annoyed. I've the honour to be a friend
of Miss King's and she was kind enough to ask
me in for half an hour. I shouldn't have thought
there was anything extraordinary about it on
Christmas Day?"

The householder did not seem to understand,
or to hear him.

"You'd best be off," she repeated, "and so I
tell yer! This is a respectable 'ouse—not meant
for the likes of 'er! Yes, *you* I'm talkin' about—
yer thing; you as don't pay your rent! I might
'ave told what it'd be when I found you was an
actress—I'd never 'ave taken you if I'd known!"

"You—ignorant—wretch!" gasped the girl,
steadying herself by the mantelpiece. "Go," she
added to Oliphant; "please, go!"

"The woman's been drinking," he said in a

low voice; "do you want me to leave you to her?"

"Yes, please!—Please!" she murmured agitatedly.

"Aha!" cried Mrs. Imms; "and you go with 'im, that's more! I won't keep you no longer. Out you go! I'll 'ave your box for what it's worth, and you don't sleep in my 'ouse, not another night!"

Oliphant looked sharply round; but the mute appeal forbade his lingering. The uproar continued as he traversed the passage—still in darkness—and fumbled with the handles at the end.

The street opened upon him quiet and bleak. The snow had ceased, but the wind blew bitterly. He hated himself for having gone in, though he could not perceive where he had been at fault. The woman's threat to turn the girl out of doors was in his ears, and weighed on his consciousness. Impossible that he could leave unless satisfied that it wasn't to be fulfilled! He made a cigarette, lit it, and sauntered to and fro, debating how long a vigil was demanded to dispel all doubt.

His capital was reduced to eighteen shillings and a few pence; his prospects were represented by the engagement at the Queen's Theatre, of which he had spoken; an engagement which would provide him with the sum of two pounds

a week—less than half the salary that he had been
receiving in the provinces. If it had been otherwise—— He sighed. He reflected that it would
have been a luxury to pay the amount of Mrs.
Imms's claim and send Miss King to an hotel
where she could dine in reality before she slept,
and have a respite from her cares. Yes, that
would have been delightful. Did rich men have
these pleasures? Or did the opportunities fall
only to men like himself, who couldn't seize them?

His cigarette was finished; he paused by a
lamp-post, and tried, with numbed fingers, to
roll another. Now she would regret that she had
met him—the oais in the desert of their London
had proved a misfortune to her! Who could have
foreseen that it would have so serious a development? All the same, she would always recall
it with abhorrence—that was only human nature.
. . . But perhaps in the morning the landlady
would apologise. He threw a glance at the house
again, and ran forward as a figure appeared on
the doorstep.

"You?" faltered the girl, shrinking.

"I couldn't go till I knew," he said. "Are you
going away?"

"Yes, don't—don't trouble, thanks. It was
good of you to wait, but there's nothing you can
do." Her tone was hard; but it could not con-

ceal that there were tears in her throat.   She looked away from him.

"Haven't you your luggage?"

"She wouldn't let me take it.   You see, I——
You understand, I owe her money—she has kept my things.   I have these."

"She hasn't the right," cried Oliphant, wincing at the handbag; "I'll make her give them up!"

"No, no! don't go back—I'd rather you didn't; I shall manage somehow. . . . Don't let me keep you any longer," she repeated; "there's nothing you can do."

"I've done enough!" said the man poignantly. "I know!"

"You mustn't think that.   You've nothing to reproach yourself for—if any one is to blame, it's I."   The restraint that she was putting on herself gave way: "You're the only living soul I've had to speak to for two months!" she exclaimed, with a hoarse sob.   "Don't think badly of me if I made a mistake."

He wished he were a woman that, for answer, he might take her in his arms; he could but express his sympathy and comprehension by halting words.   His poverty had never seemed so great a shackle as while they stood there, helpless on the pavement—the only sound, a bell that rang for evening service at some neighbouring church.

CHAPTER II

"WHAT do you mean to do?" inquired Oliphant after a brief pause. "You can't go to one of these houses on Christmas night, without any luggage, and expect to get a room."

"No, I've thought of that—I don't know yet where I shall go. There's a place where I stayed when my mother was living—the woman would remember me. If it didn't mean a bus fare every day, I'd try there."

"Where is it?"

"It's at Shepherd's Bush. Are the trains running this evening, do you know?"

"I daresay—you'll let me take you, if you go? I can't lose sight of you till I know you're settled. But how can you look for an engagement, if you're hard up, from Shepherd's Bush—you can't *walk* to the Strand? Besides, the house may be full; or perhaps the woman is dead. If she's alive, I suppose she'll want to be paid, like everybody else, won't she?" he added.

"I must get enough for the first week somehow," she declared, sauntering on; "and then she must trust me, or I must give the room up."

"Look here," said Oliphant desperately, "we haven't known each other two hours, of course; and I can see you're as proud as Lucifer. But I'm going to be as frank as if you were my sister: I've eighteen shillings—and fourpence-half-penny, I think it is—in the world. I wouldn't tell many people that, so I've a right to ask for *your* friendship in return. Let me lend you half a sovereign till you get an engagement."

"Oh no," she said under her breath. "No, thank you!"

"You won't? How can you be so unkind—so —so absurd? What's to prevent it? Isn't it any good? Or don't you respect me sufficiently?"

"Oh," she said, "that——"

"Don't you *like* me enough? You know we've been more confidential than many acquaintances of years' standing: you're refusing because it's strange that we *should* have grown so confidential in two hours. That's unworthy of a woman with a mind like yours! . . . I wish you would do what I ask, and let me get your luggage for you to-morrow. Do you propose to let that beast keep it till you can pay her?"

"I must think what to do about my trunk," she said.

"And the—it's a big word for a silly sum—the 'loan'?"

"Thank you, 'no'! Really and truly 'no'! I appreciate what you've said very much; but be tactful—and don't say any more."

"Very well," he returned. "Now where are you going?"

"I'm afraid Shepherd's Bush is too far," she sighed; "and, as you say, the woman mayn't be there now."

"Where did you stay before you went to Alfred Place?"

"I was on tour. . . . Last year I had apartments in Keppel Street; but those 'd be too dear." Her pace slackened to a standstill, and she turned impatiently: "Please don't trouble any more! There's not the least necessity for *you* to go through all this as well."

"For the first time I'm compelled to differ from you," said the young man; "I think there's every necessity."

"Well, I'd rather you went," she insisted; "you'll oblige me by saying good-night."

"I'm very sorry, indeed; but as things stand, I don't see my way to leaving you."

His decisive tone stung her helplessness to anger.

"Do you mean to say you won't go when I

wish it?" she exclaimed haughtily. "I *forbid* you to come with me, I prefer to be by myself." She stood looking in his face, her air as imperious as her words. Oliphant had not realised till now that she was so tall. "I forbid you!" she repeated. "I want to be alone."

"There's one way you can get rid of me," he said. "Here's a policeman coming; you can charge me with annoying you. I'll be hanged if I'll leave you to wander about London alone, unless you do!"

The policeman approached ponderously, his gaze attentive. The girl resumed her course, and Oliphant turned beside her. When she spoke again, her voice had no resentment, and it quivered:

"I want to beg your pardon. I was ungrateful. I'm ashamed of myself."

"Oh, please, Miss King!" he stammered. "I understand so well."

"It was only because I'm so miserable."

"I know. . . . Will you let me suggest a way out of the difficulty?"

"Oh, please do!" she cried.

"Take a room in the house where I'm staying —for a day or two at all events. The landlady's a good sort, and it's very cheap, or *I* shouldn't be there! It will avoid all bother about your having no luggage, and about a deposit, and the rest of it; and you can be 'at home' in a quarter of an hour." She was silent for a long while. "I told you just now I was going to be as frank as if you were my sister," he continued. "If you were, and another man gave you such honest advice, I should want to find him afterwards and thank him!"

"Which is our way to Burton Crescent?" she said cheerfully; "I forget." Oliphant glanced at her with admiration.

By the clock at St. Pancras it was five minutes to six as they drew near the house; they were now walking briskly. Oliphant unlocked the door, and letting Alma in, went to the top of the kitchen-stairs.

"Mrs. Tubbs!" he called. "Mrs. Tubbs, can I speak to you for a moment?"

A buxom little woman with rosy cheeks and untidy grey hair bustled up to him.

"You've got back then?" she exclaimed. "I thought p'raps you was spending the evening with your friends after all."

"No," he said; "I've brought one to you, instead. There's a lady in the hall—Miss King—who wants a room."

"*That* there isn't!" said Mrs. Tubbs; "you're joking."

"I'm not; she meant to sleep in Alfred Place; in fact, her luggage *is* there, but—— Well, I know the house isn't very nice, Mrs. Tubbs, between ourselves, and I persuaded her to come here. Mind! it's got to be cheap and 'inclusive' —no more than you charge me."

"I'm sure, Miss, I 'ope we shall make you comfortable," murmured the landlady, panting along the passage. "We're in a bit of a muddle, you know, along of Christmas Day and the girl out, but I can soon get the room to rights for you. Would you like to see it, Miss?"

"Please," said Alma.

"Bless me, I'm forgetting the candle! I couldn't very well show it you in the dark, could I? Here, Amelia, Johnny, one of you! bring me a candle, quick! In the prerfession, Miss, the same as Mr. Elephant, may I ask? Have you come up to London for long?"

"Yes, I'm an actress," said the girl; "I don't quite know how long I shall be staying. I'm sorry to put you to any trouble to-day."

"Oh, don't talk about 'trouble,' Miss; where there ain't no trouble there ain't no let! I'm sure it was fortunate as Mr. Elephant thought to bring you. It'll be awkward your not 'aving your things with you, *won't* it? But there! I dessay you'll make shift for the night."

Oliphant remained in the passage till the arrangement was concluded and Alma and the householder reappeared.

"You've settled?" he inquired. "Is it all right?"

"It's quite all right," answered Miss King brightly: "I'm glad I came!"

"And if there's anything you'd fancy, Miss," said Mrs. Tubbs, beaming, "I'll soon 'ave it up. A cup o' tea and a bit o' goose now?"

"I think we should like tea at last," said Oliphant, "if you can manage it."

"If I can manage it!" she echoed. "Go on with you! There never was such a gentleman, Miss, for fearin' to put anybody out. Your fire's in, Mr. Elephant, though I was just beginning to think I wouldn't make it up again, as more than likely your friends was keeping you."

"I wish they would, Mrs. Tubbs," he said. "Well, I expect Miss King will be glad to sit down!"

"What 'friends'?" asked Alma, as they mounted to the first floor. "I thought you said you'd nowhere to go?"

"I hadn't; but I didn't like to own it to her. She thought I'd gone to dine with some relations. What have you seen?"

"I've seen my room. It will do very well."

"Well, I'll show you some more," he said. "Enter!"

He displayed a drawing-room. It was not luxurious, but it boasted a high mirror over the mantel-shelf, and a sideboard supporting another. The furniture was upholstered in bright blue rep, and the fire leapt cheerfully.

"Is this yours?" she exclaimed, astonished.

"Oh no! 'Mine' is a bedroom the size of a cupboard. But I pay eight shillings a week, and it affords me the 'use' of this, and tea and toast twice a day. The goose this evening will be an 'extra.' "

"Do you mean——"

"I mean that you, like me, are entitled to come in here as often as you please—our terms include the 'use of sitting-room.' At present we are the only lodgers—and Mrs. Tubbs and the children have a parlour in the basement. You may sit here from pearly morn to dewy eve. Or you may shun it absolutely if you choose. If you have a preference for solitude, you can appropriate the dining-room. Only you won't find a fire in there: I buy these coals myself—a hundred-weight at a time, for a shilling. If you eventually decide upon the drawing-room, I think it would be honourable if you owed me sixpence."

She laughed. "It's extraordinary!"

"It is. But it happens to be a fact; I have practically the whole house. However, I'm willing to resign half of it to you if you want me to. Into the dining-room I will never stray."

"This evening," said Miss King, "I will share the responsibility of the 'hundred-weight.' I'll go and take off my hat."

Oliphant stretched himself in an armchair, and mechanically rolled a cigarette, and threw it away.

"Let me," he said, when she returned, "show you the extent of your possessions! These windows open on to a balcony, where Mrs. Tubbs assures me it is pleasant to sit in summer. Not having been here in summer, I cannot vouch for it personally. Beyond, lie beautiful pleasure-grounds enclosed by railings—the use of the necessary key is also yours. To our left we have Marchmont Street—on Saturday night a busy thoroughfare; stalls illumined by naptha may be found here; and the costermongers cry: 'Fine 'erring! Where yer like, laidies—three a penny!' To our right are various railway-stations, much resorted to by such of the population as are desirous of going somewhere else. Behind us, if I'm not mistaken, is Mrs. Tubbs with cold goose!"

They turned to the table, and Mrs. Tubbs said:
"Well, it *'ave* cheered Mr. Elephant up to
meet an old friend, Miss, I *must* say. I haven't
'eard 'im talk so much since 'e's been here. Might
I ask if you'll be taking a part at any of the
theatres, Miss? I ain't in the prerfession myself,
but I'm that interested in it, having 'ad a niece
as took to the stage—which her name was Billing,
and she called herself 'Clarence,' and pretty she
was!—going against her father's wishes, having
quarrelled with him, and not my pore 'usband's
or mine—though us it was that she always blamed
for spoilin' her prospecks—well, I sometimes
seem to be as good as an actress in a manner of
speaking, though I'm not."

"I'm not in an engagement now," said Alma;
"I hope I shall be before long."

"No, Miss. I 'ope you'll find the tea strong
enough. She was before your time, Miss, and—
ah, well, she's gone now, pore dear, like Tubbs
himself—though there was a coldness between
'em to the day of her death. And pretty she was.
And might have been at the Al'ambra still but
for her father's artfulness!"

"Her father didn't approve," said Oliphant;
"and Mr. Tubbs urged her to try dressmaking
instead."

"Mr. Tubbs was the tool of Mr. Billing,"

explained the widow strenuously. "Mr. Tubbs
he approved. Me and him was both very proud
to see the girl famous-an'-that. It was 'er father
as made the to-do and put 'im up to interfere—
though as fond of 'er as if she'd been 'is own—
and speaking that 'arsh she never forgot it. Mr.
Tubbs was the tool of Mr. Billing."

"I've no doubt she realised it, Mrs. Tubbs,"
said Alma; "she probably felt it in her own
mind."

"I 'ope she did, pore dear, that I do! But
lor, it'd never do to think too much about these
things, would it? Is there anything else you
fancy, Miss, or Mr. Elephant, sir? If you want
any more hot water you'll just touch the bell."

"That's quite all, Mrs. Tubbs, thank you," he
said; "we shan't want anything else. Come!"
he went on, as she withdrew; "was my recommendation so bad? There's character for you!
It's 'Mrs. Willoughby' over again; still she's a
study. . . . What are you considering?"

"That I thought it startling to be crossing the
road with you this afternoon. And behold me
now!"

"A piece more toast?" he said, passing the
plate. "You evidently don't read much fiction,
or you'd know that the distracted heroine finding
peace in the stranger's rooms is the most ordinary

thing in the world.   It's true this ought to be a handsome flat, or, at least, chambers in the Temple, but the situation is stale—absolutely."

"Talking of situations," she replied, "you must tell me the story of your play.   And the curtain's going up, and you haven't given me the title!"

"The title is *The Impostor*," said Oliphant slowly.   "The curtain rises on the hall of a country house—the house of the Countess of Plynlimmon.   At the back there's a staircase leading to an oak gallery.   She and two other women are on the stage—all seated.   Logs are burning in the grate—twilight's gathering—the women have been half-asleep; it's just before tea.   I try to convey the drowsiness and warmth of the moment—it opens very naturally.   Lady Plynlimmon's nephew lounges in; Lady Maud Elstree, her daughter, enters.   The dialogue turns on a guest there, Sir Clement Thurloe. Fourteen years before, he cut the Guards and disappeared; everyone believed him dead.   Now he has returned—causing an immense sensation —and established his identity.   Excuses are made for his youthful wildness, and Society receives him with open arms.   He is reported to have been everything in the interval, from a sheep-farmer to a sailor before the mast.   When the men return —they've been hunting, they're in 'pink'—he is,

of course, the central figure. He speaks to Maud
diffidently; with everyone else he is at his ease,
though he refers to his unfamiliarity with a
drawing-room. It's shown that he is in love with
her, and that her mother hopes to see her marry
him."

"Is 'Maud' a good part?" inquired the actress.

"Yes, as good as his, I think. You would
look it magnificently. It isn't until the act is
nearly over that it's sprung upon the audience
that he is an impostor; I think it should be a
big effect. A 'Mrs. Vaughan' has arrived to see
him—of course he's on the stage alone. He says
that her intrusion here is an outrage—he has
given her a house, an income, a carriage! what
more does she want? She says she wants their
compact fulfilled: introductions, society, the
chance to make a brilliant match. 'What's the
use of a house where nobody comes? I bore
myself to death in it!' She is an adventuress
who has been—who has been a friend of the real
man's in New Zealand, and expected to be made
his wife. When he died in delirium tremens, she
suggested to the protagonist that he should take
advantage of his likeness to Sir Clement Thurloe,
and her possession of a diary and letters, to
personate him.   Then there's an outburst of
'Clement's' in which he cries that he wishes to

God he'd never listened to her: 'I was ready
enough to take the hand, I own it! But somehow—I don't know how it is—now I come to
play it out, it's different. When a fellow calls
himself my pal—when a good woman's standing
by my side—I'd give all I've stolen to be a
beggar and a gentleman again!'"

"Well?" said the audience.

"Well, the interview is interrupted by Lady
Plynlimmon's voice: 'Oh, my fan, please; I've
forgotten it!' Rhoda Vaughan insists on her
rights. 'Clement' beseeches her. She won't
budge. Lady Plynlimmon comes down the staircase, and the act ends with the man, as white as
death, introducing the adventuress into the home
of the aristocrat he loves."

"The 'villain' is the hero?" said Miss King.

"He isn't depicted as a hero. The world's
been against him, and he sinned when he was
worn out with struggling. He felt that he owed
Society nothing—that's the idea. Then he meets
Maud!"

"You give away the element of surprise in
your title; still it's good. I don't see any actor-
manager playing 'Clement,' though. What is
the reason that the modern hero is supposed to
lose the sympathy of the audience if he isn't im-
mutably noble, while the modern heroine may

violate the Decalogue? I'm sorry 'Clement' is a
thief. Of course, he's only robbing the 'Crown'?
The Crown can afford the loss, I suppose—it
won't keep the Crown awake at night. Still, a
thief is low."

"But a rogue is human. I don't defend him;
I'm not his advocate. I show his sin and his
suffering. He is essentially weak—the girl he
loves is to be won for the asking——"

"You don't mean to say he actually marries
Maud?"

"Ah, but the temptation!" exclaimed Oliphant.
"You shall hear."

He told her the rest when they drew to the
hearth; drifted from debate to reminiscence—
recounting, with the eager egotism that is bred
of loneliness, something of his boyhood, and receiving impressions of her own life—suggestive,
feminine—in return. He felt that she was turning the pages of his history across his shoulder;
and, though he had jestingly declared her position here to be ordinary, it constantly surprised
him when he reflected that only a few hours
before they were both companionless, and had
never spoken to each other. The room, which
had always appeared to him depressing, had this
evening an air of gaiety and of home. Even
when they were silent, he found it fortifying to

look at her; and even when he did not look at her, it was delightful to know that she was there. At ten o'clock she rose and said good-night; but the magic lingered with him after she had gone. The atmosphere was for once exhilarating, and the throb of the unexpected was in it still.

CHAPTER III

A REHEARSAL of the drama in which Oliphant was to commence his siege of London had been called for eleven o'clock the following day. He saw Miss King for a few minutes only before he left the house, but received her permission to try to recover her belongings for her. This was a task which the threat of legal proceedings, and a written acknowledgment of the debt, assisted him to accomplish without much difficulty. He conveyed the trunk to Burton Crescent by means of a hansom, and then walked through the muddy streets to the Queen's Theatre.

The Queen's had recently been obtained by an actor who was assuming the management of a theatre for the first time. He had been a leading man for about fifteen years now, but the manager of only a few tours. For this production, in which the hero's part was exceedingly strong, he had selected the company with the utmost care and, excepting perhaps the Villain,

41

there wasn't a member of it in whom he had a rival to fear.

The stage was dark and draughty. When Oliphant reached it nobody had come but the prompter, who stood by a small table, overlooking the empty orchestra and the auditorium swathed in holland. His hands were plunged in the pockets of his overcoat, and he shivered. He paid small attention to the other's advent, because he was to be described on the playbills as "Assistant Stage-manager," and Oliphant was playing a small part. In the position that he had filled on tour, Oliphant would have joined him at the table; in the position that he filled here, theatrical etiquette forbade it. He walked up and down in the wings, and questioned for the hundredth time if, with such a part as this, Edmund Kean himself could have created an effect.

The other subordinates commenced to assemble, and to hang about with him. They watched the principals arrive and stroll to the table unabashed; and tried to hear what they talked about, and envied them their lustrous boots, which showed that they had come in cabs. The Villain recounted a funny incident to the leading lady, and she laughed merrily without having grasped the joke: his salary was understood to be thirty pounds a week, and *she* was only beginning. Besides, the celebrated actor under whom she had studied, and who had obtained the engagement for her, had always declared that her laugh was her strong point. The low comedian demanded of the prompter when they were "going to have the floats." There was considerable delay about this, and general expectancy; and then the footlights ameliorated the gloom a little, and the leading lady, who was very charming, bent over the blaze of light in a pretty attitude to warm her hands. The "small part women" in the wings looked additionally miserable, as they gazed at her, and the men inquired irritably among themselves "why the devil they were called for eleven." Only one, a youth who had twenty words to deliver, affected to be oblivious of his surroundings. He sauntered to and fro, muttering and gesticulating, stimulated by the secret thought that somebody of importance might comment on his enthusiasm.

A little man, with a hopeless expression, crept down to the footlights, and was greeted with cordiality—especially by the young leading lady. He was the author. He had a roll of manuscript in his hand, which represented the alterations he had been urged to make at the last rehearsal.

He was wondering what further misfortunes would befall him and his drama to-day.

Signs of impatience might be detected on the faces of the principals also now; but the actor who had a theatre for the first time felt it due to himself to keep the company waiting. He strode through the wings presently, ignoring the minor members—who scattered to let him pass—and, reaching the prompt-table, raised his hat about half an inch.

" 'Morning, ladies and gentlemen," he said curtly to the group about him. He made some remark to the author about the weather, and turned to the assistant stage-manager, whom he addressed as "Mr. Mote." He was fat, and held himself stiffly erect, endeavouring to palliate by his carriage the loss of his figure. In manner he was arrogant, and he had frequently the air of swelling—as often as he wished to assert his dignity in private, or to express emotion in a part.

"Clear the stage, please!" cried Mr. Mote, clapping his hands twice. "Act two, scene one! Sentry! Come on, Mr.—er—Williams, please— Act two, scene one!"

The youth who had been immersed in study hurried nervously to that part of the stage where he fancied he was supposed to be pacing battlements bathed in moonlight; but he was not certain that he wasn't meant to be in a corridor, looking out of a window. This lent indecision to his movements. He said:

" 'It's a fine night. How quiet it is!' "

At the same moment concealed carpenters began to hammer furiously. The youth looked disconcerted, but nobody else took any notice.

" 'How quiet it is!' " repeated the assistant stage-manager. "Enter the Colonel. 'Colonel,' please! Mr.—er—Fowler!—'How quiet it is'!"

"I beg your pardon!" The "Colonel" rushed forward. The rehearsal proceeded, and some of the women in the wings found chairs, and chatted in undertones.

The leading lady begged the Villain to advise her how she should "do her faint" when her lover was sentenced to be shot; and they moved together to where there was space for him to demonstrate his conception of a young girl's behaviour at this crisis. She confessed the fear that she would "find that flight of steps perfectly dreadful!" and he assured her cynically that there were "not many actresses who would object to be given a flight of steps to faint on." As to her train—well, it was difficult to show her! But there was a way—if she half-turned, and bent *so,* as she collapsed, it would "fall *down stage,* and the picture would be excellent." The Adventuress discussed her baby's first tooth, and the danger of convulsions, with the low comedian, who, as a family man, spoke authoritatively; and by the side of the author, who sucked his umbrella handle, the Hero sat, shouting comments, and rising from time to time to bluster with more violence.

The humble aspirants who incurred his displeasure stammered and turned pink; and one girl, whose arm he grasped so hard that he hurt her, in indicating the "business" that he desired, burst into tears. Those whose ordeal was longest were two old men. They had been in the theatres all their lives, but had sunk, from the small positions that they had once attained; to-day they were scarcely above the grade of supernumeraries. The younger might have been nearly sixty, but he remained burly and rubicund; the other, though probably not much older, appeared to be his senior by fully a decade. In his tightly buttoned frock-coat, painfully thin and shabby, he was the neatest and most pathetic little figure to be conceived, as he struggled to avoid the fiery impatience of the Hero's rebukes. The beautiful old face grew troubled by his eagerness to understand what was required of him; and occasionally, as the actor stamped and bellowed, he glanced at the spectators, as if fearing that his humiliation must excite their ridicule.

He escaped into the wings at last, and leaning against the wall of the scene-dock, consumed a sandwich, which served him for his dinner, out of a piece of newspaper.

Some hitch occurred; lines not allotted yet had to be spoken at this juncture.

"What are we waiting for?" demanded the Hero. "Get on, Mr. Mote, please."

Mr. Mote explained meekly that the part of the "Lieutenant" was not cast; and there was a few moments' consultation as to which of the actors had better "double" it. The Hero's gaze fell on Oliphant.

"Here, you!" he said, beckoning; "you can double this."

Oliphant took the type-written half-sheet among envious glances from the other "small-part men"; and glancing at the indication at the top, crossed the stage, and began to read.

He was surprised to find that, few as the lines were, they gave the player scope to distinguish himself. He was supposed to stagger on wounded, with a tale of distant disaster, and appeal to the "Colonel" to despatch aid to his comrades. The performance might have no more than the clap-trap effect of the sudden entrance

and the reel down the raking-piece; or it might
be one that would rivet the attention of every
critic in the house. He saw it more fully with
every word he delivered: the chance at that point
for a break in the voice; the effort to be strenuous,
and the exhaustion that forbade it; the horror
in the man's eyes as he described—and saw again
—the scene from which he had come! A genius
with an opportunity like this could have made
the success of the evening. He read well at sight
customarily; in his gratification he read better
than usual; and the author, who had fallen in love
with the lines as he wrote them, ceased to suck
the handle of his umbrella, and reflected with a
pleasant smile that there were "damn few men
in London who could equal his dialogue!"

The brief speech came to an end; the "Lieutenant" swooned; and Mr. Mote called "Captain
Harwood!"

"Where's 'Captain Harwood'?" he said, looking round.

"*I* play 'Captain Harwood,'" said Oliphant
blankly.

The hitch was repeated—there was renewed
consideration. It was impossible that Oliphant
could play the "Lieutenant" if he played
"Captain Harwood," for both characters had to
be on the stage at the same time.

"Well, somebody else must double the 'Lieutenant,'" said the Hero. "Mr.—er—Mortimer's
not on in this scene; *he* can do it."

Oliphant looked at him in dismay.

"Would you mind letting somebody else play
'Captain Harwood' and my keeping the 'Lieutenant'?" he asked. "I like it much the better of
the two."

The Hero made a rather lengthy pause. It
was intended to indicate amazement at the impu-
dence of questioning his decision.

"We won't discuss which of the two you like
best, if you please," he said imperiously. "Mr.
Mortimer! Come here! . . . You'll study the
part of the 'Lieutenant' by to-morrow; Mr. Mote
will give it you. . . . Go on, Mr.—er—Oliphant;
take up your cue, please—Enter 'Captain Harwood'!"

The rehearsal was resumed, and Oliphant went
through his daily task like an automaton. That
flash of hope was already extinguished. He
hadn't realised how great his delight had been
at the prospect opened to him until the speedy
disappointment revealed it. His heart felt like
lead within him, and he was glad when he was
free to efface himself, and lament and smoke
in comparative privacy at the stage-door. But

he had to go back, to speak a single line in another act.

The author observed his return, and went over to him; he regretted the Hero's high-handed arrangement, for the sake of the young man, and chiefly for the sake of the piece. Mr. Mortimer's performance in the new part would not be startling, to judge by the stolidity he displayed in the one he was rehearsing already.

"It was a pity you didn't keep the 'Lieutenant,' Mr. Oliphant, I think," he remarked; "you read it very well."

Oliphant knew the glow that comes to every young actor when one in authority praises him. And it was the first time he had been addressed by the author.

"You may imagine *I*'m sorry; but you saw what happened, Mr. Campbell," he said, shrugging his shoulders.

"Yes; but it's a pity; you were very good indeed. I'll speak about it afterwards and see what can be done."

The Hero had just been murmuring noble sentiments, which would eventually be delivered fortissimo, and as he made his exit, the sight of Oliphant and the dramatist together met his eye. He stalked across to them, with a swollen chest and distended nostrils.

"What do you mean," he exclaimed, "by appealing to Mr. Campbell against *me?* How dare you?"

"No, no," said the author, "he didn't. It was I who spoke to Mr. Oliphant."

"*I* am manager in this theatre," continued the actor passionately, disregarding the explanation. "Be good enough to understand that, Mr. Oliphant, once and for all! If you're not satisfied with the part you're playing, you're not obliged to play anything, you can resign your engagement. I have said you play 'Captain Harwood,' and that's the end of it. No, Campbell, my boy! No, no, my boy! I can't allow that sort of thing —I can't!"

There was a second in which Oliphant was tempted fiercely to answer that he did resign his engagement, but the knowledge of the straits that the indulgence would entail held him dumb. Though he had been in the theatrical profession seven years, this was his first experience of a managerial bully like the Hero, and he was sick with shame and rage.

His line in the ensuing act was no sooner uttered than he left the building. He had quite forgotten Alma King; his consciousness at the moment was only of the part that had been torn from him, and of the insult that he had been compelled to swallow. It was when five minutes had passed that the remembrance that he would find her in the lodging recurred to him; and fortified a trifle by the recollection he hastened homeward.

She was at the table in the drawing-room, writing letters—applications for engagement. A copy of *The Stage* lay near the cheap stationery and the penny bottle of ink.

"Am I in the way?" he said.

"Why should you be in the way? It's I who ought to ask that. Well?"

"Well, it isn't well! I'm angry, furious, in the blues!" He burst out with the tale of what had happened, and the sympathy in her face was sweet to him as he reached the point. "If only I could have afforded to answer the cad!" he exclaimed; "I think I'm ashamed of myself that I didn't!"

"It's at times like this that poverty scalds," she said. "I know your feeling—I've had it so often. But you were perfectly, perfectly right not to throw your part up—it would have been insane! You might have had to wait months for another chance in town."

"I suppose you're right," said Oliphant, "that *I* was right. But all the same, it's just one of those instances of his wisdom that a man isn't proud to recall."

"You're inclined to be morbid, aren't you?" said Miss King thoughtfully. "In the way you look at things generally? Just a little!"

He flushed. "I've never been told so before. It's—well, I've been a good deal alone; perhaps it's due to that, if I am."

"I *think* you are. . . . You look as if I had accused you of a crime."

"You took me aback, rather. It sounds weak, too. Do you think I'm weak?"

"I should say you are—emotional. . . . Well, 'weak' as well then, yes!—in some ways. . . . I don't think you will be spoilt by success if you get it. That's the greatest test of character."

"Poverty is supposed to be the greatest test," he said.

"Yes. But I don't believe it is. Poverty hardens a character by degrees, but success lays it bare in a flash. You would be very nice to the small people, if you were a manager, I'm sure. If *you* were the manager, for example, I should receive an answer to *this*." She pointed to one of the letters beside her.

"What is it for?" asked Oliphant; "is it anything worth having?"

"It is an appeal for a second-rate part in a fifth-rate company. If I am fortunate, I shall play in a different town every other night, and search for a new lodging every other day. The advertisement concludes: 'People who can't keep sober, save stamps!'"

"Good heavens!" cried the man; "you don't mean to say you apply for those things? They're not addressed to *you*. Have you ever travelled in a Portable?"

"No; I can imagine what it is like, though, fully."

"But they don't want an artist, Miss King; they don't want an actress! Do you know what the audience that you would play to is like? Do you know what the salary is like? Have you any idea what the company is like that you'd be with? You wouldn't be able to endure the engagement for a fortnight if you got it."

The girl's gesture had dignity as well as weariness.

"You seem to forget," she said quietly; "I am not in a position to consider these drawbacks. I'm here on your introduction—with only a few shillings in the world; and I owe money at the house I have left. I'm not afraid your landlady would turn me out in a week's time—or even in a month's: she trusts me—and you! But what

kind of woman should I be if I took advantage
of your introduction and her confidence?"

"I don't suggest you should take any advantage at all. There's such a thing as being *too*
conscientious. It would be too conscientious if
you hampered your career rather than accept a
few weeks' credit, or a friend's help. As a matter
of fact, it makes no difference to Mrs. Tubbs
whether she gets her rent every Monday or every
month; she doesn't depend on letting lodgings—
if she did, she'd be in the workhouse! She has
some share in a business that her brother has;
he's an upholsterer in Mabledon Place."

"I shan't take such an engagement if I can
get an ordinary one quickly, you may be sure,"
she said; "it will have to be my sole resource.
But I know the meaning of 'duty'!—it's my duty
to sacrifice my interests and *pay*. I've never
done anything I knew to be wrong in my life.
Oh, I don't forget I let a stranger speak to me
yesterday—and I can't complain if you think it
wasn't the first time!—and I asked him in to my
room; and it was a mistake that I shall regret
to the day I die. But it wasn't *wrong*. And *you*
know it wasn't 'wrong'; and *God* knows there
was no more of 'wrong' in my heart when I
opened that door to you than if we had both been
children. I regret it—I always shall—but I'm

not ashamed of it; if I were ashamed, I'm afraid
my goodness would go altogether, and I couldn't
live! I'm not going to despise myself now and
be a coward, and contemptible, rather than
'hamper my career,' as you put it."

"I won't urge you to do anything you're
opposed to," responded Oliphant slowly, after a
moment had passed. "But you've said one thing
I want to answer; it meant you couldn't complain
if—if I were ignorant enough to think lightly of
you. I should like you to hear me say that I
respect you more than any woman I've ever
met."

The subject of her endeavours was not resumed till the morrow, when he was leaving for
the Queen's. Then she announced an intention
of calling again on all the dramatic agents who
had her name on their books; and he walked some
part of the way to the Strand beside her.

The thought of what doubtless awaited her
in these offices, towards which scores of other
women, equally avid of employment, were hurrying from all quarters of London at the same
time, forbade boldness to them both, and Oliphant parted from her with small expectation
of hearing good news when they met at tea.

His haste to escape from the theatre the previous afternoon had left him uncertain at what

hour the rehearsal would commence this morning, but glancing at the call-board as he entered the passage, he found that he had guessed correctly. The Hero, however, was already on the stage, and it was immediately evident that his resentment was not forgotten. He stalked across to the young man without delay, his chest and nostrils expanded to their fullest capacity.

"Oh—er—I shan't want you for the piece at all, Mr. Oliphant," he said haughtily. "Give your part back to Mr. Mote, please! You—er—aren't tall enough."

CHAPTER IV

THERE was no written agreement; Oliphant
had been engaged, as hundreds of actors and
actresses are engaged every year, by word of
mouth. Even if it had been otherwise, he could
not have afforded to test the legality of the
reprisal. He was dismissed—because the author
had condoled with him on the Hero's auto-
cracy. "Nothing happens but the unforeseen":
the actor had left the lodging to attend a rehearsal, expecting to draw two pounds a week
during the run of the play; the actress had left
it, despondent, to make the round of the agents.
The man returned without a prospect; and the
girl came back with an "offer."

She was offered an engagement to go to South
Africa. The manager, who had come to London
for the purpose of organising a company, had
been in the second office that she entered—had
noticed her, asked the agent her name, and
concluded the arrangement on the spot. At
rehearsals she would have to prove herself com-

petent; but on this point she had no misgivings, and she was overjoyed.

"It was the purest chance!" she cried. "He has been here a fortnight, and Ash has never mentioned him to me—or me to him. If I had been five minutes later, he'd have gone, and I shouldn't even have known I had missed an opportunity. But, of course, I shall have to pay Ash his commission just the same—it was in his office." She paused inquiringly. "Is anything the matter?" she asked. "Has it been unpleasant again to-day?"

Oliphant told her briefly what had occurred.

What could she say? The first effect of sympathy is to weight the sympathiser's tongue, and the second is to render her self-conscious. "I am so sorry," murmured Miss King—and heard the echo of the vapid answer for ten seconds. "What shall you do?" she continued.

"I must look for something else."

"In London?"

"Oh yes, in London; at all events in London as yet. I want to get in, I want to get in! The stage-doors are stouter than the starling's bars. But I've been hurling myself against them too long to turn away and pretend the grapes are sour now. They're sweet, Miss King, they're luscious, and my mouth's watering for them!"

"You might come back to the charge all the stronger for a rest," she suggested.

"Yes, and all the older—don't forget that. I left the provinces swearing that I'd get a hearing here. I've applied everywhere. I've tramped the streets, and worn out my boots, and the sinews of war are reduced to shillings: I'm not going to feel that all that has been thrown away while I've my health and a watch and chain. London owes me for the energy I've expended. And one of these days it's going to pay me for it—with compound interest. If I returned to the provinces now, I should feel that I had made a bad debt, and the thought that I'd made a bad debt would make me a bad actor, and if I were a bad actor, I should have no excuse for existing in this overcrowded world at all! If I'm not an actor, I'm nothing, and—— This isn't strength of character, it's hysteria, to be perfectly truthful; I don't suppose I could get a provincial engagement before the spring if I tried."

"Haven't you any friends?"

"Haven't I any friends?" he repeated meditatively. "Well, I've relations; I go to see them occasionally—when I've a new suit of clothes. They aren't in the profession—nor in England, at the present time—so we needn't take them

into account. But, yes, I have a friend—I've
an extraordinary friend—I've a friend who, I
honestly believe, would lend me a thousand
pounds if I asked him for it."

She looked to see if he was serious. "Is this
hysteria too?"

"No, this is a sober fact. I was at Oxford
with him and we were very chummy. He had
leanings towards literature, and every qualifica-
tion for embracing it, including the most important—it didn't matter to him in the least if
he never made it pay. He was worth about ten
thousand a year when he was nine years old.
We haven't met very often lately, but I'm bound
to admit that that's entirely my fault. When I
do dine with him, I find him as good a fellow as
ever he was. I should be very fond of him if he
hadn't untold wealth like the prince in a fairy
tale; I struggled with the ten thousand a year,
but the accumulations of his minority were the
last straw."

"You don't expect me to believe that, of
course?" she said.

"Why not—does it sound petty? Perhaps I
didn't express myself very well; I mean we
should still be pals if he weren't so rich. Two
men whose lives are antithetical can't be very
'pally,' you know. A very rich man and a very

poor one may like each other extremely—they
may find each other very estimable and interesting—but they can't find each other so companionable as if they were both flush, or both beggars.
Otho Fairbairn keeps racehorses, and—and is a
dear good fellow. But *I* find it difficult to keep
myself; and though we've points in common, I'm
perfectly aware that by the time we've finished a
cigar each, he begins to feel the evening would
be livelier if he'd asked a 'chappie' who was going
down to Kempton, too, next day. Abstractions
pall. I can talk to you much more freely than
I can to Fairbairn, though I've known him for
years. . . . Tell me—you go to the Cape with a
répertoire, of course. What are the pieces?"

She named them—one was running at a West
End house. "I'm to go to see it; I shall write
in to-day. If you like I'll ask for two seats, and
we might go together."

"I'd like it very much; I was thinking of writing in myself. What line are you playing?"

"Oh, lead," she said.

"Really?"

"Oh yes, I'm engaged for lead; and the parts
are excellent, aren't they? It will be splendid
experience, too, with a répertoire. It's a good
thing I have my trunk; but even as it is . . .
I have to find the modern wardrobe myself, you

know! Still I shall be all right for the first fortnight, and I can get one or two frocks in Cape
Town."

She did not mention what her salary was to be,
though; and in view of the circumstances, and
her general frankness, the peculiarity of the
reservation struck Oliphant as forcibly as if he
were again a novice. He remembered living with
an actor years before and listening to his domestic
anxieties until three o'clock in the morning and
there was nothing the actor hadn't communicated
when the tour came to an end excepting how
much a week he received. Past salaries were
quoted; and there were confidences about his
mother's intemperance and the shortcomings of
his wife; but his "terms" of to-day were tacitly
understood to be a sacred matter.

With this single exception—the only professional trait he had observed in her—Miss King
was candour personified. The tickets for the
theatre arrived, "With the acting manager's
compliments," and she and Oliphant spent an
evening in the dress-circle. Both enjoyed it. To
be able to lounge in a velvet fauteuil in evening
dress, when he can ill afford the sixpence for the
programme, is the one advantage that the actor
out of work possesses over the rest of the un-
employed. His dinner may have been a sausage,

and for supper nothing may await him at all;
but a draught of oblivion is, at least, permitted
him by the kindly etiquette of "the profession";
and many a hopeless heart has been fortified
by it.

Yet it is tantalising, sometimes maddening.
Sometimes it fills the breast of the actor out of
work with such longings that he wrings his hands
with desire—this view, from the Delectable
Mountains, of the Celestial City whose gates are
closed.   Oliphant enjoyed the performance—to
watch good acting gave him as keen a delight as
a musician derives from a superb instrumentalist;
but to him the pleasure of the evening was alloyed
by the craving that assailed him in the entr'actes.
To Miss King there was no alloy.   The girl foresaw herself in the part of the favourite actress
whom she had come to study and to criticise; and
it was almost like witnessing her own success.
She sat recalling the "business," debating
whether it could be improved, and thrilling with
the anticipation of delivering certain lines.

The epoch of the drama was admirably
adapted to her.   She seemed created to wear the
robes of a bygone age—almost any bygone age—
and move among great deeds.   She would have
looked lovely as Juliet, which she wanted to play;
as Hypatia, which she hadn't thought of, she

would have been ideal; the intense earnestness
of the part was there in her face. Oliphant was
again conscious of this when they left the theatre,
and turned homeward through the wet streets.
He was also conscious that not one woman in a
hundred, trembling with thanksgiving, would
have divined his mood and troubled to assuage
it by the first remark she made:

"I daresay you'll be playing there one day!"

"I?" he exclaimed.

"I daresay. If you were as sure of your future
as I am, you'd be happier."

"But why?"

"How shall I define? You're an enthusiast—
there aren't so many of them in our profession!
But it isn't that either—I suppose enthusiasts fail
too. You impress me with the idea that you'll
succeed, and I've never had the conviction about
any one else. If I've been curious about people
at all, it has been to wonder why on earth they
ever took to the stage."

"Because it's the laziest life."

"Say it *may* be; don't you study?"

"Oh, *I* do; but have you been on many tours
where the people did?"

"Of course one can take it easy, if one likes,
now there are no more stock companies. It
couldn't have been very 'lazy' in the old days

when one had to master three or four parts a
week. Those were the times to make actresses—
when one sat up all night studying with a wet
towel round one's head! when one was Lady
Macbeth on Monday, and Lady Gay Spanker on
Tuesday. Ah, heavenly times! Yes, to people
who don't work at home it *is* the laziest life now,
I suppose—during an engagement; they're fairly
busy when they're 'resting.' What are you going
to try for to-morrow?"

"I'm going to try to see Townsend," he said.
"You know they are producing a piece of his at
the West Central. I once went out in one of his
things; and he rehearsed the company. He was
kind enough to think me good."

"Will he remember you?"

"An author never remembers anything except
his grudge against the critic who gave him a bad
notice, but I shall remind him who I am. I hear
they have only engaged the principals so far, and
the first call is for twelve o'clock to-morrow. I
mean to waylay him as he goes in."

To waylay a man as he goes in; to scheme for
an introduction to another who doesn't want to
know you; to submit to rudeness, and disguise
privation under well-cut clothes; to smile in the
Strand and break your heart in private, are the
essential preliminaries to success on the stage,

unless you have money, or your father was a favourite actor.

Miss King was rehearsing in a large room over a public-house in Covent Garden, and after accompanying her there next day, Oliphant proceeded to his destination. The stage-door of the West Central was in a narrow court not more than five minutes distant, and he reached it too early. Rather than incur the risk of missing the dramatist, though, he remained; and casting eager glances in the direction in which the man must come, endeavoured to persuade himself that he was hopeful. To be hopeful is to wear a cheerful expression, and a cheerful expression is valuable to the applicant for favours.

When Mr. Townsend appeared he was walking at a swift pace. He passed Oliphant without any sign of recognition, and, hastening after him, the young man said diffidently:

"Mr. Townsend!"

"Eh? Yes; what is it?"

"You don't remember me; my name's Royce Oliphant; I played 'Albert Kenyon' in *Don Quixote of Belgravia*—the Number 1 Company."

"Oh y-e-s, yes. How d'ye do, Mr. Oliphant?"

"Is there any part open in this? I should be

immensely glad to get a chance at the West Central."

"I'm afraid the cast is complete. You—er—might drop me a reminder when the tour starts. I'm afraid there's nothing open in the production."

"Not a small part? To come to town I'd take twenty lines."

The author mused.

"Well, there's a—I don't know; I'll see. It's just possible that I *can* offer you something. You might wait a second, will you?"

He plunged into the gloomy entrance, and clattered down the stairs. And a quarter of an hour went by.

When he emerged he was with the stage-manager. Oliphant's momentary expectation, however, faded into blankness as he saw that Mr. Townsend had forgotten all about him. He stopped him again:

"Mr. Townsend!"

"Eh? Oh, yes, yes. I have to go round to the front with Mr. Bensusan now. I'll see you when I come back. Don't go away; I shan't be ten minutes."

The actor made a cigarette, and stood before the door like a sentinel. An hour passed. He would have liked to sit down, but there was nowhere to sit. Two hours passed—two hours and a half. Still Mr. Townsend did not return. In desperation at last Oliphant went in search of him. At the box-office it was believed that he would be found at lunch in the restaurant across the road; and he was discovered eating oysters. He looked up as Oliphant approached him.

"Oh—oh, Mr. Oliphant! yes, of course! I mentioned the matter to Mr. Bensusan; but there are wheels within wheels, you know, my boy!— I can't work it. I'm sorry."

"It can't be helped," said Oliphant. "Thanks for doing what you could."

He turned away, and paused among the turmoil of the Strand, considering what to try for next. The odour of the restaurant lurked in his nostrils enticingly, and a passing omnibus threw a clot of mud in his face.

CHAPTER V

A FEW days later Miss King sailed for the Cape. She had contrived to discharge her debt to Mrs. Tubbs—probably by the sacrifice of something from her trunk: Oliphant did not hear how the payment was accomplished—and the widow deplored her departure on every occasion that she appeared with the remaining lodger's tea and toast.

Oliphant missed the girl too—more than he would have believed was possible considering how brief a time she had lived there. He felt lonelier than ever now when he returned to the empty drawing-room after tramping the pavements in vain. It is one of the painful features of the theatrical life that the friends of to-day are so often strangers to-morrow; every tour sees intimacies formed among people who, after the company is disbanded, may not meet one another again for years. But Miss King had been met in an unusual way, and in this case his own environment remained the same. Its sameness emphasised her absence, and lent a pathos to it.

It was about a week after their farewell that something unlooked for happened—something that promised to alter the whole complexion of his affairs. A letter lay on his hot-water can one morning, and a letter was sufficiently rare for him to open it with eagerness. When he had read it his eyes sparkled, and the attic looked lovelier. London had a heart after all, and he could hear it beating. London was human! The agent with whom he had left *The Impostor* wrote that he could place it for immediate production at a West End house. The percentage offered was very fair in view of the author's obscurity; and a hundred pounds, on account of fees, would be paid when the contract was signed. Oliphant was asked to reply at once, stating whether he was prepared to accept the terms. He stood still and laughed.

Yes, he was "prepared"! His hands shook as he dressed. He would reply in person. That the drama had been accepted three times already and that three contracts for it had been broken, did not damp his exhilaration, for the offer of money on account showed that business was meant, and besides, the production was to be "immediate." For once he left Burton Crescent buoyantly. Like the attic, the familiar windows of Marchmont Street had an unfamiliar air. The confectioner's which had recently appeared to mock him with its display of unattainable short-bread decorated with New Year's greetings in citron and sugar-plums—the little toy-shop, lower down, where he bought his papers—the oranges and tomatoes, and apples and chestnuts, on a stall under the tarpaulin—everything smiled to him to-day; he contemplated the landmarks with affection. Even the Strand—though he could never love the Strand—he was able, at least, to forgive. He remembered the sufferings it had inflicted without resentment. He had got the better of the Strand at last!

What a good fellow was the agent! though he had never struck him in that light before. How difficult, as the brilliant details were imparted, to disguise that the thing appeared incredible, something too marvellous to be true. "Clement" was to be played by Herbert Rayne, who hoped to obtain a lease of the Dominion. Herbert Rayne would be excellent as "Clement." And he had a reputation—the part of the hero was in first-rate hands. Would Oliphant meet him here on the morrow at, say, one o'clock? Yes, he would not fail; it was an appointment. His blood bubbled in his veins as he proposed a drink. There was a flicker of feeble sunlight on the puddles when they stood outside, and he saw a blaze that dazzled him.

How charming was Herbert Rayne when the interview took place and signatures were written! How novel it was to be deferred to by a popular actor, with astrakhan on his overcoat, and to discuss with him the qualifications of other popular actors! What did the author think of Miss Proctor for "Lady Maud"? The author, astonished at his boldness, confessed that he had always thought Miss Proctor lacked sympathy. Rayne agreed with him—she did. And she asked thirty pounds a week, which was absurd. He suggested somebody else, and they walked down the Strand together arm in arm. And they were seen by two persons to whom Oliphant was known! He was mortal and the fact gratified him.

"You're an actor yourself, Mr. Oliphant, eh?" said Rayne. "How about playing in the piece?"

"I don't think so, thanks," laughed the young man; "I shall be nervous enough as it is!"

"It would be good business for you—author's fees and a salary too! But, of course, you're right; it'd be a mistake. I think I shall be able to get the Dominion—I shall know this week. I've made them a fair offer. The rent they ask is a hundred and fifty, but that's all pickles!"

No longer compelled to husband the few
sovereigns that remained from the loan on his
watch and chain, Oliphant proposed luncheon,
and Rayne did not decline the invitation.   On
the contrary, he declared there was only one place
to lunch at, and that was Dolibo's.

"It's the best cooking in London, *I* say; and
then it saves time—as everybody goes there, one
meets all the people one has to see.   I must introduce you to Ravioli."

So they jumped into a hansom, and drove to
Dolibo's; and Oliphant was duly introduced to
ravioli, which he had presumed was a composer,
but which turned out to be a mess that tasted of
nothing but the tomatoes.   Nevertheless it was
a delightful day.   And the fact that the agent,
after deducting the amount of the commission,
had given him a crossed cheque, was the only
alloy to his satisfaction.

Rayne's confidence was justified and the Dominion was secured.   There were various hopes
that were not fulfilled—either the salaries asked
were prohibitive, or it was found that the artists
would not be disengaged soon enough.   The
"Lady Maud" on whom Oliphant had set his
heart was attacked by pleurisy three days before
the date of the first rehearsal, and in her place
was Miss Blanche Ellerton, whom he had never

seen, and who was by comparison unknown. The morning arrived, however, when the company assembled at the theatre to hear Royce Oliphant read his play.

He arrived early. It was at this period his constant endeavour to avoid all the faults and affectations that he had execrated in others. He had rendered himself rather a nuisance by the earnestness of his attempts to obtain small parts for his acquaintances, who, from the moment the earliest announcement was made, besieged him with written and oral reminders of their exist-ence. That he had not succeeded in a single instance was due to circumstances that he could not help; but the failure troubled him, and he had felt that his explanations must sound as hollow to his former colleagues as the explana-tions of his present associates had hitherto ap-peared to himself. He arrived early.

The others were before him, though. A semi-circle of chairs had been formed on the stage, as if in readiness for a minstrel entertainment; and facing it, under the T-piece, was the one reserved for himself. Mr. Rayne made several remarks to him, which he believed he answered: he had the vaguest idea of their tenor. He noted a pretty, fair girl, who wore a feather boa, lifting attentive eyes to him, and hoped she could act. He saw the manuscript and a glass of water on the prompt-table, and shivered as the patient at the dentist's shivers at the sight of the forceps. He approached the prompt-table—and put his umbrella on it! He had touched the apex.

"Good-morning, ladies and gentlemen," he said, in a voice that he didn't recognise.

The remembrance assailed him that more than one of these people to whom he was about to read bore names that were household words among playgoers, and he turned suddenly giddy. He wished that Rayne had not known he was an actor, for he was certain he should read like an amateur of the worst kind. He fumbled with the leaves of the manuscript, and cleared his throat, and sipped the water.

"*The Impostor,*" he began.

He dashed into the stage-directions, which gave him a moment to accustom himself to the situation; and he gabbled them vilely. It seemed to him five minutes—in reality it was less than thirty seconds—before he had his voice under control at all. His predominant and paralysing thought was that everybody would be bored to death hours before he had finished.

To read a play well is an achievement of which very few are capable; for to read a play well means to render perhaps fifteen parts, and the more thoroughly one character may be realised, the more difficult it becomes to change instantaneously to the next. When the reader is the author too, sensitive to each movement of every member of his audience, strained to sickness with the double responsibility, the ordeal is beyond description. It was twelve o'clock when Oliphant sat down; it was four o'clock when, after three brief intervals, he closed the covers of the last act. During two hours he knew that he had done the best of which he was capable. He looked up at the girl with the feather boa, and he saw that to her thinking, at all events, *The Impostor* spelt success.

There was a hum of congratulation. Everybody had a smile; the girl exclaimed feelingly, "Oh, it's beautiful!" And an elderly woman, who, Oliphant assumed was cast for "Lady Plynlimmon," said with quiet authority, "The play is sure—oh, sure!" at which Rayne looked much pleased.

Then there were introductions, and more flattering comments made. And at last, not quite certain whether he was awake or in a dream, Oliphant escaped to gulp the air, after hearing that everyone was expected at twelve again the following morning.

It might be imagined that the rehearsals would

prove no novelty to him, but they were astound-
ingly new. Familiar things were all at once presented to him in a fresh light—just as light had
been shed already on Mr. Townsend's behaviour
at the West Central. A rehearsal here was as
different from the rehearsals to which he was
used—as different from a rehearsal at the
Queen's, for example—as the captain's impression of the voyage is from a passenger's.
Hitherto his sole anxiety had been his own performance—now he was anxious about everyone's;
and, too diffident to pull up the artists publicly
in order to obtain the inflections he desired, his
brain swam in trying to remember the thousand-
and-one suggestions he wanted to make to them
in private. He was harassed day and night by
the remembrance of warnings about something
which somebody had felt it "only right" to utter.
He was drawn aside by "Lady Plynlimmon" to
be cautioned that the stage-management was
ruining her most important scene; Voysey, the
stage-manager, informed him that his refusal to
have incidental music was going to "damn the
show"; and Rayne came down to the theatre one
morning with the opinion that the "hero was an
unmitigated blackguard." Even when the incidental music was conceded, it was not the end of
the matter. Oliphant derived his principal com-

pensation from watching the rehearsals of the
girl with the feather boa, who had proved to be
Blanche Ellerton. Though she was not more
than three or four and twenty, her performance
promised to be admirable—in fact, she was an
ideal "Maud." Her girlishness was so "natural,"
her pathos was so unforced, that she delighted
him. So when she turned to him one day in
excitement and despair, he was ready to take
her side before he had heard what her grievance
was.

"Oh, Mr. Oliphant," she exclaimed, "please,
please tell Mr. Voysey that that awful number
they play through my soliloquy won't do! It
kills it. I simply can't act if they play it. The
situation wants something plaintive, and Mr.
Van Putten has written a jig!"

Oliphant hadn't remarked the incongruity, and
said so.

"Well, ask him to let you hear it. Will you?
Do!"

"Certainly I will," he answered; "I'll ask him
now."

The conductor was sitting by the piano at the
opposite corner of the stage, and Oliphant went
over to him.

"Mr. Van Putten," he said, "I wish you'd let

me hear one of the numbers you've written. Do you mind?"

"Zo?" said the conductor coldly. He inquired which number it was.

Miss Ellerton joined them. "Number three," she said.

"Ha, ha!" said Mr. Van Putten; "dee lady find zomeding wrong mid it, yes? Ha, ha! Zir, I 'ave gombosed dee music for all dee brincibal deatres in London; but dee gombany knows best, ain't it? Zo, I vill blay it!"

He did. In describing it as a "jig" the actress had exaggerated, but not more wildly than was pardonable in the artistic temperament.

"It's very fine," said Oliphant; "yes, thank you. Still, I fancy that for the situation something a little slower would be better; it doesn't quite fit the lines. Perhaps you've noticed it yourself?"

"What's the matter?" demanded Mr. Voysey.

"Dee audor and dee lady gomblain of dee music."

Without any premonitory symptoms Mr. Voysey exploded. The conductor posed resignedly, with the offending number drooping from his hand. The rehearsal was stopped, and a heated argument continued for five minutes. Rayne agreed with everybody all at once.

"It's Miss Ellerton's scene," repeated Oliphant, "and if she doesn't feel the number it ought to be changed. We can't sacrifice the actress to the incidental music!"

"Oh, that's enough, Mr. Oliphant!" cried the stage-manager. "All right, all right, all right! I've had thirty-five years' experience in the profession, but I'm always ready to learn. Produce the piece *your* way! I may as well go home, as I don't know my business."

However, he picked up the manuscript again at the same moment. Miss Ellerton had gained her point, and the rehearsal was resumed.

"You got me into nice trouble," Oliphant said to her by and by.

"Oh, it was so good of you!" she answered radiantly. "But wasn't it *hideous?* It set one's teeth on edge."

"It was a trifle weird," he agreed.

"You don't know how grateful I am! I couldn't, I simply *couldn't* have acted to that ghastly noise. . . . Have you seen the boy anywhere lately?"

"Do you want anything?"

"I want him to fetch me a bun. I'm famished, and we shan't get away till five if we're going through the last act."

"Let *me* go for you. What shall I bring?"

"Will you? Oh, just a bun, please; that's all. Thanks awfully!"

So he brought a box of cakes from a neighbouring confectioner's, and she handed it round to the other women, and then came back to offer it again to him. She stood beside him in the wings, eating chocolate éclairs, and discussing the frocks she was to wear in the part. She was pretty enough to be attractive, even while she ate a chocolate éclair.

CHAPTER VI

WHEN the Wednesday dawned for which the dress-rehearsal was fixed, Oliphant rose in a state of tension which he knew was to continue for thirty-six hours—until the curtain fell the following night on the production. His remembrance of these thirty-six hours was always vague. A salient feature was Mr. Voysey's silk hat at the back of his head, as he stood, on Wednesday morning, doing nothing anxiously in the centre of "Lady Plynlimmon's" hall; the brilliantly-lighted scene, in which he was the solitary figure, and the gloom of the auditorium formed a striking contrast. There was a sprinkling of curious strangers in the stalls. And when the rehearsal began at last, everything went wrong—everything except the performance of Miss Ellerton. Even Rayne was not so good as the author had expected him to be; and others did not know their parts; and terrible omissions were discovered which could never be remedied in time. At five o'clock, when Oliphant went back to Burton Crescent, he was bowed with despondence.

Thursday drew towards dusk tardily. He had strolled about the streets till he was tired, and, still too restless to sit down, he now paced the drawing-room, staring with strained eyes at the darkening enclosure beyond the windows. He thought that he wanted somebody—anybody—to talk to; but when Mrs. Tubbs brought in the inevitable tea and toast, her chatter drove him to the verge of frenzy.

"I suppose you can't help thinking about it, Mr. Elephant," she said, "and being a bit worried like? Well, you're fine and large on the bills, that you are! Mrs. Johnson she was saying only yesterday—you've heard me speak o' Mrs. Johnson?—the lady as does your washing—she was saying only yesterday she never see a strikinger bill in her life; and she's what you may call a reg'lar playgoer, mind yer! Is it a laughable piece?"

"No," he said huskily; "it isn't meant to be comic. I don't think I want any tea, thank you."

"Lor, you must eat a bit—whatever are you talking about! I suppose if it takes, you'll be making a lot o' money, won't you? I do wonder you ain't acting in it yourself—seems so strange. Mrs. Johnson she was asking me which of the parts you took, and when I said you hadn't got nothin' to do with it, she was that surprised!

Well, me and her 'll both be there, anyhow; I give her a ticket, and we mean to clap like one o'clock, *I* can tell yer!"

"For heaven's sake," he exclaimed agitatedly, "don't go clapping all by yourselves! Don't, I beg you!" The toast choked him, and it was necessary to obtain a respite. "I'll go and dress," he declared.

"Better 'ad," said Mrs. Tubbs; "Mrs. Johnson she 'as took especial pains with your shirt—you'll find it at the top of the parcel. *I* know the sinking you've got, Mr. Elephant—'aving 'ad it myself. Never shall I forget the night as 'er as is gone left this very 'ouse to make her first appearance before the public, with me and 'er uncle a-followin' of her, a mask o' perspiration in the bus! And the talent o' that gal was astonishin', though little more than showing of 'erself off 'ad she got to do. And if it 'adn't been that Mr. Tubbs was the tool of Mr. Billing, it's at the Al'ambra or somewhere she'd 'ave——"

The quiet and coolness of the bedroom was refreshing. By maddening degrees another hour crept by. Presently it wasn't ridiculous to consider starting for the theatre. He had intended to take a hansom, as befitting the occasion, but suddenly he preferred to walk. He did not mean to go behind the scenes until after the performance; to show himself earlier would be only to increase the nervousness of the company. In the Strand he had a liqueur of brandy, and bought a cigar, and consulted his watch, which he had taken out of pawn, a dozen times.

The crowd outside the pit and gallery was large—he wondered with a pang how many orders it might represent. The people surged forward as he speculated on the point, and a flood of light was cast upon the pavement from the centre doors, which opened noisily and displayed the foyer. The commissionaire who opened them was very tall and fat, and his buttons shone; Oliphant noticed that. The gleam of the acting-manager's shirt-front, and the blue scarf over the head of an early arrival in a four-wheel cab, also impressed him, like the artificial redness of a bank of roses at the foot of a gilt looking-glass when he entered. There was a telegram for him in the box-office, and it slipped from his fingers three times before he mastered it. It ran: "I'm drinking your health. Heartiest wishes for a thundering success to-night—Otho." It was sent from Paris. At the top of the stairs he handed it to the programme-girl instead of his ticket, and tried to smile when the mistake was pointed out; his lips felt very stiff.

He sat in the dress-circle, and listened to the

clatter of feet overhead, as the gallery-patrons
stumbled down the wooden steps.   After an
eternity, when the orchestra appeared, and the
first preliminary scrape of a fiddle wrung his
heart, he understood the sickness of the soul
which so often prevents a dramatist attending
the production of his play.   Hitherto he had
ridiculed it; now he understood.   Momentarily
he entertained the idea of going away, but a
feeling of physical weakness, as much as curiosity, held him chained.

The stalls were rapidly filling, and occasionally
there was the sharp rattle of rings, as an attendant preceded a party into a private box.   Mr.
Van Putten emerged; he settled his coat-tails.
He tapped with the bâton, and collected eyes.
The orchestra emitted a feeble wail.   It grew
louder; it acquired time, and tune; it culminated
in a crash.   The author gripped the arms of his
chair—and the curtain rose.

The scene glowed before him as it had done
yesterday; the women were there—and they
spoke; so much he knew.   Whether they spoke
the lines well, or whether they spoke the words
that he had written, he did not know in the
least.   He thought that if the actresses' nervousness had equalled his own they would have been
tongue-tied; but they had—as he had always

had till now—the stimulus of the footlights. . . .
Gradually his mind became acuter; he waited
for an inflection, and looked for the next "entrance." It was "Maud's"; God! was Maud
late?

"'Maud is here, mother; and very impatient
for tea!'"

Ah! she was on the staircase—she came down
it slowly, her finger-tips trailing the balustrade.
How graceful she was! How charming a figure,
as she smiled across the table! . . . There was
a ripple of laughter as "Lady Plynlimmon" let
fall an epigram with an air of unconsciousness
that gave it twice its point. . . . Rayne—looking very handsome in "pink"—was welcomed en-
thusiastically. . . . To find that "Sir Clement"
wasn't Sir Clement at all startled the audience
as it was meant to do, and an audible stir ran
through the theatre. The author's agitation had
a throb of enjoyment in it now; yesterday's
blunders were avoided—the piece was going
without a hitch!

He did not go to smoke in the interval; nor
in the next. He sat longing to grip Rayne and
everybody else by the hand. He had misjudged
Rayne! The whole company was doing valiant
work, and the applause had been of the warmest
description.

The act-drop went up for the third time, and "Maud" and the man who called himself Sir Clement Thurloe were "discovered" on the anniversary of their wedding-day. Rayne and Miss Ellerton were both excellent here. His hunger for the love of the wife whom he had bought by his fraud, and her own awakening tenderness, were depicted admirably. Soon her dislike of "Mrs. Vaughan"—the man's embarrassment when questioned—fanned a mistaken fear to jealousy. The girl's voice as she turned to "Lady Plynlimmon" with the cry of "Mother! *You* made me marry him—tell me if it's true!" brought Oliphant's heart into his throat. She was displaying an intensity that astonished even him. For the end of the act—the whirlwind of despair—he relied on Rayne. But another scene had to come first: the "scene of the two women," when "Maud" declined to receive "Mrs. Vaughan," and the adventuress, in retaliation, flung the truth in her hostess's face and told her that she was the wife of an impostor. The scene came which was to be made or marred by Miss Blanche Ellerton.

And now she held the house; and Oliphant worshipped her. The girl who had eaten chocolate éclairs, and talked theatrical slang in the wings, bore herself like a queen. Every word she uttered, every quiver of the proudly-set lips, struck a chord in his own being. His life seemed a part of her—to flutter with her breath. The act—the play—ended somehow; he thought of no one but her.

He fancied there was a cry of "Author" when he made his way "behind" after the curtain fell. The artists were all on the stage—all with their nerves strung high; the eyes that some of the women turned to him were wet as he stammered his thanks. He loved everybody; the members of the company were his brothers and sisters! Rayne clapped him on the shoulder, and sounded imperative—Oliphant didn't understand about what. All he realised vividly was that Blanche Ellerton was standing among the group, waiting for him to reach her. He took both her hands and could have fallen at her feet.

"Oh, God bless you!" he gasped.

"Was I what you meant?"

"You were great—what can I say?—you were great!"

"For Heaven's sake, man, come!" Rayne wrenched him round; "they want the author—take your call!"

He was dragged before the audience, and made his bow.

She was there when he came off—not queenly

any longer, but a girl with paint on her face, and a tear trickling down it. "Good-night," she said. "I think it's a success?"

"Thanks to *you*," he muttered. He caught her hands to his mouth, and kissed them violently. "There are no words to tell you how grateful I am—no words! Good night, Miss Ellerton."

It occurred to him afterwards that a diplomatist would have bestowed his superlative benediction on the manager; but he didn't care!

CHAPTER VII

W HEN Mrs. Tubbs came into his room with the bundle of newspapers that he had ordered overnight, Oliphant sat up in bed and grabbed them; and the more he read the blanker grew his dismay. Not one of the Press opinions of *The Impostor* was wholly favourable, and the majority were decidedly the reverse. The actors and actresses, of course, were complimented, especially Miss Ellerton—*The Daily Telegraph* was reminded of Aimée Desclée—but the dramatic critics were not so diffident of disparaging the author; and after breakfast, when the evening papers were published, one of the notices was headed, "CLAUDE MELNOTTE IN A CHIMNEY-POT HAT."

The author walked down to the Dominion in the morning, because he felt that it would be cowardly to stay away; and he had a brief, dejected chat with Rayne in the office. To go to the theatre at night, however, and see the company flat, and the house three-parts empty, was beyond him. He wondered if Miss Ellerton was sympathising with him in his failure. She could afford to do so; *The Impostor* had at any rate been a triumph for *her*. He would go to-morrow! He fancied what she would say and what he would answer, and foresaw her reply to that. He found that he was looking forward to their conversation very eagerly.

But it was not quite so charming as he had expected. She said that "the bad notices of the piece were an awful shame," but he could not avoid perceiving that her mind was chiefly occupied by the good notices of herself. The conversation approached his imaginary picture more closely when he congratulated her on her success; then she was again animated. He was relieved to hear that the audience was not so scanty as he had feared it would be; and when the acting-manager came round with the returns Rayne perked up, and spoke hopefully of "pulling the thing together yet."

It was his first play; the atmosphere of a theatre had grown essential to him; and man knows no wilder adoration than a dramatist may feel for the actress who realises his heroine—the Dominion drew Royce Oliphant like a loadstone. He watched Blanche Ellerton from the wings while she was on the stage, and talked to her in the wings when she came off, and found the wings a void when she was in her dressing-room. The not uncommon delusion that to obtain disenchantment it is only needful to view the make-up on an actress's face at close quarters, is the reverse of the truth instead of a fact. She is probably far better-looking so—there in that light—than she is by nature—and the consciousness that she is made up, moreover, is by no means active in the spectator's mind. At the rehearsals Miss Ellerton had been a pretty girl; here she was a beautiful woman. Very soon, indeed, Oliphant came to remember her as she was here and altogether forgot the comparatively insipid face which belonged to her by rights. It was a little shock to him the first time he saw her again in her own person—they had met in Oxford Street. But for the glamour of her identity, which nothing could destroy—the knowledge that she was the girl who inside the theatre affected him so powerfully—he would have felt the meeting sad.

None the less he was delighted a few evenings later when she mentioned that her home was at Earl's Court and it was understood that he was to call there some afternoon.

He went the following Sunday—he would have gone before but for the dread of showing himself impatient. The house that sheltered the goddess when he reached it was not imposing; but as he waited in the little drawing-room, with its dyed grasses, and photographs of Blanche Ellerton on the mantelpiece, he smoothed his hair a trifle nervously.

She came in to him a moment afterwards, and they exchanged preliminary platitudes. She was followed by her parents, and a sallow, unattractive girl of about twenty, with high shoulders and a flat chest, who, he learnt with surprise, was her sister. There was tea, and, on his part at least, uneasiness.

Mrs. Ellerton was a thin, simple-looking woman, prematurely grey. Her destiny was to write novelettes to order. Novelettes that filled a couple of pages—longer novelettes issued at a halfpenny, between blue, pink, and green wrappers—novelettes that were "To be continued in our next," all came alike to her pen. She took pleasure in the work, and was ashamed to be pleased by it, for she was keenly sensitive to ridicule. She was consoled by remembering that the money she obtained was indispensable. Blanche had earned a little as a child-actress before she was eleven, but the five pounds a week she was drawing from the Dominion was the highest salary to which she had attained, and there were many months in which she earned nothing at all.

The head of the family—the husband of the lady novelettist—was James Ellerton; he frequently reminded her of it—in fact, it was his misfortune that he could never forget it himself. He had formerly been a provincial actor—a calling he loathed—and as a provincial actor he might have contributed towards the household expenses to-day. Unhappily, some ten years since, he had written a very clever novel, which evoked most excellent reviews, and of which the publishers sold the fewest possible number of copies. For a writer who had been likened to Balzac—and he *was*—to continue to make a fool of himself on third-rate theatrical tours, or to say, "The dinner is served, madam," in London, he had felt to be incongruous. James Ellerton, in the *Saturday Review,* was "a distinguished novelist"; James Ellerton, in the theatre, was a nonentity to be snubbed and bullied. His success in literature gained him no jot of consideration from stage-managers and dramatic-agents— as the adaptation of a French melodrama would have done—for the simple reason that none of them knew anything whatever about it. He had, therefore, retired from the theatrical profession; and at very lengthy intervals produced two further novels, which were reviewed highly also, and much admired—by the reviewers. Few other persons had heard of them. He was supported, fitfully by the exertions of his elder daughter, and for the most part by his wife's novelettes, whose literary quality caused him acute disgust. She mentioned them in his presence deprecatingly.

"It's so nice to see you, Mr. Oliphant," she said. "We were all in front the first night, of course. I do hope it will go on! Do you think it will?"

"I think that Miss Ellerton's performance alone ought to be enough to draw all London," he said.

"Oh, how lovely of you to say so! She's worked so hard, Blanche has; and she's never had what I call a 'real chance' till now. But the drama is so good in itself! I'm sure it ought to run. Mr. Ellerton thought highly of it; didn't you, James?"

Mr. Ellerton had been considering—as he always did consider on being introduced to anyone—how to intimate that he was "a distinguished novelist"; and he was grateful to her for making the opportunity. It would have been beneath his dignity to let her see it, however; the fiction of his importance—the importance of his fiction—was maintained on the domestic hearth.

"The *literary* quality of the dialogue," he said impressively, "of course appealed to me. There are lines that I would have written myself."

"I'm glad you liked it," said Oliphant; "yes." He saw that the others were of the opinion that the elderly gentleman had paid him a great compliment, and was a little puzzled. The father wrote, then?—that was why he wore a brown velvet jacket.

"Papa doesn't often praise a piece, I can tell you!" said Blanche. "He's so fiendishly critical. You know his books?"

"I—I know the books in a sense," murmured Oliphant. "I'm ashamed to say I haven't read them."

"There are some millions," said Mr. Ellerton with a fine smile, "in the same position." He always said this, and said it rather well. "I am *not*—er—popular, Mr. Oliphant—I won't say 'successful,' for, as a detail, my novels obtain their—er—columns of eulogy in all the important papers." He waved the papers aside. "I have never consented to cheapen my style from commercial motives. It may be a weakness. I may be wrong."

"I think it's the reverse," declared Oliphant;

"very much the reverse. To know he can afford to do his best work must be a literary man's greatest joy."

Mr. Ellerton bent his head, and smiled again—ineffably.

"It *is*," he said.

"Oh, we're a very brilliant family," laughed the actress; "you've no idea!"

"Do *you* write as well, Mrs. Ellerton?"

"Oh, only a little," she faltered; "*my* writing is—— My husband is the author. *I* write for papers; I've no time to think about a book."

"You write more than a 'little' then?"

"Well, they keep me busy," she confessed nervously; "don't they, James? Did I tell you that there's a note from Mr. Trussell asking for a ten-thousand-word story as soon as I can let him have it?"

"How long does a story like that take to do?" Oliphant inquired.

Under the influence of polite interest—an influence to which she was so unaccustomed—the simple woman grew expansive. "Oh, not very long, if I keep at it; and I do when I've begun! Of course my tales aren't—aren't—what is the word, James?"

" 'Serious,' " said the authority carelessly.

"Yes, aren't 'serious,' " she continued, wincing—"in a literary sense my husband means. They're—they're written to suit the class of papers that want me; but they take hold of me while I'm doing them; and I don't like to put them down."

"I can understand the fascination very well," answered the young man. "To keep seeing one-self in print, too, must be jolly!"

"The characters seem quite real to *me*," she said, "and—and it's exciting when one gets them into some dreadful trouble, and doesn't quite know how they're going to get out of it. One doesn't worry, you know! There are nights when I can't sleep because I keep asking myself how the heroine's going to be saved, and——" She saw her husband's expression, and changed colour pathetically. "But it's absurd to talk about *my* writing in front of Mr. Ellerton! *I* only play at it."

"My wife's work has—er—has its merits," admitted the introspective novelist whom it kept. "It really isn't so bad as some of the stuff these papers trade in; I hope to see both her and Blanche advance considerably. And—if you persevere, Mr. Oliphant—I think there's somebody else I shall have to congratulate one of these days!"

"It won't be on my plays," said Oliphant

shortly; "I'm an actor." He was sorry to be
conscious that he felt the visit was proving very
dull.

All this time the girl in the background had
said nothing except "How do you do?" but sat
regarding Oliphant with hungry eyes. Though
she was accustomed to men ignoring her, she
yearned to be noticed by them, and she had
always a passionate hope that the last one introduced would be the exception to the rule. The
attention secured by her sister's brightness, her
father's self-assertion, even by her mother's small
talk, accentuated the force of her secret mortification. Life contained for her but one brief
excitement. It was when she stood up in company and played, in an amateurish, untrained
way, some simple air on her violin, trembling to
know that now, at least, men looked at her. At
these moments there was, in the breast of the
semi-deformed girl, the tumult of triumph and
despair that belongs to a Paganini. But her skill
was of the slightest, and nobody suspected, as
she scraped "The Last Rose of Summer," that
she felt much more than a mechanical toy.

"Gertrude," said Mrs. Ellerton now, with a
glance in her direction, "came home from the
Dominion hysterical. How she cried there! So
did I—I always do—but Gertrude sobbed."

"Did you, Miss Ellerton?"

She turned sick with the intensity of her desire to say something "good"—something that should stimulate his interest. She clasped her hands in her lap with an unspoken prayer.

"Yes," she said huskily, her face suffused with an unbecoming blush.

"I wish it had been your business to write some of the notices. You'd have dealt more kindly with me."

"Yes," she said.

"The receipts are going up a little every evening, though, lately; perhaps it may turn out well after all—it's possible. One can't say."

"No," she said.

"I wonder how much money Rayne has got?" exclaimed the leading lady; "do you think he can afford to wait till it works up into a draw? But I oughtn't to ask you that."

"As a matter of fact I don't know," Oliphant answered.

"He ought to advertise it more. There are no advertisements—none to speak of. And—oh, these managers, these managers!"

"What were you going to say?"

"Well, the advertisements he does put in— look at all the lines from the notices that he quotes! They're not the best, they're not the finest by any means: because the best notices were got by *me,* and he doesn't want to advertise anybody but himself. 'Herbert Rayne's Latest Success!' And what of the author of the piece, and poor Blanche Ellerton?"

"I'm afraid the author of the piece can't lay claim to many good notices," he laughed.

Her mother despatched a warning glance. "Blanche is so frank, Mr. Oliphant," she murmured; "she says too much sometimes."

"Oh, Mr. Oliphant won't tell tales out of school, *I* know! *Have* I been indiscreet, Mr. Oliphant?" She smiled bewitchingly.

"Why, I thought we were friends?" he said.

"I feel perfectly safe in Mr. Oliphant's hands —I'm not alarmed! But isn't it so? The lines that would tell go into the waste-paper basket. You know what the critics said of me! Did you see *The World?* Oh, did you see *The World?* I must show it you! Where is it, mother?"

"Yes, I saw it," he said; "I brought you the cutting, if you remember."

"Oh, so you did—so kind of you! Well"— her gesture was perhaps a little unrestrained for a room—"these things aren't advertised, and there ought to be half a column of them in all the papers! I've suffered in the same way all through my career. They won't, they *won't* let you get a better adjective than themselves—the vanity of a management is simply appalling!"

"*I* have never written for the theatre on that account," observed the novelist; "I wouldn't do it. I would *not* consent to stultify my intention because an actor-manager demanded that he should be in the centre of the stage when he ought to be in his dressing-room. I always say one thing; I say: 'Come to me when you can forget that you are managing this house for your own glorification——and then I'll write you a play. In the meanwhile, my dear sir, no! You don't suit me, and *I* shouldn't suit *you.*' They may be offended; but I say what I mean."

"My husband won't give in," boasted Mrs. Ellerton feebly. "He'll never give in."

"No! Those are my principles, and I shall keep true to them. Possibly"—he lifted his eyebrows and his shoulders—"possibly I may be unwise!" The doubt troubled him less because he had never been asked for a play in his life.

"I know something of the difficulties of the profession, naturally," said Oliphant, addressing himself to the actress; "but surely *you* have nothing to be dejected about? You've done wonders."

"Oh," she sighed, "if you knew what I've had to contend with in my career—the obstacles that would have crushed an ordinary girl! I daresay

I shall take things more lightly in ten years'
time; I suppose a woman does take them more
lightly than a young girl"—her tone suggested
that she was sixteen—"but, do you know, I
simply writhe to-day at an injustice! Shall I
ever forget when I went to New York with Mrs.
Sweet-Esmond? She got me for twelve pounds
a week, between ourselves—I accepted the offer,
as I accepted these ridiculous terms at the
Dominion, because the engagement meant an
opportunity—and then she simply hated me because I rehearsed the part well. 'Miss Ellerton,'
she said, '*I* have come to New York to make the
success—not *you!*' Cat! I think that tour with
Mrs. Sweet-Esmond did more to—to destroy
my childish trustfulness than anything in my
career."

He caught himself wishing that she would be
satisfied to call it her "life" occasionally, but he
sympathised with her nevertheless.

If her conversation had been phonographed
and reproduced in his hearing without the play
of her eyes, and the magic that her presence
exercised upon him now, he would have judged
it as fairly as anybody else. Had he gone to the
house as the friend of another man who admired
her, he would have judged it fairly too; and—if
he had been a fool—he would have attempted

to convince the other man when they left that, apart from the inexplicable histrionic gift, there was "nothing in her." As it was, the blemishes which he could not overlook were only spots on the sun. They did distress him on his way home, but for the veriest instant. He even persuaded himself that they had a charm, because they implied a glimpse of the girl's real self—the thing which every man honestly in love, every man not a sybarite in the emotions, constantly tempts her to expose, instead of assisting her to veil. The man honestly in love is the eternal justification of the parable concerning the goose with the golden eggs. In truth, the longer the girl takes to become "real" to his sight, the longer his homage will last, though she may be able to display as many virtues as eyelashes; for nearly every educated man is unconsciously an idealist in relation to the opposite sex, and rarely falls in love with a girl at all, but with a character quite different which her face suggests to him. That there are contented husbands is less a testimonial to men's wisdom than to women's adaptability and tact. "Familiarity breeds contempt" was a man's adage; as a reflection on feminine character it is a lie. Women are idealists too, but they idealise their possessors; men idealise only what they seek to possess. The longer the

average woman lives with a man, assuming he
is not a brute—and often when he is—the fonder
of him she becomes; and on their silver-wedding
she can kiss his hand if his finger-nails are dirty.
But it is a severe chill to the average man's
adoration the first time the woman he worships
has a cold in the head. Royce Oliphant, however,
was wooing severer chills.

It was seven o'clock when he reached home,
and Mrs. Tubbs, whom he met on the stairs,
informed him that at about four o'clock a boy
had brought a note for him. Oliphant opened
it hastily, and read the pencilled message with
astonishment. It was from Mr. Voysey, and
stated that Rayne had been thrown from a cab,
and rather seriously hurt. Would Oliphant play
"Clement" the following evening? Voysey
would be at the Eccentric Club till eleven, and
must know to-night.

He did not hesitate a second. To appear in
the piece himself would no longer imperil its
prospects, and now he would be able to show
what he could do in a leading part. His chance
had come. But this was not his paramount consciousness as he caught his breath. The thought
that intoxicated him was that he was required
to make passionate love to Blanche Ellerton.

Of course Rayne had an understudy—a novice

who was filling a minor rôle, and receiving two
pounds a week; and of course the aggrieved
understudy was almost the only person in the
theatre who was surprised that he wasn't called
upon to play the part now occasion arose.   The
understudy is frequently given cause for such
surprise.   But to substitute his unknown name
for a favourite's if it can be avoided would be
folly.   If *The Impostor* had been a success, Oliphant would not have been thought of either.
The receipts, however, did not warrant another
forty pounds being added to the salary list, and
the actor-author was chosen as a compromise
between a man with a reputation and the indignant tyro who had been praying that Rayne
might be taken ill ever since the dress-rehearsal.

Oliphant left the Eccentric Club with the part
in his pocket, and walked about among the blue
rep furniture of the Burton Crescent drawing-
room, studying, till four in the morning.   He
really knew the lines almost as well as Rayne
himself, and his chief anxiety was the "business."
He was now painfully alive to the importance of
his opportunity, and when he permitted himself
to realise that he was on the eve of appearing as
leading man in London he shook.

Mr. Voysey had written to all the principals
whose addresses he remembered, and early next

day telegrams were despatched to the rest. At
one o'clock Royce went through his scenes with
them—nobody doing more than murmur the
words—and then clothes had to be decided on,
and a visit made to Shaftesbury Avenue to
remedy defects; and his hair had to be trimmed,
and some dress-ties bought, and a moustache
selected; and dinner had to be swallowed—with
the part propped against the cruet—and shoes
had to be varnished, and his make-up box ex-
amined, and a portmanteau packed; and after
that he had to stretch himself on the sofa and
try to sleep, tortured by the thought that some
ghastly oversight would paralyse him when it
was too late.

When Edmund Kean walked into Drury Lane
Theatre "with Shylock's costume in a bundle on
his arm," he found it necessary to dress among
the supernumeraries; when Royce Oliphant
arrived at the Dominion, he was given the star
room, and Rayne's dresser, and all the appur-
tenances of a position that he hadn't won. On
the whole he thought he would rather have been
without them, though he appreciated the blessing
of a room to himself; he felt that if he made a
failure, he would look doubly foolish for the
grandeur. He was made up and dressed half
an hour before his first entrance, and lay back

in an armchair beside the mirror, listening to the vague sounds from the passages and stage that crept through his nerves. A first performance in a company that are already at home in their parts is a far greater ordeal to an actor than a first night. At a first night the nervousness is general, and the artists do not criticise one another; but when one actor alone is new to the piece, his nervousness is quadrupled by his fear of his companions' opinions.

"Curtain's up, sir!" remarked the dresser, returning with a box of cigarettes.

"Thank you," said Oliphant; "how long have I got now?"

"About twelve minutes—it's just on a quarter to nine when Mr. Rayne's called. Will you want anything after the first hact, sir?"

"Yes, you might get me a small bottle of stout. But for heaven's sake don't be late for my change!"

He lit a cigarette, and waited for the call-boy's summons. . . .

" 'Clement!' Mr. Rayne, sir!"

The wings seemed brighter and hotter than usual this evening; the glances that he caught looked anxious. He had still nearly two minutes. He walked round to the door in the canvas "flat" that he was to open, and stood listening intently. What was the prompter hanging about for? he knew what the cue was well enough! "Lady Plynlimmon's" voice thrilled him—she ought to get a laugh here. . . . Yes, it came! A line from "Maud," and it would be the instant for him to burst into speech and enter. "My God," he said, "help me!" The cue fell; and he turned the handle.

CHAPTER VIII

A FURTHER contrast to the Edmund Kean night was the fact that it *wasn't* "marvellous so few of them could kick up such a row," but the applause was hearty notwithstanding, and Oliphant left the theatre a happy man. He had succeeded; he knew it; and the cordial congratulations of the company buzzed in his ears. Naturally the success lacked the splendour it would have had on the night of the production, before rows of Press men; still it effected a great deal. *The Stage* gave him a glowing paragraph in the next issue; *The Era* was equally generous on Saturday; and *The Referee* sweetened his Sunday bloater by its hope that the managers would take care Mr. Royce Oliphant did not return to the provinces in a hurry—he had been hidden there too long.

These things mean that many people drop into the theatre who would not go otherwise; though, as the majority of them gain admission by the presentation of their cards, their attendance is of less value to the box-office than to the artist

they come to see. The dramatic-agents, for
instance, went to the Dominion; and those on
whose books Mr. Royce Oliphant's name was
not registered were loudest in advising him to
put his trust in them. Two offers of "leading
business" were made to him speedily; but one
was for a spring tour, and the other was to support an actress who was going to "star" in
America; and he held fast to his resolution to
remain in town. It looked as if he should be able
to do so now! At any rate he had obtained a
hearing, and he had been very fortunate.

He had, indeed, been more fortunate than he
quite realised, for not only had the opportunity
not come too late, but—what was nearly as important—it had not come too soon. Though he
had much to master still, he had now gained the
experience without which his talent could have
made little or no impression. He had conquered
the hardest of all histrionic tasks: he had learned
to convey emotion as well as to feel it. Many
other things he had had to learn: things unteach-
able, and things that he might have been taught
with ease—but which he had picked up with difficulty. The actor is taught nothing. When he
blunders at rehearsal, the stage-manager tells
him to "do it the other way," and he obeys; and
in a different situation the "other way" may be

a clumsy way. If he is astute and assiduous, and an enthusiast, he may, by acquiring one wrinkle from the part he plays in January, and another from the next, which he plays in June, know very nearly as much in five years of the "tricks" of the stage, as they are foolishly termed, as he could have been shown at a Conservatoire in three weeks. He has attained by this time qualities which no Conservatoire could have conferred, but he is like an author beginning to make effects with a language while he is still ignorant of its grammar.

However, Oliphant had profited more than most young men by the seven years that he had served for his Ideal, and such excellent accounts of his performance reached Herbert Rayne that the invalid suffered a twinge of professional jealousy. Royce himself was radiant. Miss Ellerton filled his thoughts—Miss Ellerton more than ever confused with her assumption of "Lady Maud Elstree"—and elation and love rendered these days the most delicious that he had known in his life.

When he had been playing "Clement" rather more than a week, he congratulated her one evening, during their first conversation.

"What about?" she inquired, opening surprised blue eyes.

"I'm told that Rayne will be able to come back very soon." He laughed. "You'll have somebody to act up to you again!"

"M-mm!" she said.

"You know you're relieved to hear it?"

"Am I?"

"Well, *aren't* you—truth?"

"What do you want to know for?"

"Because I'm so conceited; I want to be praised."

"Well—go and read your notices!"

"I could write them to you. Tell me; aren't you glad Rayne is coming back?"

"Look out," she exclaimed, starting forward; "there's my cue!"

He moved to the prompt-entrance, and watched her—a different woman in an instant, with dignity in her bearing and sorrow in her face. Familiar as he was with the environment, he was momentarily sensible of the strangeness of the thing. When they were both in the wings again—it was after the act-drop had fallen, and she was hurrying towards her dressing-room— she flashed a glance over her shoulder and threw him her answer:

"No—I'm sorry!" she said, with a smile that blinded him. He would have overtaken her, though she ran swiftly, but staggering scene-shifters intervened, and the walls of "Lady Plynlimmon's" dismembered mansion blocked his way. Behind the footlights all was chaos now, and there was his own change of costume to be made. The dresser said: "It's a good 'ouse to-night, ain't it, Mr. Holiphant?" but he scarcely heard the question, nor the depressed addendum that "No doubt a deal of it was piper!" He was engrossed by the knowledge that she would be "sorry," and that *he* would be sorry—sorrier even than he had understood.

But when he attempted to tell her so, she declined to be sentimental, and he returned to the dresser's ministrations sadly.

There was a card stuck in the looking-glass now, and he saw with surprise that the name on it was Otho Fairbairn. At the back was scribbled: "I'm in the stalls, and want to come round afterwards."

"Tucker," he said.

"Yes, sir."

"Tell the doorkeeper that when Mr. Fairbairn asks for me, he is to come in, please."

Oliphant was in his vest and trousers, removing his make-up, when Mr. Fairbairn was conducted to the room.

"Don't shake hands with me—I'm all vaseline," said Oliphant. "How are you, old man? When did you come back?"

"My dear fellow," cried Fairbairn, beaming, "you're perfectly 'immense'! I do congratulate you, upon my word! I didn't dream you had it in you. I say, you *are* going it, with your own piece, too! What did they cut it up for? I think it's very good. Well, how are you, eh?"

"I'm all right," said Oliphant; "awfully glad to see you again. Sit down somewhere—Tucker, clear a chair, will you? Have you come from Paris?"

"Yes; I was going to Cairo, but I don't think I shall. You've got to come and have supper with me at the club; I want to hear all the news, don't you know. Don't say you aren't free!"

His evident pleasure at the meeting would have been infectious even if the sight of his fair boyish face had not been agreeable to Oliphant always. He still looked so rosily, peacefully young; and his affectations were so innocent, because he was deceived by them himself. Perhaps because he was conscious of the weakness of his character, he was perpetually adopting a new one—for an hour or a season. A year or two before, the Turf had been the only thing worth living for—he avowed the opinion frankly, and gloried in it; but six months later he was attempting to demonstrate to his associates the hollowness of their pursuits and talking earnestly of the responsibilities of wealth, and the beauty of a self-sacrificing life in the East End. The phase lasted the entire autumn, and was succeeded by an interval of Schopenhauer-worship, in which he expressed his preference for solitude, with a pipe and his bookshelves, in such perfervid terms as to offend several of his dearest friends. Allusions to the latest character that he had resigned were received by him with disapproval; and the still eligible women whom he took down to dinner once in six months were frequently embarrassed by their doubt whether to approach him on the subject of Theosophy or golf.

One of the truest sentiments that he had uttered sprang to his girlish lips when he and Oliphant had supped, and, having lighted cigars, lolled opposite each other before a fire.

"I do envy your having an aim in life!" he exclaimed.

"Yes; it's a very good thing if your aim is true. It means a big disappointment if it isn't," said Oliphant, rather startled.

"It's a good thing anyhow, Royce. The secret of enjoyment is Endeavour and Purpose. Look at me—what *am* I? I'm miserable. I'll take my oath I'd change with a happy mechanic."

"Rot!" said Oliphant. "This is new, isn't it? You've always struck me as appreciating your advantages very thoroughly."

"What I want," said Fairbairn, emitting circlets of smoke and contemplating them, "is love, Royce. Believe me, everything else is a bubble. The happiest man isn't the wealthy man, or the famous man, but the man who has the love of a good woman. There's no blessing so great."

"No," said the lover; "no; there I'm with you."

"Mais cherchez la femme! Oof's a big drawback, old man. I never get a woman who cares for *me;* other chaps do! I want a big passion, Oliphant; I want a woman to renounce the world or something for me. I suppose there *are* women who renounce things for fellows? But damned if I see 'em! There are plenty to pretend, if I like to pay for the amusement—some want jewellery, and some want settlements—but I don't get near the middle lot who would love me if I were a Government clerk."

"Why don't you read for the Bar, or do something like that?" said Oliphant. "And you used to write; have you quite given that up?"

Fairbairn nodded. "Let's have a whisky-and-soda!" he said. "Yes; I get nothing but disillusions. I see a girl—beautiful girl; good family, nice figure, not a point to find fault with. Well,

perhaps I think I'd like to make that girl my
wife. But she wants to marry me. How can a
fellow fall in love with a girl who wants to marry
him? I was at the Opera Ball the night before
I left——"

"You didn't see her there, did you?"

"Don't chaff, old man—I feel very deeply on
the subject; I do, really. I say I was at the
Opera Ball the other night, and I saw another
girl—well, she'd the face of a goddess, a face to
die for! I can't tell you how intensely she affected
me as I watched her. She was standing alone;
but I didn't go over to her, because I knew that
to hear her speak would be disenchantment. It
struck me that that was typical of everything in
my life, Oliphant! Is this the Scotch, waiter?
Yes, the Scotch for *me*. I wrote some verses
when I got back to the hotel. 'Don't take off
your mask——' No! What is it? I forget the
beginning. . . . One of them goes like this—

"Do not speak, I pray, ma mignonne,
For 'Things are not what they seem',
And I know your voice would surely
Dissipate my drunken dream.
Muse a moment mutely so, dear,
With your cheek upon your hand,
While I worship what you are not—
What you would not understand!"

"It's very pretty," said Oliphant.

"I wish I could remember the rest," said Fairbairn more cheerfully; "I think the sadness underlying the cynicism is rather—— Eh? Oh, everything's a sell! The world's grown too old to be lively—how our sons will amuse themselves Heaven alone knows! Paris is a sell—where are the grisettes and the romance? When you expect the descriptions you've always received to be realised, they say, 'Ah, that *used* to be!' It never was in *my* time, though. And in New York, when you want to see the things you've heard of all your life, they say, 'Ah, that was *once!*' It seems to me you and I were born too late. I was at Brighton last season—I believe the most beautiful women in Europe were to be found at Brighton during the season 'once.' I said I should like to see one or two of them this time. 'Ah, people don't come here as they did!' *I'*m trying to find the place that exists *to-day*. But if I give Cairo a chance I know it'll be a fraud, and when I complain I shall be told, 'Ah, you're talking of twenty years ago!' "

"Is that why you are here?"

"Well, I should have seen your piece, anyhow; I meant to stay in town a night on purpose. I say, that girl who plays 'Maud,' Miss—what's her name?—is good-looking.   She's a clever actress, too."

"Miss Ellerton," said the actor, gazing at the fire.

"Yes, 'Ellerton,' that's it! Is she—er——"

"She's a very fine actress indeed, and a lady; and—and her father's a literary man," broke in Oliphant hurriedly.   "A charming family altogether."

"I suppose you meet everybody now, eh—all the celebrities?   It must be a change from the provinces, by Jove!   You'll go to the top of the tree with a rush, I expect.   Well, you deserve it!"

" 'Go to the top with a rush'—what are you talking about?   I'm likelier to be 'up a tree' than at the top of it; there are more difficulties in the way than you imagine."

"Oh, bosh!" said the other, with the easy assurance of the friend who knows nothing of the matter; "you're always so doubtful of yourself. You're miles ahead of half the best men in London.   You don't appear to be acting, that's what fetched me.   Why don't you take a theatre?"

"Why don't I what?" said Oliphant, staring.

"Why don't you take a theatre?" repeated Fairbairn in the tone in which he might have said, "Why don't you take a cab?" "It's the thing to do, isn't it? *I'll* go in with you."

"My dear fellow, do you regard me as the most conceited man of your acquaintance? It's very kind of you to suggest such a thing; but I shouldn't draw twopence, and I know it."

"You're a damned fool," said his host casually. "The men who get on are the chaps who don't know what modesty means. 'You must stir it, and stump it, and blow your own trumpet, or trust me you haven't a chance.' Wouldn't you like to have your own theatre, and play Hamlet? You used to talk enough about it, I remember. Bored us to death!"

"Ah," murmured Royce, "that's another question! Would I 'like it'? Oh yes, I'd 'like it.' I'd like to play Hamlet, and I'd like to have my own theatre. Both. Either. Whether I shall ever realise the dream—or half the dream—only the good gods know. Hamlet!—in London! . . ." He shook himself and laughed. "Oh, man, why send me home dissatisfied? I was rather puffed up by my present advance when I came."

"But I'm perfectly serious!" protested Fairbairn. "If you'd like to have a shot at a theatre, I'll go in with you. I won't make you any presents—you needn't be afraid of that. We'll

do it on commercial lines. We'll find out the
square thing, and——"

Oliphant extended his hand, with a flush on his
face. "You're a trump, Otho!" he exclaimed:
"you're a friend in a million! The idea is preposterous, I assure you. It's—it's years too
soon; one takes a theatre when one has a following. But—well, you're a pal!"

He did not make his way towards home "dissatisfied," nevertheless. The proposal, wild as
it was, had excited him temporarily; and with
the effervescence of fancy, his mood was gay.
London—already the City of Recollections to
him—pulsed with promise. Overhead the stars
were brilliant, and an artificial radiance tinged
the puddles on the road. In the stillness of
Southampton Row his reverie broke into voice:
" 'O, speak again, bright angel!' " he cried; and
an unexpected policeman scrutinised him as he
passed. Heavens, how absurd he was! But he
returned to Bloomsbury for a moment only, and
in the next he was under the balcony again, where
Blanche Ellerton leant as Juliet. And he spoke
Romeo's lines—beyond the hearing of the policeman—until he trembled at the Burton Crescent
door.

"Mr. Rayne will resume the part to-morrow
evening." There was no exultance in his mood

then. Could he ever have exulted? The theatre
has heartaches "peculiarly its own"—which was
the phrase by which Mrs. Ellerton habitually
described the grace of her heroines. To see a
part that has been played during months by the
woman he loves represented by her successor
means a heartache to an actor; and a bad heartache, accentuated by every familiar line the new-
comer delivers—in such different tones from the
voice he is used to hear. Often she wears the
same frocks—which are eloquent to him by asso-
ciation—and mocks him with a poignant resemblance to the woman who is miles away, or dead,
until she turns her face. Perhaps this is the
worst. It hurts, though, on the eve of leaving
the company himself to act with a girl who is
dear to him. To-morrow night the story will
be played again—she will be listening as she is
listening now; only, he will be absent, and another man will speak the words to her instead.
No child sits in the dress-circle to whom the
scenery says so much as to the young actor who
is bidding it good-bye at a time like this; he tries
to impress the picture on his brain, that not a
detail may be missing from his memory of her,
and feels for the rooms of canvas all the tenderness with which one quits a home.

Certainly Royce would retain the advantage

of being the author—he could still talk to Miss Ellerton during her waits, as he had done before the eventful Monday; but when he entered the Dominion for his last performance there he was wretched.

As the piece progressed, sentimentality swayed him wholly. He might never act with her any more. He felt as if he were falling from heaven to a blank. Each minute was precious, and he would have caught it and prevented its escape. The result might have been foretold, though it was unpremeditated—he confessed in the love-scenes all that he longed to confess in the wings; and in the situation where he had to clasp her to him in despair, and swear he wouldn't let her go, he lost control of himself in reality. The approval of the audience was ardent—there was the loudest round of applause that had been heard in the house since *The Impostor* was produced. But when Oliphant led Miss Ellerton before the curtain and they made their bows, they didn't look at each other.

"May I speak to you?" he said presently, when she came downstairs dressed to leave the theatre.

"Mr. Oliphant?"

"Yes, I've been waiting to speak to you; I can't go without speaking to you." Yet for a moment he could find nothing to say. "You know, don't you? Blanche, I love you!"

She was at the foot of the staircase. The stage was so dark now that her pale face was indistinct; he could see little more than that it was hers. "Do you care for me at all? If I get on, will you marry me?" Some of his life seemed to leave his mouth with the last question. He touched her hand diffidently—there was a glove on it, and the cold suède chilled him. "Blanche?"

After a long silence she said:

"You've surprised me very much. I—— Oh, no; I don't mean to marry for years and years!"

"Why not?" he asked in a dreary voice.

"It would hamper me frightfully. And besides——"

"And besides I'm nothing to you?"

"Oh, you're not to say that," she returned; "you're a friend; and I hope you'll keep one. Our friendship has been so charming and so interesting, hasn't it? It would be simply horrid if we could never talk together again just because of this." She smiled. "You will forget, I'm sure."

"No," he said, "I shan't forget. If—if I remember long enough—if I succeed—will there be a chance for me then?"

"Oh," she exclaimed, "but I'm not going to

marry for years and years and years, I tell you! Marriage is a mistake for a young girl in the profession, unless she marries somebody very influential."

"But—but if you loved me, Blanche?"

"Don't let us talk nonsense; very likely I shan't marry at all; I shall live and die an old maid. Can you see me? with a cap, and pepper-and-salt ringlets! . . . We *shall* remain friends, shan't we? I must say 'Good-night'—I've my train to catch."

"May I walk to the station with you?"

"Yes, if you like. But you're not to be foolish, mind!"

They passed through the passage and turned into the Strand—which was henceforth to have to him yet another memory. The bright decision of her tones at once intensified his suffering, and precluded the possibility of his finding further words; he did not disobey her verbally. On the Temple platform he closed the door of the first-class compartment that she selected, and yearned at her with wide eyes through the glass till the train rushed on. She was praying meanwhile that it would be quick to start, for she held only a third-class ticket.

Now she was gone. The line was empty; and he moved heavily away into the street.

CHAPTER IX

HE determined not to go near the Dominion for a week, and it was two days before he did go. Then he denied himself the stage-door and went into the dress-circle. It was delicious pain. It is, of course, desirable to bear "the pangs of despised love" for any woman—"the beautiful time when one was so unhappy" cannot, in fact, be repeated too often—but to be wretched for an actress is best of all; the emotion is richer and more varied than being miserable for a girl in Society. A man refused by a girl in Society, for example, cannot feast his eyes on her features and get intoxicated on the sweetness of her voice for two hours and a half without her knowing he is there. Oliphant availed himself of the opportunities of his position for a fortnight to the fullest extent.

That he did not avail himself of them longer was because they temporarily ceased to exist. *The Impostor* was withdrawn, and Miss Ellerton, like himself, was out of an engagement. In her advertisements in *The Era* she called it "resting."

He now regretted that he had not gone "behind" oftener after the evening of his declaration. He could see her from the dress-circle when she played another part; but when would he be able to stand beside her in the wings again? Perhaps never!

Fortunately there were other matters to occupy his mind. Excepting that enough remained of the hundred pounds to spare him pecuniary anxiety, his situation really appeared much the same as before *The Impostor* was produced. That his performance of "Clement" had borne good fruit he knew; but the fruit was not ripe— or he could not reach it. Momentarily he seemed no better off than if there had not been any fruit at all. The Press had said that the London managers ought to snap him up; but they didn't. Nobody displayed the least eagerness to prevent his returning to the provinces; the agents talked about the provinces as persistently as ever. Much better parts, much better salaries, were offered to him, but always for tour.

Then at last he did obtain an engagement in the West End; and once more the criticisms he received were excellent; but the piece had as short a run as his own, and he was not needed for the next. All the same he might now have remained in town. He was not wanted as a hero, because so many of the theatres are in the hands of actor-managers, who are their own heroes; but he could have remained in town, and earned ten or even fifteen pounds a week before the year ended, for there are very few professions better paid than the stage when once one turns the corner. His stumbling-block was love.

It happened that in the Green Room Club, one afternoon, he met Rayne. Rayne had lost a good deal of money by Oliphant's drama; and as "The Great *Dominion* Success," he was hoping it would put something back in his pocket by means of an autumn tour. There were about half a dozen dramas "on the road" at this time described as "The Great *Dominion* Success"; some of them had run there a whole month.

"How are you?" he said. "I was just going to drop you a line about the play. I suppose you wouldn't care to go out with it?"

"Oh, no; I don't want to go on tour," said Oliphant.

"Well, it's for the autumn, you know; everybody will be on tour in the autumn. I go on tour myself, with Erskine."

"Oh, *you* don't go out with it then?"

"I can't afford it—I can't afford to throw

away a big salary, my boy. No, I'm sending it
out with the cheapest company I can get together. It occurred to me that it might be worth
your while to play 'Clement' for the sake of the
piece. The better it goes, the better for you
as the author."

"Humph!" said Oliphant.

"If it does well, there are your fees for years;
if it does badly, that's the end of it—short, sharp,
and decisive. I've no more money to lose, I can
tell you; by George, the Dominion nearly ruined
me!"

"The cheapest company you can get together?"
said Oliphant ruefully. "*The Impostor* wants
acting; it won't play to great business with a
cheap crowd, I'm afraid."

"It must take its chance. I did all I could for
it here, and then what was the business like? I
haven't got back the hundred I put down on the
contract. I'm not sure the wisest course wouldn't
be to accept the loss and let the whole thing slide;
I'm not sure of it by any means!"

Oliphant looked round the room without
speaking. It was Saturday and the tables were
already laid for the house-dinner, though it was
only three o'clock. A few actors were playing
poker near the small fire-place; a few others
lounged by the big one, puffing cigarettes; but

not many members were present yet—the room
would fill after the matinées finished.

Rayne shifted his cigar between his teeth, and
continued with elaborate carelessness:

"Of course 'Clement' and 'Maud' *ought* to be
in good hands—and 'Maud' I've got. If you
had seen your way to play 'Clement' at very low
terms, I think the tour would have been safe."

"You've got 'Maud'?" asked Oliphant.
"What's she like?"

"Oh, Miss Ellerton goes out with the piece;
I've managed that. I thought you knew."

He knew perfectly that he did *not* know; he
had been leading up to the announcement from
the beginning of the conversation. That Oliphant had been in love with Blanche Ellerton,
and that Blanche Ellerton might have been fond
of Oliphant, had meant a possibility of obtaining
two good artists at much less than their ordinary
salaries. He had been on the stage too long to
overlook it. With the girl, however, he had
failed; she did not reduce her terms a pound when
he mentioned that Mr. Oliphant—whom he had
not seen then—had "practically settled with
him." Oliphant, therefore, would have to reduce
his tremendously! In his heart, indeed, Rayne
was a shade sorry for Oliphant. "Still, as Ellerton was engaged at her own figure, it was only

fair that some of it should be contributed by her mash!" That was how he put it afterwards to the lady he loved.

"All right," said Oliphant, "I'll go. How much do you want to pay?"

"My dear boy," answered Rayne, "I'm ashamed to tell you. Upon my soul I am!"

He overcame his reluctance; and even the lover started before he said "Yes." However, he did say "Yes." He would have said "Yes" to thirty shillings a week in view of the inducement offered. On tour with Blanche! He walked down Bedford Street intoxicated by the prospect.

To the ordinary person there would seem little that is attractive in a mode of life that involves occupying different lodgings every six days, and undertaking a railway journey to another town every Sunday, and indeed Oliphant had come to dislike it himself; but a goddess can change discomfort to delight as easily as a fairy turns a pumpkin into a chariot.

The tour commenced at Northampton on the August Bank Holiday. The evenings, of course, were much the same as the evenings at the Dominion; but now there was no need to wait until evening for a glimpse of Miss Ellerton. Almost every fine morning, if he were patient

enough, he could be certain of meeting her in the
Drapery; and then what more natural than that
he should accompany her on her way? Occasionally they forsook the shop-windows—the
shop-windows of Northampton are not the most
alluring—and wandered through Hardingstone
Fields, where there is nothing to remind the
pedestrian of shoe manufactories and pork-pies,
and the country is as sylvan as if there were not
a chimney within a hundred miles.

From Northampton *The Impostor* proceeded
to Leicester, but the name, the industry, of the
town they happened to be in was really of very
slight consequence to the players. Whether the
chief thoroughfare was called the "Drapery" or
the "High Street," whether the theatre was
known as the "Royal" or the "Grand," their
habits and the pursuits remained the same. A
touring actor's world moves with him on Sunday.
On Monday when he wakes up in another city,
his surroundings are to all intents and purposes
what they were in the last city the day before.
The characteristics of the streets impress him
very little—he views so many new streets—and
the myriad dwellings contain nothing but strangers to him wherever he may be. The population
is merely the "public," whose raison d'être is
to go to see the "show." His friendships, his

quarrels, his interests are in the theatrical company in which he is engaged.

The drama did not attract the provincial playgoers in large numbers, but the author was not severely chagrined. So long as he could saunter beside Blanche Ellerton in the morning, and now and again call upon her in the afternoon, he was able to pardon the box-office record. The afternoon visits, indeed, with tea in the twilight, were the rarest privileges of all, and by and by they held moments in which he was convinced it wasn't conceited to feel that she was fond of him.

And he was right. When this conviction convulsed him it was the middle of October. For nearly three months they had been constantly in each other's society. They had been in each other's arms on the stage at night, and walked and talked together during the day. When the towns afforded opportunities, they had made little excursions—to the Castle from Leamington; to Jesmond Dene from Newcastle-on-Tyne. Because he was curious about her Juliet, they had read the Balcony Scene together in her lodgings; her Juliet perhaps would not have pleased him quite so much if it had been anybody's else, but then her ambition did not lie in the direction of Shakespeare and blank verse. He had shown her he adored her in the most flattering way—

by endeavouring to conceal it in obedience to her command. She was a very practical young woman; she had erected as many "warnings" for her guidance through life as disfigure Hampstead Heath; but, being a woman and young, it was not astonishing that her feelings should have trespassed.

She did not succumb to the weakness without a struggle, and she mourned the circumstances by which the weakness was caused. She had always hoped to marry an influential man possessing a large income; influential, because she did not wish to contract a marriage that would necessitate her leaving the theatre, but longed for notoriety; possessing a large income, because she loved luxury—more, had a passion for it; thirsted to see her figure in silk petticoats and satin corsets, and to let them fall to the floor indifferently when she undressed, since she had so many of them; wanted to lie in a perfumed bath, and have her maid bring her chocolate; and be surprised by a friend as she nestled over her bedroom fire in a wrapper that cost more than her best frocks today. It had been her aim to avoid any errors of judgment that would increase her difficulties; and now she had been idiotic enough to become fond of an actor without reputation or means. Yes, Blanche Ellerton regretted having signed for the tour of *The Impostor* very keenly when she was calm; only she was not always calm, and these moments in which she yielded to sentiment were as exquisite to herself as to the man she loved.

Nevertheless she had no intention of yielding to it unreservedly, and she wondered if it would take her long to forget him when they separated; if the nonsensical ache would be bad to bear. The tour was drawing to a close, and after it finished, of course, they would scarcely meet. That was well! Perhaps he might come out to Earl's Court once or twice, but not oftener certainly. Once or twice couldn't be helped. If she had not asked him to call when they were at the Dominion, however, she need never have seen him again at all. How stupid she had been to ask him! Still she had acted from business motives; he had been very taken with her, and how could she know but what he might have another play produced in London soon? Yes, she had been quite right—that she would be a fool about him later was a thing she couldn't foresee. She stretched her arms above her head and yawned. Heigho, these beastly rooms!

Oh, she was dull! What a shame it was that a woman like herself should be moped in poky lodgings, and have to buy two-and-elevenpenny house-shoes! And she had such pretty feet! Royce would . . . yes, Royce would like her feet. . . . How ridiculously he thought of her! —and she had really been quite candid that night when he popped. Perhaps not quite so candid since. When one liked a man, of course one did, naturally, take a little pose of—— ˙Well, one sympathetically adopted his favourite key. A woman, though, would have known her for ever after that night. . . . Men were very much nicer than women. If—— He was a darling! Why wasn't she a woman who could afford to be absurd? it would be lovely to marry him! Wouldn't it be *lovely?* She wasn't yearning now, she was smiling. The street-door bell rang, and she quivered with a hope which she felt to be childish, for he never came unless he was invited.

It *was* his voice! She sprang up, and dragged the powder-puff from her pocket, and pulled at her favourite curl, and threw herself back in a graceful position before he had wiped his boots.

"Come in," she said languidly. Then on a note of surprise: "*You?*"

"Am I in the way?" asked Oliphant, his eyes devouring her. "I've had good news, and I—I wanted to tell you about it."

"Good news? No; sit down, do! What is it?"

"It's an offer."

"For London?"

"Yes, more! I go to the Pantheon. Greatorex offers me Faust!"

It does not merit contempt that her first emotion was a pang of jealousy; or, if you must be contemptuous, despise human nature and not Blanche Ellerton. It was inevitable that she should be envious. For an actor to be chosen from the provinces to play "seconds" to Greatorex—to create such a part as Faust before a first-night audience at the Pantheon—was almost the highest conceivable compliment. *The Impostor* company had been shaken to the core recently when the whisper ran round the dressing-rooms that "Greatorex was in front." They had watched him from the wings, and acted at him from the stage; they had all—even to the humblest among them—dreamed their dreams in secret for a day or two and pictured the opening of a note that would mean that their abilities were recognised at last. And the unlikely honour of an "offer" from Greatorex *had* fallen —but on *him;* and she remained where she was.

"I am so glad," she murmured. "Well, you are simply made now ?"

"I'm on the road, I think," he said. "I ought never to look back after this if I'm all right in the part. Of course I'm already quaking with the ghastly misgiving that I *shan't* be found all right."

"What nonsense! Besides, it will be all Mephistopheles, you may be sure." She couldn't help saying that, and after it was uttered she felt more generous towards him. "You'll be a success," she added; "I'm certain of it. I'll come and see you."

"Will you? Not the first night? Good heavens, how nervous I shall be!"

"I don't suppose I could get seats for the first night if I tried. You may send me a couple if you like; but I daresay you won't be able to get them either. I say, you *will* be a swell now; how you'll look down on us poor people!"

Oliphant laughed, with a reproach on his face. "If I'm anxious to get on, it's that you may like me better."

"What a cruel thing to say!" she replied, smiling. "And what a story, too! Didn't you want to get on before we knew each other?"

"Not so much."

"Now you're making fun of me—that's unkind. When did you hear? You must tell me all about it!"

She did not want to talk herself yet; she wanted to think. She looked musingly at the "Weighing of the Deer," surmounted by a Japa-

nese fan, between the windows. The question in
her mind was, How much difference did this piece
of luck make? Common-sense answered "None,"
firmly. His engagement might be a thing of
the past in six months, and have left him just
what he was now, excepting that for the rest of
his life he would pepper his conversation with
inapposite remarks, beginning, "That reminds
me of an experience I had when I was with
Greatorex." No, it could make no difference
to anybody who wasn't a love-sick girl eager to
find an excuse for being silly! A few months'
rapture. And the price? Two-and-elevenpenny
slippers to the day she died; a cheap existence
burdened with babies, and enlivened by the
perusal of panegyrics passed on the women who
had outstripped her in the race!

"Supposing," said Oliphant, "I get good
notices, and I remain there for the next production, and for years?"

"I hope you will."

"It would be a grand engagement—one could
scarcely hope for anything finer."

"You'd have been very fortunate indeed."

He left his seat, and went over to her side.

"You said if you married, it would have to be
a successful man. Blanche, I *am* succeeding;

and with *you*—— Oh, we should go right to the top together!"

She bit her lip, and her eyelids fell.

"Blanche—may I call you Blanche?"

"Yes," she said, almost inaudibly.

"Blanche, my darling, be kind to me! Oh, marry me, for God's sake—now, to-morrow! Let's risk everything! You shall never regret it. I swear you shan't! Will you?"

She shook her head; she didn't wish to trust her voice again just yet.

"Don't you like me at all?" he demanded impetuously. "Not a little bit?" Her silence continued, but her head was motionless. He dropped on to the stool beside her armchair and seized her hands, and showered kisses on them till she snatched them away because they were playing her false.

"Oh, be sensible!" she exclaimed. "In a year we should hate each other!"

"I would worship you! You don't know me if you think I could ever love you less."

"I know myself. I wasn't meant for domesticity in the back-parlour—I wasn't meant for domesticity at all. I'm an artist; I've my own life to live, my own ambitions to satisfy. I want to be paragraphed, and interviewed, and photographed, and run after. You couldn't give me

one of these things I want. I know it—I know it
as well as if I'd been your wife ten years. Quite
the reverse! You'd make everything more difficult for me—impossible for me! If you do get
on, what then? What good will it do *me?*"

"I'd buy the world for you!"

"With good intentions? You can never be a
rich man, my dear boy——and if you marry, you
will always be a poor one. You may succeed—
I think you *will* succeed—but your success will
mean a name, not a fortune. Then what have
you to offer for spoiling my career? Am I to be
content to sit in the stalls all my life, and hear
you applauded?" She beat the treacherous hands
in her lap, the bitterer because she was fighting
against her heart. "What can any ordinary man
offer a girl who has a future without him? Marriage is all very well for women with no profession—as a Home for the Helpless—they were
nonentities anyhow. But what does it give to
a woman like me in return for all it costs? *I*
don't need to be presented with shelter. I should
be a lunatic!"

"Plenty of married women have been famous
actresses," urged Royce; "very few famous
actresses *haven't* married. And I may have a
theatre one day; I know a man who would help
me."

She had small faith in the man.

"Do you think marriage made the struggle any easier for them?" she retorted.

"Yes, I do, if their husbands loved them, and could sympathise with their ideas. Besides, to be an artist, a woman *must* love!"

"Yes," she said, "but to be a poor man's wife she must be a fool."

He choked with mortification and pain.

"You care nothing about me, of course, or you couldn't argue so."

"No," she said, inwardly triumphant, "I suppose that's true."

He left, cursing the vanity by which he had deceived himself. And she bit a hole in her handkerchief and cried.

CHAPTER X

THEY spoke together in the wings briefly that evening; indeed for two or three evenings there was restraint between them. Perhaps it would have lasted longer, but on Saturday night he happened to hear that by a chapter of accidents she had been unable to arrange for apartments in the next town and would have to look for some when she arrived. Even the worst-paid members of a theatrical company engage their rooms by letter; for the trifling reduction in the rent that may be obtained by a personal application does not compensate for the dreariness of tramping from address to address after a long journey until a vacant lodging is found. He begged her to take his. She refused; and "vowing she would ne'er consent, consented."

As it was now Oliphant who had no rooms and no dinner awaiting him, the lady insisted that he should dine with her and share the chicken which he had been the one to order. The circumstances precluded formality, and the estrangement was at an end. He was thankful that it had been a chicken. It might easily have been half a pound of steak, which would have been awkward.

Still he was resolved never to revert to the subject of his love for her again; and he kept his resolution so well that she grew hungry for the music of the tale tabooed. Perhaps that was why she did not hesitate when he suggested another excursion. It may not have been so, but even if it was, her inconsistency was equalled by his own, for this excursion that he meditated was a veritable sentimental journey, aggravated by the proposed companionship.

A few miles distant lay a country town which was intimately associated with his boyhood. He had gone there with his father seventeen years ago, and never seen it since. He had scarcely seen it, in fact, when he bade it good-bye, for he had bidden good-bye to his first sweetheart at the same time, and been blind with tears. The maiden had been twelve, and he a stout thirteen. During a long heartache he had made abortive efforts to paint the scene of this early romance in water-colours on cartridge paper. He failed, not because his memory of the spot had weakened, but because he had never painted anything hitherto excepting a dog kennel. The best picture was the intangible one that disappeared when he woke; for he dreamed of arriving at the little station, and surprising Mary Page in the orchard—her name was Mary Page—vividly and often; and he could never eat his breakfast on the morning after the dream occurred, so sick was he with the longings of his little soul, the craving for the sight of Mary Page's plaits. He now found himself as a man in the vicinity of the place for which he had yearned so desperately as a child, and he wanted to look at it again with Blanche Ellerton by his side.

They had an hour's journey, for the train travelled with intense deliberation, and stopped at every opportunity. At last, however, they arrived, and Royce, who discovered that the hallowed station had been enlarged, inquired the way to some wooden steps.

"There are some wooden steps leading to a road with a hedge on each side, aren't there?" he asked.

He was told there were not, and was disconcerted.

"If there aren't," he said to Miss Ellerton, "I'm afraid it's a failure. There were two houses in a private lane, but I don't know what the lane was called—I don't think it was called anything. The houses were Mowbray Lodge and Rose Villa. *I* lived at Mowbray Lodge. I could walk there blindfolded from the top of those steps. They should be just here—I've stood on them a thousand times, and watched the sails of a windmill go round."

"Did your First Love lean there with you?" asked the actress; "it sounds like it."

"No, I don't remember her there; she was always in the orchard opposite the two houses."

"Eating green apples!"

"They were ripe—and the best apples I've ever tasted. Here's somebody else! There are," he repeated, "some wooden steps close by, lead- ing to a road with a hedge on each side, aren't there?"

"Lord love yer," answered the native, "there ain't been no steps 'ere this ten year!" He seemed to think the question very foolish, and continued his way.

"Rip Van Winkle, the steps have vanished," said Miss Ellerton. "What next?"

Royce pondered, and looked about him.

"Well, the road can't be gone, at any rate," he said. "Perhaps it's at the top of this slope? I didn't notice we were on a slope, did you? Shall we try?"

She thought it a good idea; and the road was there.

"Ha," cried the young man radiantly, "how

it all comes back to me! I hear my own moun-
tain-goats bleating aloft, and know the sweet
strain that the corn-reapers sing. But I'm sorry
they've taken away those steps! We go over
the bridge, and the lane is on the right. Isn't it
pretty? I wish we'd come in summer, though!"

"It's very pretty now," she said.

The entrance to the lane occurred unexpect-
edly, at least to her; the low wall above which the
trees waved made a quick curve, and was lost
in a laurel-bush. Oliphant urged her forward
joyously, and then they were on the other side
of the wall, and opposite a gate which divided
them from a weed-grown carriage-drive. He
said: "Mowbray Lodge!" And when he lifted
the growth of encroaching creeper, the name was
indeed visible—which was to him like a kiss from
the past. After a minute they came to another
house, also lying back from the lane behind a gate
and carriage-drive; and this time he said "Rose
Villa!"

"Are you satisfied?" she smiled.

"I am sad," he declared quite truthfully,
though a moment before he had been delighted.
"Do you see that fence? It separates the Mowbray Lodge and Rose Villa gardens. It was
across that fence I first saw her. Come, I'll show
you the orchard that I used to try to paint. But

—oh, this is quite different! None of that glass was there; it was all open—it had nothing, nothing at all, except the apple-trees and two children. Look, there's a man in his shirt-sleeves, digging. Let's go over to him!"

The ground had been acquired by Mr. 'Obbs, the florist in the 'Igh Street, they learnt; and both the houses were to let. "Page"? Yes, the man remembered the name of Page. The father had been a doctor, hadn't he? They had been gone—oh, a matter of nine years.

"I believe you're sorry you came," said Miss Ellerton gaily. "Did you expect to find Mary waiting for you?"

"It would have been romantic to find her living here still, wouldn't it? Though, of course, she wouldn't have known me. But I don't think it's Mary I'm melancholy about so much as——"

"As what?"

He sighed. "I don't know—it's so pathetic to be 'grown up.' "

She accepted it as a jest, and laughed; but he had spoken quite seriously. Thoughts of his childhood crowded on him. His father used to stroll along this lane in the sunset, with a pipe between his lips. There was no sunset now, and the lips were cold, but the dead day lived again to Oliphant. His sweetheart, Mary with the

golden plaits, must be—how old? Nine-and-
twenty! He realised it with a shock. If it had
been nineteen! But nine and twenty! There
was tragedy in the difference between such an age
and twelve. And the boy he recalled so tenderly,
where was *he?* Gone too. He would have loved
to commune with him, as the boy had always
looked forward to his doing. How beautiful a
comrade! But life was so large, and the boy
had been lost, somewhere among the years, and
was only a memory.

"At this point," said Miss Ellerton, "an extraordinary thing happens! You see the figure
of a young and lovely woman in a contemplative
attitude. And she is Mary Page revisiting her
old home. It would act well. Could you play
the scene?"

"The heroine would speak first," said Royce,
rousing himself. "What would she say?"

"Oh, she begins with a question. She says:
'Excuse me, but can you tell me if there is a
caretaker here?—I see the house is to let.'"

" 'I am a stranger,'" answered Oliphant; "I
am sorry I don't know.'"

" 'I saw you coming from the garden. I
fancied perhaps——'"

" 'I've been guilty of trespassing. I knew that
garden well once; I couldn't pass it by.'"

" '*You* knew it? You?' "

" 'Dr. Page lived here in the days I speak of.' "

" 'Dr. Page was my father's name.' "

" 'Your father? *Mary!* Oh, forgive me! But —am I quite forgotten?' "

" 'You—are—Royce—Oliphant? Oh, this is wonderful indeed!' "

They looked in each other's eyes and laughed together. Then a shadow crossed the girl's face, and she said half playfully, half in earnest:

"I do believe that's just what you'd really like!"

"What is?"

"To see Mary here and make love to her. But I daresay she's fat and ugly, and you'd be disappointed."

"She had a beautiful nature," said Oliphant. "I hope *that* hasn't got ugly."

"A 'beautiful nature'—a brat of twelve! What did she do—always give you the lemon-peel off her cake? I should look for her and marry her if I were you."

"I expect she married long ago. Why have you turned cross all of a sudden?"

"Cross?" she echoed with amazement. "I'm not in the least cross. . . . Only this is rather dull, you know, standing about a wet lane and pretending to be somebody else."

"Why," he cried, paling, "it was you who suggested that! If I'd guessed it bored you——
Let's go! I'm ever so sorry."

"I don't want to go; I'm tired. I want," she said imperiously, "to sit down on that bench, and have some buns and lemonade."

"Won't you come and have some tea?"

"No, thank you," she said. . . . "Well, shall we go home?"

"Will you stay here half an hour alone?"

"What for?"

"As well as I remember there isn't a shop anywhere near; but if you don't mind waiting, I'll race into the town."

"Very well," she assented. "I'll wait for you."

Although the task that she had set him was a troublesome one to fulfil, and though she looked triumphant when he returned in a heat to minister to her requirements, she ate only a fragment of bun, and sipped but little of the lemonade. This puzzled him very much. He decided, at last, that she must have grown faint during the delay; and he said so. And then she seemed to smile involuntarily, which puzzled him more. However, her amiability was restored.

Presently she said in a careless tone:

"What do you call a 'beautiful nature'? I mean in a woman?"

"I don't follow you."

"You used the expression about something. Oh yes! You said that that child had a beautiful nature, that was it!"

"Well, it's rather difficult to define," replied Oliphant.

"You mean 'unpractical,' I suppose?"

"Say 'unworldly.'"

"It's the same thing—let's keep to 'unpractical'! Why—why should men look down on a woman for being practical? They don't look down on one another, do they?"

"I don't think it's true that they do look down on her."

"Yes, it is," she said; "they want women to be fools."

"Only men who are fools themselves."

"Do you think *you're* a fool?"

"I *don't* want women to be fools."

"But you despise a girl for being sensible."

"I don't know what you mean." He was beginning to be troubled.

"You do," she said with a catch in her voice. "You despise *me!*"

The gardener in his shirt-sleeves had disappeared. Where they sat, Oliphant could see nothing but the trees and her distress. Emotion for an instant held him dumb; but it was for an instant only.

Then it was she who was troubled by the blaze she had made, though warmed at the same time by the ardour of it.

"No, no," she said, "I told you it was impossible."

"But you shall—you shall! I won't let you go till you say 'Yes.'"

"You are mad to want me. I'm a piece of stone."

"I'd kiss you into life if you were!"

"I'm not good enough for you. Oh, believe, believe I'm not!"

"My God, there's nobody on earth like you! Tell me you love me."

"I don't!"

"You do! and you shall say it. Tell me!"

"No."

"Tell me you love me!"

"I'm stronger than you think—I won't!"

He began to fear that she never would; and indeed she did not say it. But the next second her face turned whiter, and she flung her arms round his neck. And after all they were engaged.

CHAPTER XI

AND the moment when she first regretted it was seven hours later, after the candle was out, when she lay thinking. But the next morning, when she was in his arms, she was reckless again and happy.

They did not love each other, but both were violently *in* love, and thought they did. But the woman's self-knowledge was at least greater than the man's, and she knew that there could never be any person in the world whom she loved quite so dearly as herself. Therefore she was exigent and imperious, and if he had been less infatuated, would have appeared unreasonable in the demands she made upon his time; for she wished to stifle the knowledge and the voice of wisdom, and when he was with her she succeeded.

As he asked no better than to be with her all day long, it was only when the candle was out that the voice of wisdom had a listener.

And then she argued with it, and said that it was maligning her, and that she was a much nicer

girl than it knew.   It was a fact that she was
forsaking her faith, but since it had been a false
faith she was acting wisely to desert it.   She was
converted!

Of course at home they wouldn't rejoice!   She
hesitated to write the news; and then decided to
write it quickly, so that they might have time to
accustom themselves to the idea before she saw
them.   It would mean more novelettes, or increased economy; she wasn't going to continue
to help them after she was married—it wouldn't
be fair to Royce.   A woman's first duty was to
her husband.   Besides, it would be horrid to
have to admit to him that her people were in
such straitened circumstances.   No; Royce, poor
boy, was burdening his back to win her—every
shilling that she earned belonged to *him!* . . .
Mother—who would feel the difference most—
would behave best about it.   Father would
advise her to take years to make up her mind,
and be doubly disagreeable to mother.   Gertrude?   Gertrude would be jealous of her as
usual.   On the whole the house would be none
too pleasant during her engagement; she was
sorry she had to return to it. . . . How Royce,
though, would loathe taking her salary, the dear!
And going to the Pantheon as he was, he could
certainly do without it—at all events if she didn't

have a baby. Probably he would refuse to touch
a penny of it and tell her to keep it for pocket-
money. Really their life would be quite charming! With nothing to do with her salary but
buy frocks and hats—— And then Royce would
want to give her frocks and hats as well! Oh,
she was glad, glad she was being brave, and
marrying for love—God had been very good to
her!

The Impostor company disbanded at St. Pancras a few Sundays later. Sunday was additionally tedious to her and Oliphant now, for—the
men and women being divided when they
travelled—this was the day on which they saw
least of each other. When St. Pancras was
gained, the lovers had not spoken together for
more than two minutes during three hours. Oliphant hurried to her compartment at once.
There were general handshakes amid the clamour
for cabs. Many of the company who had become
staunch friends would not meet again for years,
as has been said before, and names and faces
alike would be forgotten; but this afternoon they
were still comrades, and the men exclaimed: "Ta,
ta, dear boy! I suppose you turn up in the
Strand?" and the women kissed one another
affectionately, and repeated, "Now, mind you
write!"

Royce and the girl stood on the platform con-
ferring. It had been arranged that he should
not go out to Earl's Court before the morrow;
but all at once both felt the manner of their
parting to be melancholy, and he begged that
instead of their separating at the station, she
would at least let him drive some of the way with
her. She said "yes" readily enough, so he had
his own luggage deposited in the cloak-room, and
got into her hansom.

Needless to say, she had made use of her
powder-puff before the train stopped; and she
was one of the women who knew how to tie a
veil. She put on her gloves well, too. She could
not help their quality, but she didn't commit the
infamy of buying them tight, and skipping the
first button. Women's hands were meant to be
squeezed, but she knew they were not meant to
be squeezed into gloves. Oliphant took Blanche
Ellerton's hand, and thought what a wonderful
thing it was to be a woman. There was no power
like it! What a delicate little nose she had; and
how tempting her lips were under the net!

"Darling!" he said; "put your veil up."

"Oh, I can't! People would see us."

"The street's empty; look!"

So for ten seconds she put up her veil.

"I've been miserable all the journey," he said.

She confessed coquettishly that she also had found it dull; and after he had rhapsodised:

"I wish this fellow wouldn't drive so fast!" he exclaimed; "I don't know how I shall get through this evening. *You*'ll have your people; but *I* shall have nothing—only your likenesses."

" 'Only' indeed! Give 'em back to me if you don't appreciate them."

"Oh, you know what I mean!"

"Do I?"

"I shall spend the time writing you a letter."

"Silly Billy! You won't? Not really?"

"I believe I shall! Blanche, you're quite sure they won't make obstacles to-morrow when I come? You won't keep me waiting a year for you?"

"Is a year long?" she murmured, gleaming with mischief.

"Oh," he cried, "a year! It's going to be soon, isn't it?"

"Well, we'll see how good you are! Why are you in such a hurry?"

"Because I love you! love you! love you! . . . Have I torn it?—oh, I'm so sorry! Why did you pull it down again? . . . Blanche!"

"M-m?"

"Where shall we live?"

"My dear!" she laughed. "This is *very* previous!"

"No, it isn't; what have we to wait for? We could take a little house somewhere to-morrow; we could furnish it on the hire-system. And we can save a heap out of my salary. Even if I left the Pantheon after *Faust* we should have plenty to live on till I got something else."

"Yes," she said; "we shouldn't starve, I know. Don't forget there's *my* salary as well."

"Yours?" he exclaimed; "yes, there's yours, of course; but I don't want you to buy your own bread-and-butter, sweetheart. It isn't as if I were still getting five pounds a week and we couldn't marry unless we clubbed together."

"Don't be so ridiculous," she answered, warm with happiness; "what do you suppose I'm going to do with the money then? You'll tell me next you want me to leave the profession!"

"I won't do that—because I know how wretched you'd be. But there's one thing I want; I want you to remain in town. You won't go on tour if I'm in London, Blanche?"

She hesitated. "Not from choice, naturally. I should like London shops myself."

"But I mean assuming you can't get one, and you are offered a tour; you wouldn't accept it?"

"But if I didn't, I might be out for a year at

a stretch; to all intents and purposes I *should* be leaving the profession."

"Oh, nonsense!" he said cheerfully; "if *I* can stop in town, *you* can certainly! It's easier for a girl to get on than for a man."

"They say it is, as a rule. But there are exceptions to every rule, aren't there?"

"The proper thing would be joint engagements."

"Yes, that would be simply charming," she said. "Do you think you could get me into the Pantheon? Oh, Royce, wouldn't it be simply sweet if you could get me into the Pantheon!"

"I'll try, you may be sure; but, of course, it's a difficult theatre for a woman—I don't quite know what you could do at the Pantheon. Still I shan't be there for ever; we'll go to a house where you can be lead—although as *I* shan't be lead, that won't be unalloyed bliss either. I don't want to see another fellow making love to you in every part you play!"

"As if it mattered!" she said scornfully. "I shouldn't know he was there."

"Wouldn't you? *I* should! It sounds a selfish sentiment, Blanche, but upon my soul I almost begin to wish you hadn't been an actress at all."

"How abominable! Oh!" She turned astonished eyes. "What a perfectly philistine thing to say!"

"Yes, I know," returned Oliphant with a helpless smile; "I know it's very philistine—that's exactly what I thought you'd call it. But I worship the ground you walk on, and the hat that's been on your head, and—and that veil I've torn on your face. My dear, you don't know what you are to me. I shall be green with jealousy every time the hero puts his arm around your waist."

She drooped a little, so that her shoulder thrilled him.

"And what about *me*," she said, "when you make love to the ingénue?"

"Oh, Blanche, you know that's quite different!"

"Is it—why?"

He could not explain precisely why; so he held her hand again behind the apron of the cab. At last he said:

"Well, when we have that theatre of our own, 'all will be gas and gaiters'!"

"Ah!" she said; "and drive home together to Cadogan Square or somewhere in our brougham!"

"Can you see it—you and me in management?"

She *had* seen it. She saw Cadogan Square and a brougham.

"Not Shakespeare all the time, dearest boy," she said, "eh?"

"No, not Shakespeare all the time—rather not; very little Shakespeare. But I think you and I would do good work together for all that; shouldn't we? We shall have it—I shall get on! All I needed was to meet you—to encourage me, and keep me up to the mark. If I'm ever tempted to sink the artist, refuse to live with me, and say I won you by false pretences. No, seriously, you'll be the making of me. A man by himself is apt to get his ideals blunted—the world's hard, and it takes the edge off them; but a girl like you would keep a fellow an artist to the end of time."

She could never quite understand what his ideals were, though she had often listened to him on the subject. Now, however, when he said that a girl like herself was such a boon and a blessing his meaning seemed momentarily clearer. She gave a sigh of response, and felt holy.

It is an error to suppose that Earl's Court is never adjacent to St. Pancras. They had stopped at the corner of the street. Having ascertained that the trap in the roof was down, Oliphant said good-bye to her, and then got out, and was astonished that so very short a drive could be more than a shilling fare. She waved her hand to him a second time, and the pleasure within her had scarcely faded when she saw her home.

Mrs. Ellerton, who had been watching for her arrival, behind the spiræa in the window, ran to the door herself, and kissed her in the passage almost as warmly as she desired to do. She had not for years kissed her quite so warmly as she desired to do; the girl confessed that she was not demonstrative, and since the summer when she put her hair up, her mother had always been a little afraid of a repulse.

Blanche followed her into the drawing-room. As it was Sunday, and there might possibly be callers, a fire had been lighted there.

"Tea will be ready directly," said Mrs. Ellerton; "I told Flora not to make it till you came. Are you tired? Well, dear, I'm very pleased—what I wrote you is quite true, I'm very, very pleased. I wish we'd seen more of him; but, of course, all that's to come. When you're rested, you must tell us everything."

"Where are the others?" asked her daughter, unpinning her hat, and plucking at her hair. "What does father say about it?"

"Well, dear," said Mrs. Ellerton evasively, "of course we shall have to manage a little better, shan't we? And it's only proper that we should!

You'll have your own home to think of, and we can't expect things to be quite the same. But we couldn't hope to keep you with us always; it was only to be supposed that this would happen some day. And I do, do hope you've chosen well, Blanche, and that he'll make you very happy!" She half opened her arms, but the girl was still arranging her hair in the looking-glass and did not seem to see.

The novelist and Gertrude joined them now, followed by the general servant with the teapot.

"I think I'll go upstairs and get my boots off," said Blanche after the greetings. "Can Flora take up my basket? Gertie, you might help her."

"That's a new coat," observed Gertrude, regarding her enviously; "you're always buying new things! *I* can't help her with that great basket—I've been ill again. Why didn't you ask the cabman?"

"Leave it till to-morrow, dear," said her mother; "one of the tradesmen will carry it up in the morning. You can take out what you want for to-night; I'll come and help you presently."

"I'll get my boots off at once; I shan't be a minute. Is that toast? Don't let Gertie eat it all before I come back—I'm hungry."

"How unromantic!" said Gertrude; "we

thought perhaps you'd eat less now you're in love. And my frocks are all on one side of the wardrobe again, and I've left you have the chest of drawers; so don't go taking pegs that don't belong to you! I'm very glad to see you again, Blanche, but you do make a difference to the bedroom, I must say."

"Never mind," said Blanche; "you'll soon have one all to yourself for the rest of your life!"

The toast was in the fender when she returned; and her father, a moment afterwards, approached the momentous subject facetiously.

"So we are going to be married?" he said, stirring his tea. " 'There is nothing half so sweet in life——' Is the happy day fixed?"

"No; it isn't fixed. Mr. Oliphant is coming to see you all to-morrow."

"What time, my dear?" inquired her mother with anxiety. "Will he come to dinner? We've been dining at two since you've been away; I suppose while you're not doing anything, we may as well keep to it?"

"It's a funny time to dine, isn't it? What was wrong with five?"

"Well, dear, so is five a funny time for anybody who hasn't to play at night. And you've no idea how much cheaper middle-day dinner comes out; we have a haddock or eggs at seven, and it only means a meat meal once a day. If you don't mind——"

"Oh, it doesn't matter," said the girl, shrugging her shoulders; "do as you please—ask him to stay to eggs!"

"We shall be glad to see Mr. Oliphant," said the author. "But is he—I hesitate to express myself, Blanche! Is he coming to ask my opinion? I inquire because I'm reluctant to tell you my opinion. We can't, among ourselves, ignore the fact that you have, from time to time, been of—er—assistance to the household. My opinion might, on that account, be misconstrued."

"I suppose you mean you don't think I ought to marry him?" she said for answer.

He made a gesture expressive of helplessness.

"As I say, I hesitate to tell you what I think. It *seems* to me to be a rash step, on both sides. You have always been a clever girl. You've the right to expect a husband in a first-rate position —your good looks, your talent, all give you the right. If you waited, there is no doubt you *would* marry into a good position. In choosing a young man, an unknown young man, in an exceptionally precarious calling, you seem to me to be throwing yourself away. But though this *is* my opinion, it's perhaps not worth uttering, because—it's painful to say—because you may believe it to be the outcome of self-interest."

"But she loves him, James," said her mother weakly.

"My dear!" replied Mr. Ellerton with a fine smile, "we are not discussing the plot of a penny novelette."

"I don't suppose I should marry into Park Lane if I waited till I was grey," murmured the fiancée.

"I don't suppose you would; but between Park Lane and penury there are a great many grades. I should have been satisfied to see you engaged to a man with influence, who could give you the chance in the profession that you deserve. You would have been a celebrated woman then; I am sure of it! Now—— You may be happy now, if domestic life can content you; but I fear you'll never be celebrated. You may go on struggling, but you're handicapping yourself; instead of marriage helping you forward, it will drag you back. I've heard you express your own views of marriages like this; why have they changed all of a sudden?" He regarded her with an air of innocent surprise. "Why have they changed all of a sudden?" he repeated. "And further, I am sorry for Mr. Oliphant! For him, too, it's a blunder. Marriage is the end of a man's youth.

By himself Mr. Oliphant might rise, but you
and your babies will be a weight that'll ruin him.
Don't *I* know what it is—the strain of supporting a wife and family? Don't *I* know what it
is to be crippled for life by an early marriage?
My dear girl, the best woman becomes a burden
to a man!" The wife who was keeping him
winced, and her eyes filled. She did not speak,
however. "No, Blanche, since you really want
to know what I think, I think you are behaving
like a short-sighted child. The difference your
marriage will make to *us* is not vital—I shall
have to write a little more, that is all—but the
difference it will make to *you*, to say nothing of
him, I regret. Yes; I regret it."

"I thought you would," she said insolently.
"Well, I'm going to marry him! And you may
talk till you're tired—and I shall marry him!"

There was a long silence in the room. Gertrude's attention reverted to the coat, which had
been tossed on to the sofa, and she wondered how
much it had cost, and mentally compared it with
some coats that had been "marked down" last
month at a local sale. Mr. Ellerton lit a pipe
with dignified deliberation, and the mother bent
her wet eyes on the fire, pitying everybody except
herself. She would have liked to feel the girl's
head in her lonely lap, and receive confidences

and caresses, and plan the trousseau; but that was how things happened in her novelettes at which they all laughed.

"Won't you have some more tea, James?" she said at last, with a nervous effort to sound at ease.

"No, thank you," replied the novelist, rising with a heavy sigh; "no more. I'm afraid I can't spare the time; I must go back to the study, my dear, and work!"

CHAPTER XII

WHEN Royce, rehearsing Faust at the Pantheon, dwelt on the fact that only a year before he had been reduced to sixpenny dinners, while he awaited his first London "appearance" at a salary of two pounds a week, he thought how amazed he ought to feel at his progress. This is as near to being amazed at our progress as we ever get.

He had removed to rooms in Brunswick Square, which is a better address than Burton Crescent, and where he was on the whole less comfortable, though he paid more rent. However, he did not propose to stay there long. Unless his Faust proved a failure and he received his dismissal, Blanche and he might as well be happy soon as late. The girl no longer demurred, and it was arranged that they should marry early in February soon after the play was produced.

The usual honeymoon would, of course, be impossible, and they meant to have the ceremony on a Saturday, and go by the eleven fifty-five

173

train at night to Brighton, where they could
remain till Monday afternoon.

Mr. Ellerton had spared the young man the
arguments that he had wasted on the fiancée,
realising that since they had failed with his
daughter, it would be futile to repeat them to her
lover. Excepting that his air was rather gran-
diose indeed, Oliphant had found nothing to complain of in his future father-in-law. Gertrude
was monosyllabic, and apparently characterless;
and Mrs. Ellerton he liked. It was with her that
he and Blanche discussed where they should live.

She considered that they would be very unwise
to take a house, even the cheapest; for though
they might expect to stay in town, who could say
but what they would both be on tour again together before long?—desirous as they were of
playing in the same theatre, it was likely enough!
Blanche inclined towards a small flat, but the
same objection applied to this; so they agreed
that, after all, the only plan was to make themselves comfortable in furnished apartments at
first. Furnished apartments where they would
put out their photographs and not have to pack
them up again at the end of a week, would really
be quite like home, she said. She privately determined that they should not be at Earl's Court,
however. She meant, when she married, to begin

to form a circle of useful people, and she didn't want her family dropping in on her at inopportune moments: father, who always referred to his books, which nobody knew, and made one feel so ashamed! and mother, with her ridiculous novelettes in papers that no one had heard of either! and Gertrude, who as soon as she learnt that a man was expected, would always be fishing for an invitation to come and play her fiddle! Oh no, Earl's Court would be simply hateful! It was a pity that a flat was out of the question —a flat somehow suggested a circle. But the privilege of living on the fourth floor or in the basement, and viewing a blank wall from every window, was very expensive, and if they were to be away eight or nine months of the year, the establishment would certainly be a white elephant. It would not do for Royce to assume too heavy responsibilities; preserve her from leaving one atmosphere of money worries for another!—she wanted a respite from hearing about the bills. Besides, remembering their profession, nice apartments would look natural enough.

The date on which the first performance of *Faust* was to take place found Oliphant sick with suspense. There was no rehearsal, and he went out to the Ellertons' in the morning, and gath-

ered encouragement from the mouth of his Be-
loved. Although, when he received the offer, he
had declared that he would tremble to know she
was present on the first night, he had since re-
canted. They were engaged, and so it was
different; it was essential that she should be
there! He had brought four dress-circle tickets
to the house a few days earlier, and this morning
Blanche gave him a bunch of violets from her
bodice for luck.

In a tumbler of water it stood all the evening
on his dressing-table among the sticks of grease-
paint; and after each act, when he came off the
stage, he touched it. And though her violets
were not responsible, he liked to think they had
had something to do with his success when he
read his notices on the morrow. For finally and
with certainty he had "arrived." He could not
have acknowledged it to Blanche—though he
objected to perceive that he couldn't—but in a
fervour of thanksgiving he dropped on his knees
among the newspapers and muttered to God.

The girl's felicitations were wholly sincere this
time—he pertained to her now; and had not pertained to her sufficiently long for her to begin to
say: "So much we are one—and so much I am I,
and you are you!"

And it was with pride that she asked the

Editors of *The Era* and *The Stage* to insert
paragraphs announcing that Miss Blanche Ellerton, who had "created" the part of "Lady Maud
Elstree" in Mr. Royce Oliphant's drama *The
Impostor,* was engaged to be married to him.
Oliphant asked her why she did it, and she replied: "Silly Billy, isn't it always a free advertisement for us both?"

And it was two or three weeks after *The
Speaker* and *The World* had confirmed the pronouncement of all the dailies, that he and she
went to Brighton by the eleven fifty-five.

The wedding had been the quietest possible.
For one thing the Ellertons could not afford an
expensive breakfast, and for another, neither the
bride nor the groom had many intimate friends.
So simple had it been that Royce even lacked a
best man; the men whom he knew best were married and ineligible for the post. As for Otho
Fairbairn, apart from the objection that to ask
him would be to ask for an expensive present,
he had been heard of only once—full of a yacht
and vague projects—since the night when he
came "behind" at the Dominion. After the service there was cold chicken and a sort of champagne in the drawing-room; and maternal tears
and a literary speech. And then Royce went
away, leaving his wife with her family. He

could not see her from the stage during the evening, but he knew she was up in the dress-circle again; and when the curtain fell she went round to the stage-door and waited for him. And it wasn't a hansom in which he drove with her to Victoria, it was a celestial car, and the occupants of the ordinary cabs in the Strand received his compassion. Poor people who were not just married! She was his wife, his wife, his wife! This was the moment when both first realised it. Emotion kept him voiceless, and while they sped between the passing lights to the jingle of the horse's bell, the girl herself asked nothing better than to be allowed to dream.

It wasn't a celestial car in which he drove with her from Victoria to their apartments when they returned, it was a hansom; still they were both very happy. They had decided upon Maddox Street; and when they entered their drawing-room the table was laid for five-o'clock dinner, for which they were a little late. A few things went wrong—not quite so agreeable as the hotel! But that was natural; and the landlady and the servant would soon fall into their ways. The photographs, and a plant or two put about, would give the room a homely air. And they would have some cut flowers on the mantel-piece every morning. With Bond Street on one side and

Regent Street on the other, it would be quite
easy to obtain a plentiful supply.

About half-past six her husband left for the
theatre, and then Blanche lay on the sofa before
the fire and mused. Her first reflection was that
they must buy a couple of cushions; and next
she perceived that if they hired an upright piano,
it would improve the aspect of the room very
much. A good piano, left open, always looked
well. She thought she would have a black one,
and get a gilt basket of red azaleas to stand carelessly on the top.

So she was married—it was very wonderful!
He was a dear fellow. Would she ever be sorry?
. . . N-no.

Ah, she knew there was something she had
meant to do! A cab accident that they witnessed
in the King's Road had suggested the idea. She
rang the bell, and borrowed a bottle of ink from
the landlady, and went into the bedroom and
unpacked her writing materials. While she was
in the bedroom, though, she might as well get
into her dressing-gown. When Royce came back
she would look nice lying on the sofa in her
dressing-gown. Its tint was pale blue, and she
had a pair of slippers to match it, embellished
with little paste buckles. When she had put on
the wrapper, and the slippers, she pulled all the

pins from her hair, and shook it over her shoulders, smiling in the glass at her folly. She did indeed look very charming so; and she returned to the drawing-room complacently. She drew a chair to the table, and dipped her pen in the ink, and meditated. . . . "An accident which might have turned a joyful occasion into a tragedy——" No, that wasn't good; and she wanted to begin with her name—the name always stood out more then. "Miss Blanche Ellerton, who was married on Saturday last to Mr. Royce Oliphant, narrowly escaped having no honeymoon——" She nibbled the penholder; "narrowly escaped having no honeymoon" didn't sound right—was it, or wasn't it, what she meant? An accident like the one that had occurred to somebody else in Brighton might easily have happened to her and him when they were driving from the Pantheon on Saturday night—she might have been taken to a hospital instead of to Brighton. "Miss Blanche Ellerton, who was married on Saturday last to Mr. Royce Oliphant"—what a pity she couldn't say at St. Peter's, Eaton Square—"had an experience which fortunately does not fall to many brides. As the newly-married pair were driving to the station the horse fell down, and——" Fell down? Should one say "fell down" or only "fell"? Cross out the "down" anyhow! "The horse fell, and——" Well, and what? It was a beastly difficult thing to write a paragraph!

She plunged her fingers into the unpinned hair, and stared at her paper, with a frown.

She had only just completed the task when Oliphant came in.

"Look!" she said triumphantly.

"I *am* looking," said he; "what a vision!"

"Oh," she murmured against his mouth, "that's not what I meant; I meant what I've written! I'm going to post it in the morning."

His expression was less proud when he had read the paragraph.

"Do you—do you think that's necessary?" he said. "I can't say it's the sort of thing I believe in! It's very questionable if they'll print it; and if they do——"

"If they do, what?"

"The taste is questionable still."

"Why, Royce," she exclaimed with surprise, "what do you mean? You know the value of a paragraph surely? The more one can get, the better; and poor me, I seldom get *one!*"

"But this isn't true. I hate lies even if they don't hurt anybody."

" 'Lies' is a *werry* big word to use about it.

And don't *you* ever say anything that isn't quite true, milord?"

"I suppose I've told a good many 'polite' lies; I've never told one for my own advantage that I remember."

She gave him a little kiss on the cheek, and held up a finger laughingly.

"It's a good thing you have a business woman to take care of you at last. *Oh,* Silly Billy! Well, what have you got to tell me? I suppose you had a packed house as usual?"

She found the evenings dull during his absence, and was eager for another engagement. Sometimes, however, she took a hansom up to the Pantheon about eleven o'clock, and they went to supper at a restaurant. This was jolly. They seldom chose the same place twice, because the restaurants were new to them both, and they wished to gain experience. Royce took her to Dolibo's first of all. It was his second visit there, and when he had gone with Rayne, he and she had never met. So they were bound to drink champagne! And on subsequent evenings when they went to supper, if they had not had champagne, the jaunt would have seemed rather a falling-off.

The proximity of Bond Street provided them with a very pleasant thoroughfare to stroll in on

fine afternoons. It did not cost two persons the
amount of Royce's salary to live, even with occa-
sional suppers in restaurants, and so they could
look at the shop-windows and buy hats. It was
not a solitary occurrence for them to disagree
as to which hat became her better; and when he
had yielded to her opinion, he begged her to yield
to his—and she said that it was "simply prodigal"
of him, and that she wouldn't hear of such a
thing. But he came out victorious. They liked
to saunter through the Burlington Arcade also.
The early illumination of the windows there often
lured them in from the cold daylight of Piccadilly; and the gloves, and the garters, and the
notepaper were attractive trifles to a man with
a fascinating woman by his side. After all, they
were practically on their honeymoon, though they
were in town; and a very cosy honeymoon it was.
Just as they had prophesied, the landlady "fell
into their ways" with the ready perception that
distinguishes the genus—and the "extras" in
their bills were a sight to see.

When they had been in Maddox Street about
six weeks Blanche was offered an engagement at
the Sceptre. She was to receive eight pounds a
week. This did not seem so startling to her as it
would have done before Oliphant went to the
Pantheon, but she still counted it high terms, and

she was very much elated. Royce was pleased
by the news because it pleased *her,* and it was
not until after she had come home with the part
folded in her muff that their first difference arose.

From a professional point of view it was an
extremely good part; from Oliphant's, it was a
very offensive one. She was to play a courtesan;
and as courtesans in drama are much more brilliant than courtesans in life, she had to utter
several epigrams which he objected to his wife's
delivering. He tried to induce her to cancel the
engagement, and their argument grew heated.

"I never heard anything so ridiculous!" she
exclaimed; "it is simply philistine! I—— Really
I'm surprised at you! Cancel it? Why, my dear
boy, if I make a hit at the Sceptre, just look what
it means! One would think you were I don't
know what."

"I'm your husband," he replied; "that's what
I am. I respect you, darling; the greater the
hit you made, the worse I should feel."

"Thank you," she said indignantly.

"Don't misunderstand me on purpose. The
point is——"

"The point is that you're being philistine,
simply philistine!"

"Yes, you said that before. It's always you
who find me philistine—I don't think I was

thought so by anyone else. Come, don't let's wrangle, Blanche"—he sat down on the couch, and put his arm round her waist—"you know yourself it isn't a nice part; now, is it?"

"I don't think that's the way to look at it at all; I didn't know you did look at things in that way. I've heard you say that a dramatist should be free to take any characters he pleased—the most abandoned. Haven't you?"

"I never said I wanted my wife to play them," answered Oliphant doggedly.

"Oh!" She left his side, and walked about the room. "You're not consistent. I'm an artist. I don't recognise such rotten suburban distinctions! I thought you were an actor, Royce. Upon my word you make me gasp!"

"Put yourself in my place! Is it astonishing that I should blush to know my wife was sneering at decency every evening to make a crowd titter? I hope I *am* an actor, but I was a man first."

"Oh, yes—and you were going to be a parson first! To hear you talk, I—I almost think it's a pity you changed your mind."

Oliphant did not reply for some seconds. The colour had gone out of his face, and his eyes were angry.

"As a matter of fact," he said in a sharp voice,

"there is no question of my consistency here, for the part has nothing to do with art."

"You know a great deal about the piece, don't you," she retorted, "considering you didn't hear it read?"

"I know what the man is capable of who wrote it, and I know this character. 'Character'? There's no character in it, only cheap cynicism. 'There is some soul of goodness in things evil'! But what does this teach; what is it *for?*—she isn't a woman. She came out of a writing-table to wear Paris frocks and amuse the stalls."

"Oh!" she cried; " 'Teach'? 'For'? She's for eight pounds a week and to get big notices! Don't be a fool."

"Blanche!"

"Well, you shouldn't irritate me. I think it's very cruel of you to make childish difficulties, instead of being nice and congratulating me on my good luck. I do, Royce"—she whimpered a little, and pressed her handkerchief to her eyes— "I think it's very cruel!"

"Blanche!" It was a different "Blanche" this time.

"You—you've disappointed me very much. I came home so happy."

"Oh, dearest, don't say that—that hurts."

"I thought we were *one;* I thought we entered

into each other's hopes so thoroughly," she faltered behind the handkerchief.

"We do; we always shall," he said, trying to take her hand.

"And this engagement—you know what it might mean to me?"

"But you might get another just as good. You might——"

"No, I should be turning my back on fortune; it would never come again—or not for years. *Do* good engagements keep knocking at one's door? I didn't want to feel that our marriage was going to hinder me in any, any way—I *didn't!*"

She suffered him to capture the hand now, and draw her to him; to dry her tears—and bring a smile to her pathetic lips by the assurance that he "wouldn't say any more."

CHAPTER XIII

AND being a decidedly clever actress, she made a success at the Sceptre. Her name became familiar to London playgoers, who, knowing nothing of the apprenticeship that she and her husband had served in the provinces, while their hearts grew sick with hope deferred, spoke—as playgoers do speak—of Royce Oliphant and Blanche Ellerton having "come out at the Dominion last year." To the actor, who is so fortunate as Oliphant only in exceptional cases, and has often grown grey in his calling before he obtains recognition in London, this phrase "come out" has its humour.

The earliest days of June brought Royce his first professional worry since his marriage. *The Impostor,* which he fervently wished would sink into oblivion, had been sent on tour again. Rayne was now deriving a small profit from it, and there were insignificant author's fees. One morning when Oliphant received the Chester-le-Street notices from the Press-cutting agency to which he had subscribed, he was astonished to discover that the last act of his play had been entirely rewritten. He could scarcely believe his eyes.

"I won't stand it!" he cried, rising excitedly; "the thing's monstrous; I'll have it stopped! Rayne has turned *The Impostor* into a burlesque —he's holding me up to ridicule all over England!"

"What do you mean?" asked Blanche. "Turned it into a burlesque?"

"Look at this! He, or some other ass, has written a new act. Clement is sent to Portland, and escapes to France. And Maud and Mrs. Vaughan fight a duel—fight a duel!—about him with swords. They fight a duel—two English ladies!—here it is in print!"

"Why the man must be insane!" she exclaimed. "Maud and Mrs. Vaughan fight a duel? You should go and see him at once."

But Rayne was not visible; and being in a theatre every evening for three hours, he thought himself much too busy a man to answer a letter. Then Oliphant sought Counsel's opinion, and there was, of course, no doubt that he could obtain an injunction. Theatrical advisers, however, pointed out that if he took the matter into court, Rayne would probably declare that the drama, as it left Mr. Oliphant's hands, had proved so disastrous that "there wasn't a manager who would give it a date." The statement might not be accurate, but it would be damaging. And after all, the company was only visiting the "smalls," where not more than two persons in five hundred would observe who wrote the play, or remember, if they observed. On the whole he was recommended—for various reasons—to submit to the outrage until Rayne's rights in the property expired.

So the hero continued to escape to France, and two English ladies continued to fight a duel about him; and those among the audience who had the sense to laugh, continued to imagine that the author whose name stood on the play-bill was the ignoramus that they were entitled to laugh at.

"And at any rate," said Blanche, "if it plays to better business with the alteration—and I suppose Rayne reckons it will—you'll get bigger fees; don't forget that!"

Royce looked at her without answering; and though the subject burned within him, he never mentioned it at home any more.

Four months of matrimony had been ample to display the disparity of their points of view. He had a pretty wife, and—as she would be judged in "the profession"—a talented wife; but he had no companion, and never would have one.

It was his own fault, he was quite aware of it. He had made a mistake; but that it was a mistake for which he would have to suffer all his life did not lessen the weight upon his mind as he realised it. She was fond of describing herself as an artist, and when they disagreed upon practical matters, she insisted also that she was a business woman; but to him she appeared a business woman always, and an artist only when she was behind the footlights. She was an actress, he did not deny that—and it was a puzzle to him how she was able to project herself into a part— but her taste in dramatic literature was *nil*. She cared no more about the quality of a play in which she was engaged than did the scene-painters. For a piece to "run" was everything that she had imagined anybody could ask of it. "Success" to her was the last word; and *succès d'estime* was the French for failure. Money was spent freely in the Maddox Street rooms, but he never saw her spend a shilling on a book, and rarely saw her read one. Their conversation yielded nothing, was barren, dry as ashes in his mouth. He could not talk to her as he wanted to talk to someone, because the references, the comparisons he made, had no significance to her, and she found his attitude towards the theatre wholly incomprehensible. They had at this period only two interests in common. One was the removal they were about to make to a small furnished flat in Victoria Street—she wanted a flat, and it was a more sensible arrangement than living in lodgings and wasting half his salary outside; the other was the child that was expected to be born to them at the end of November.

It may be thought that these meant a good deal, but wherever their home might be, Oliphant must live chiefly within himself; and as to the child—well, she had hurt him very much about the child, and though he tried to forget it, the pride of anticipation that he might have felt was absent. She was now resigning herself to the idea of becoming a mother; but he had known nothing until she had suffered in secret, and made herself ill; and when he reproached her, she had turned from him, crying passionately that "This would prevent her following up her Sceptre success, and now she would be out of a shop all through the autumn!"

Of her parents and sister he saw little. No mother-in-law could have been less obtrusive than was Mrs. Ellerton. Oliphant had gathered enough of the family's circumstances to understand that they must miss their daughter's help, and he assumed that some of Blanche's eight pounds went to Earl's Court every week. She did not tell him that it was so, and he did not inquire; nor, if he had been better versed in the prices of West End dressmakers, would any question have been necessary.

They moved into the flat on the 4th of June. Blanche's engagement at the Sceptre would soon terminate, but at the Pantheon *Faust* was running still. Next month the house would be temporarily sub-let, while the annual tour was made. Whether he would be offered a re-engagement for Greatorex's next production, Oliphant did not know; he only hoped. It was reported that this was to be *Romeo and Juliet.*

The photographs and sofa-cushions had not been transferred to Victoria Street quite a week when he received a note at the theatre from Otho Fairbairn, apologising for so long a silence, and begging him to make an appointment. They lunched together two days later, and Fairbairn was found paler and older-looking than when Royce had seen him last. He wrung the actor's hand heartily, and said how delighted he had been to discover the name "Oliphant" in the Pantheon cast.

"I thought you might be acting in town, and was going to read all the names 'under the clock' on the chance. Lo, you were high in the list! You've done well, Royce!"

"Where have you been?" asked Oliphant.

"I'm a pig—I've made fifty resolutions to write to you; but I—I've been in a good deal of trouble, old fellow; you must forgive me."

"I'm sorry to hear that! May I know—is it private?"

"Well, I was engaged to be married," said Fairbairn, "and the lady changed her mind. I've been in New York, you know—she was an American girl. I was very fond of her; but she discovered that she liked somebody else better. It leaves one rather raw, that sort of thing." He laughed drearily. "She didn't treat me well, but my dollars weren't so startling on the other side —lots of the Americans have more—it was a pity the governor didn't live to buy a title! . . . Never mind about *me*—I want to hear about yourself. What have *you* been doing?"

Oliphant hesitated. "Well," he said, "I—I *have* married."

"No? Is that a fact? My warmest congratulations! Married!"

"I married Miss Ellerton—she played in my piece at the Dominion. We're living in Victoria Street. You must come and dine with us; or lunch with us—our dinner-hour would be rather barbaric to you. We don't do things in style, but we can give you an edible lunch—there's a restaurant downstairs, and they feed us."

"It must be devilish jolly," said the other. "So you married an——"

"I married an actress, yes; and a very clever actress."

"The wisest thing you could do, of course! A wife in one's own profession must be ideal. When was it?"

"We were married at the beginning of February. What day will you come?—the sooner the better."

Fairbairn was free to go the next afternoon, and Blanche put on the frock that suited her best for his subjugation. She had learnt the details of his offer to back Royce in a theatre, and she intended that he should develop into a constant visitor now that he had returned to England.

He found his hostess informal and charming; and Oliphant was in high spirits, perceiving that she had made a good impression. Conversation did not flag, and soon became frankly professional in tone; for Fairbairn was interested in their prospects, and put a good many questions, and, although he now believed himself a misogynist, there was a fascination to him, an outsider, in hearing an actress chatter about the stage. To Blanche it was even more novel to

entertain a young man who possessed a splendid
income; and when he inadvertently said he must
have been "staying at Brookhill" at the date some
comedy was produced, and she discovered that
he meant the place of a peer, she dared not look
at him lest she should betray the sensation that
the announcement had caused her.

He took leave of her with the consciousness
of having spent three hours as agreeable as misogyny permitted, and his assurance that he would
drop in upon them often was no less sincere than
the lady's petition that he would do so.   She
regarded Royce respectfully for being the friend
of "such a swell"; and when they received a note
in which Fairbairn trusted that it wasn't too late
to send a wedding present, and they found that
the present was silver suitable for a prince's
dinner-party, her "lively sense of favours to
come" knew literally no bounds.

"How much money does one need to take a
theatre?" she inquired eagerly.   "Do you think
he would be just as ready to do it as he was?
Well, do you think he will be just as ready when
you want him to?—people's ideas change.   Why
shouldn't you ask him now—why not make use
of him while he's here?"

"We're not well enough known," said Royce.
"We don't want to have a theatre for three

months—I want to open it, and keep it open. Besides, it wouldn't be a fair proposal in our present position."

"He has lots to lose," she argued; "it wouldn't hurt him if it *were* a frost. Which house should we take? Perhaps—perhaps he'd *build* you a theatre! You're very stupid to take it so easy, my boy—when you want him, he may have cooled off. And he may marry—men are such mugs—I daresay he'll go and marry and want all his money for his wife. You may be sure there are heaps of women trying for him—he'll fall in love directly."

"He was engaged in New York. The girl broke it off."

"Broke it off? The *girl* did?"

"So he told me."

"Good Lord! Heaven was kind to us to make her such a fool!"

"Don't!" said Royce; "I think he's cut up about it."

She lifted her eyebrows protestingly. "I hope he understands we are genuine," she said, "and won't be afraid of taking us by surprise. If he doesn't call soon, you must fix a day—or *I* shall. I want him to be very much at home in this flat, I can tell you; he means our future!"

This was all very distasteful to Oliphant; it

jarred upon him terribly, but to say so would
entail another altercation. He held his peace,
and let the subject drop. The woman's ardour
was chilled by the coldness of its reception. She
reflected that he was not companionable. How
different he had been before he got her! She
might have done better for herself even if Fairbairn did start them in a theatre! And momentarily she felt that he never would—Royce was
so impossible! Now how nice the hour would
have been if he had been sympathetic, and could
have shared her enthusiasm, and made plans with
her for their advancement! That would have
been marriage. She could understand that in a
marriage like that a girl might be happy although
she was not rich. Royce was only enthusiastic
about matters that didn't concern him; what
affair was it of his whether a play was "literature," or whether it wasn't, if the parts were
good, and it caught on? He was a dreamer.
His ideals were very fine, she supposed; but high
ideals were a dreadful strain to live with. She
did not ridicule his theories—she knew that many
dreary subjects were deep and admirable—but
the proper place for them was Exeter Hall, or
the Birkbeck Institute, or somewhere; she could
not pretend to want them rammed down her
throat with her meals. If he felt aggrieved, she

couldn't help it—she had not yawned often, and he had bored her to death. No, Royce was unpractical—a crank. He was—he was— She tapped her foot restlessly, and shook her head to herself behind *The Era*. She had blundered with the wrong man!

The following day, however, she had another triumph. A fancy fair was being held at the Botanical Gardens for the benefit of—— The visitors were not quite certain what it was to benefit; but a number of more or less prominent actresses had given their services, and a large contingent of the gilded youth sped to Regent's Park from Clubland, curious to see Miss this and Miss the other off the stage. There were several Society women too, being charitable in elaborate toilettes, and it was possible for quite inferior young men to acquire a chance to win a tea-cosy, or buy a baby's comforter from a lady who had a title.

Blanche was assisting at the Burmah Stall, captivating in a frock which Oliphant mentally described as "a shower of lace without a figure." When he joined her there, he found her radiant.

"Oh," she exclaimed, "I've been talking to Lady Fleck, and she wants to be introduced to you! They say she knows everybody in the profession—the authors and critics and everyone.

She's ever so gone on *you*—says you're the coming man, and I don't know what. There she is! Come over now."

Lady Fleck was emerging from a group upon the lawn, smiling vaguely. As she saw Oliphant and Blanche approaching, her smile gained expectation. She was not pretty and she was not young, but actors and authors and musicians found her charming—she liked them so much. She gave Sunday luncheon parties, which she called "bohemian," and which sometimes cost two hundred pounds.

"I'm *so* delighted to meet you, Mr. Oliphant," she said; "I've been telling your wife how I've looked forward to knowing you both. Such an interesting couple I've always thought you—so romantic!"

The last word completed his embarrassment; it was his earliest experience of social adulation. Blanche covered his awkwardness by the playful assumption of a shyness that she did not feel.

"Oh, don't say that, Lady Fleck," she cried, hiding her face affectedly; "you'll make us so vain of each other!"

"But I must say it," declared Lady Fleck; "such an interesting couple! Oh, your Faust, Mr. Oliphant! it impressed me so deeply. You revealed *Faust* to me. How you must have

thought"—she half closed her eyes to convey
thought—"how you must have *lived* in the character to portray it as you do!"

"I'm glad it pleased you," he murmured.

"Of course I'm an enthusiast about the Stage,
I confess it! My passion is the Theatre. When
I see a performance like yours, I want to *thank*
the actor—I want to *go* to him—to tell him what
I *owe* him for the intellectual and emotional treat
he has given me!"

He contrived a response with great labour.
She discovered it to be "so original, so suggestive." Blanche felt rather in the way, but hesitated to make an excuse and vanish, not knowing
whether a lady in Society would consider it tactful or rude. She was relieved when they were
interrupted. Lady Fleck pressed them to go
to see her, and repeated her "day" twice, with
much warmth.

In the bedroom that night Royce was entreated
to realise the responsibility that rested on him.

"You must make the most of this chance,"
insisted the girl; "*say things* when we go! If
she takes us up, we shall meet no end of people.
And gaze at her as if you thought she was good-
looking—that's more important than all; she
knows already you're clever. I know what
women are—*you're* the draw with Lady Fleck,

because you're a man. It wouldn't hurt"—she raised her bare foot contemplatively and admired it, as she always did when she undressed—"it wouldn't hurt if you make up to her a little. Not ridiculously, because her husband mightn't like it, and then we shouldn't be asked any more; but plain women are so easily flattered, dear boy— Gertrude smirked in the Zoo when a monkey looked after her—you needn't go far. . . . Do baronets' wives know duchesses?"

CHAPTER XIV

IF their marriage had sprung from love instead of from infatuation—even if one of them had ever truly loved the other—their life would have been very enviable. The child was born early in December, and at the end of February Blanche was fulfilling another engagement in town, and at the Pantheon Oliphant had won approval as Mercutio. They were young, the man had had great luck, and they were in a profession which pays the fortunate lavishly while making small demand upon their time. It is true that every day Oliphant studied—shutting himself in a room and striving to attain the control over the muscles of his face that a musician seeks over his instrument; taking his voice note by note, and practising with it as a singer practises his scales—but this was only in the morning, and by no means during the entire morning. He did not work for hours at a stretch as do authors, painters, civil engineers, city clerks, and other men. He was free to go out with his wife whenever she wished

him to do so; and although she had met far fewer
titles at Lady Fleck's than she had expected,
there were, by the summer, several "Tuesdays"
and "Thursdays" on which she claimed his company.

She did not disguise that she was very ambitious of extending their circle of people worth
knowing; by "people worth knowing" she already
meant people in Society. Scheming to extend it,
she never missed an opportunity of being agreeable to her own sex; men only paid compliments,
she realised—it was to women she must look for
the magic words "I shall be so pleased if you'll
come and see me." From this cause she accepted
the former's attentions with such composure that
she was pronounced by masculine admirers to
be "a bit cold, don't you know," and gained
among women—to whom she listened with an air
of enchained interest—the reputation of being
devoted to her husband. To a "romantic couple"
in the most popular profession an invitation to
one house led to the drawing-room of another
if tact and patience were employed.

Otho Fairbairn also had his social uses, though
as a bachelor they were limited. He had not
become quite the constant visitor that Blanche
had hoped to see him; still he would drop in upon
them sometimes at odd hours now, and she had

made herself very sympathetic in a tête-à-tête once on the subject of his misogyny. Otho had found it a pleasant matter to discuss with her. She had assured him that he was only temporarily embittered, and prophesied that some day he would come across a pretty girl who would completely change his views. He denied the possibility. Between his heart and him the Atlantic rolled. Nevertheless the conversation had a charm, and he was more than ever of the opinion that Royce had married a very nice woman.

The year for which the flat had been obtained had expired, and Oliphant and she had just taken one a shade more commodious, on the same side of the street. Since the advent of the baby and a nurse their recent quarters had been rather inconvenient. Now that the child was here, and could be brought to her arms in white embroidery, and carried away if he cried obstreperously, Blanche showed an interest in the little being— even in moments displayed tenderness for him. He had been christened Hugh, the name that had been Royce's father's. Oliphant, still half-frightened of breaking him if he picked him up, loved to sit and look at the mite. He did not remember looking at a baby before, and the helplessness of this tiny thing that was his son awoke extraordinary emotions in him. If Blanche's tenderness had not been capricious, if her interest in the undesired child had been more than a liking, there would now have been a firm link between him and her.

Excepting during the few weeks in the previous autumn when he had toured with the Pantheon company, they had not been separated since their wedding. They had, however, never played on the same stage since then. Each had a nightly world apart from the other. The fact to a well-mated pair might have furnished food for cheerful chatter across the supper-table, but only to a pair very happily mated indeed. Gossip about those who are strangers to the listener is rarely amusing, and it sounds dull to the one who gossips also. The listener generally says the wrong thing, and the anecdote falls flat. Oliphant and his wife rarely touched upon the incidents of the evening to each other.

While Royce remained at the Pantheon there was no prospect of a joint engagement. Even when he was wanted for a matinée at the Mirror, he knew nothing about it until the women's parts were cast. Blanche had asked him to ascertain if there was a chance for her there, and he returned with the news that all the arrangements were made.

"How about *you?*" she inquired. "Has Greatorex given you permission?"

"Yes, that's all right. I spoke to him last night. What are those—the proofs of your likenesses? Let me look."

She gave them to him one by one, scrutinising them herself across his shoulder. She had a passion for having her likeness taken, and, not having arrived at the position where photographers wrote offering sittings for nothing, she spent a good deal of money upon it, although, of course, she obtained the "professional reduction." There were here various presentments of her: she stood triumphant, showing her bosom and her teeth; she sat thinking high thoughts, with her cheek upon her hand; she had her face in profile and her hands behind her back; and her hands full of flowers and her face bent. She laughed; she mused; she yearned—she was beautiful in all of them; and her husband's paramount reflection was how little they resembled her.

"Which do you think is best?" she said.

"They're all exquisite; I don't know. Perhaps this . . . but it's so difficult to say."

"The 'soulful' one—I think I like that best myself. You know it ought to sell, that—I do want an agent who would push me on; I wish I could get hold of Bernstein!—What do I look as if I'm thinking about?" She held the photograph out, and viewed it critically. "Now suppose you'd never spoken to me—suppose you were somebody else and saw it in the shop-windows—what would you think I was like?"

"My dear girl," said Oliphant, checking a sigh, "I can't imagine!"

"Well, you'd be curious to know me, wouldn't you? It would stand out among the other women's? Wouldn't it—isn't it uncommon? What do you say? Or do you think there's too much shadow about it? What does it suggest—what kind of girl? I meant to look all aspiration and religion in this; very Bible-y! as if my eyes were fixed on Heaven. You know what I mean. I think I shall have a dozen of this, and a dozen of the one in the low-neck, and . . . I don't know that any of them are *really* very good—I don't look my best. The one with the hat on is a perfect beast! . . . No, he must give me another sitting. Don't tell 'em at home I'm having any done—I want to save them for particular people."

"Where's Baby?" asked Oliphant. "Is he out still?"

"No, it's in the nursery," she said, disposing the mounted proofs in a line along the mantelpiece; "do you want it in?"

"I may as well go to him, if he's awake."

"It was awake just now—I heard it crying."

"Well, I'll go and say 'How d'ye do' to him in his own domain."

The nurse said she had "never seen a gentleman take such notice of his baby as Mr. Oliphant." He inquired if the eyes were likely to remain that glorious blue; was despondent when he heard that " 'most every baby was born with blue eyes"; and knew restored hope when she added that, "as Madam's eyes was blue, there was no saying but what they might." · It pleased him to imagine that the infant looked at him with a different expression from that awakened by others; and because he felt embarrassed under the nurse's surveillance, he was always glad when she withdrew, leaving him at liberty to behave as ridiculously as he pleased. How he wished that "Hugh" could talk already, and that he could take him out, holding his warm little hand, and dazzle him with toys! How funny and jolly it would be! . . . And unless he had all his own feeling for the art, he should never be an actor. Oh no! he should be a doctor, or go to the Bar. And—he shouldn't take a wife until he was quite, quite sure. Poor little Hugh—the nurse *had* withdrawn, and he touched the baby's face with his own. If only his father could have lived to see Hugh! . . . He wondered if he knew about him now. It was an awful thing, poor little Hugh, to choose the wrong girl. O God, grant that the child would find nothing lacking in Blanche!—how piteous if he couldn't love her, either!

The matinée for which Oliphant's services had been sought was designed to introduce the first dramatic experiment of a novelist of the introspective school. For a reason that was not known he awaited the verdict on his earliest play with deep anxiety. When he had married, a year or two before, his mother had been very indignant. Some mothers do consider matrimony the one unpardonable offence that their sons can commit. The indignation of the novelist's mother, however, had placed him in a peculiar predicament; the first time after his marriage that he drew an unlovable woman, she called on all their friends, and said that "Arthur had discovered his wife's real character at last!" And when, in his next book, he drew the failings of a totally different woman, she exclaimed that "poor Arthur was finding out more about his wife every day!" As a consequence he was terrified to describe any woman who wasn't a born angel, and his career in fiction seemed over.

He read a play as badly as most novices, and resembled dramatists more eminent by cherishing the delusion that few persons read one so well. Oliphant received his part the day before the reading was to take place, and to a cursory perusal it looked promising: some of the speeches a little long perhaps; here and there a line that "didn't speak"—awkward when one came to utter it; but the man seemed alive, he evidently meant something. To an admirer of the author's novels the production of the drama was an interesting experiment.

Arthur Mundey was on the stage, and made himself known, when Oliphant reached the Mirror. He said he was glad that it had proved possible to obtain Mr. Oliphant for the protagonist, and the actor was gratified. Whatever significance the public might attach to the matinée, it was to the organisers decidedly important—the outcome of a movement with which he was in cordial sympathy. The company had not all arrived, and as he lounged under the T-piece his gaze met a face that was familiar, though he did not instantaneously remember how he knew it. The woman, who was seated in the prompt-entrance, had been looking towards him at the same moment, and he saw in her eyes the diffident expression of one who waits to be recog-

nised. Now, her identity flashed upon him, and
he went to her quickly. But her name escaped
him still; so extending his hand, and in a tone
of pleasure that was not feigned, he exclaimed:

"How d'ye do? We meet again at last!"

She rose, with a murmured greeting. "You
didn't expect to find me here, Mr. Oliphant?"

"Indeed, no; I—I didn't know who was in it
at all. Have you been back from South Africa
long?"

"I came back in January," she said. "I saw
you looking across—I wondered if you'd remember me."

"Of course I do!" The name touched his
tongue. "I'm very glad to see you again, Miss
King. What are you playing—is it any good?"

" 'Patience Banfield,' " she said; "it's a small
character-part. You—you have fulfilled my
prophecy, Mr. Oliphant—may I congratulate
you? I was at the Pantheon last night."

Her manner was graver than it had been, he
fancied. He recalled a girl, and here she was a
woman. How long ago was it? Two years—
two years and a half. No time! But what a
change it had made in his position!—Pathetic, as
he stood before her, that she had not risen too.
He paused with a little embarrassment. The
questions that he would have asked were impos-

sible, but he felt that he was appearing formal,
even that the situation imparted to him, against
his will, an air of patronage. He was distinctly
relieved when Mundey sat down at the table,
and they had to listen to the play.

It disappointed him; yet how clever it was!
though half its cleverness was missed by the
assembly to whom it was read. It was a novel
in dialogue. It would have been admirable under
the library lamp, but the flare of the footlights
would kill it. It was delicate, subtle, undramatic
—it was the scenery painted by an Impressionist.
A great regret possessed him as the reading went
on, Mundey perspiring and growing hoarse. He
felt the pity of it that a fine talent should be
frustrated by an unskilful hand. He glanced
round as much of the semi-circle as was within
his view—the listless heads, the disposal of the
limbs, signified nothing but weariness. Yes! one
face spoke the emotion that stirred himself—one
woman understood: Miss King was thinking his
own thoughts.

He spoke to her again as she was hastening
up the steps, after a few insincere compliments
had been made upon the work. She had bowed,
and vanished, but he had overtaken her. That
she should leave without saying "Good-afternoon," without approaching him, revived the

mental discomfort he had experienced. Circumstances had once flung them into an intimate, if short-lived, friendship, and though in the interval he had forgotten all about her, it hurt him to see that she felt they no longer met upon terms of equality. He was a leading man, and she remained an obscure actress: so she did not speak to him unless she was addressed! He could not bear that—it distressed him.

"You're not going to run away before we've said ten words to each other, are you?" he asked. "How do you like the play?"

"I——" she hesitated. "I should like very much to read it quietly by myself. Do you think it will succeed, Mr. Oliphant?"

"I think my opinion of it's the same as your own."

"The same as my own?"

"Yes; I saw you while it was being read."

She looked surprised, and a little dismayed; "I hope Mundey didn't see!"

"You needn't be alarmed! But shall I tell you what you thought? You thought what a good novel it would have made."

"That's true," she acknowledged; "I did." They were at the corner of the street, and she stopped.

"Am I in the way?" inquired Oliphant. "Do you want me to say 'Good-bye'?"

"Not if we're going the same road; I go through Drury Lane."

"So do I, if you'll let me. But it isn't about the play I want to talk to you; I want to hear about yourself. I thought perhaps you'd have written to me after you went to the Cape, to tell me how you got on. Why didn't you?"

"I didn't like to," she said. "Did it look ungrateful?"

"'Ungrateful'? What on earth had you to be grateful for? No; but I should have been pleased to hear! When did you say you came back—in January?"

"I've been back six months. It was a very good engagement, in a sense—it lasted much longer than I had expected; I was out there two years. I didn't look forward to staying anything like that time. I played in Cape Town and Kimberley and Johannesburg, and became quite an Afrikander."

"Was it pleasant?"

"I don't like the country. The Colony and Johannesburg aren't so bad, but Kimberley is loathsome. It's none of it very agreeable, though, after the novelty wears off; and, oh, how dear! One's salary goes nowhere! After we left Cape

Town I used to pay a shilling for *The Stage*—
when I bought it."

"I suppose that wasn't often?"

She laughed. "There were weeks when I
missed it, if nobody had had a copy from home
to lend me."

"And since you have been back?"

"I've been on tour with *A Lilac Chain*—not
much of a company, of course! That's what I
meant when I said it was a good engagement 'in
a sense': the Cape doesn't lead to anything—I'm
just where I was when I went away. You've
been marvellously fortunate, Mr. Oliphant, if I
may say so."

"Oh, please don't say 'if you *may* say'!—why
shouldn't you? Of course I've been fortunate.
Luck's everything. It was *The Impostor* that
gave me my opportunity, you know; Rayne had
an accident, and I got the chance to play lead
in town *by* accident. But for that I daresay I
shouldn't be any better off than when we last
met. I suppose you saw that *The Impostor* was
produced soon after you left England?"

"Yes, that was one of the weeks when I did
see a paper—I was so glad! You mustn't say
luck is everything, though. Luck gave you your
chance, but you had the talent to make use of
it. I never thought, when you told me the plot

of your drama that evening, that I should be
reading a criticism of it in Cape Town two or
three months later—it seemed so funny! That
was when I was really tempted to write to you;
but—oh, I don't know!—I hadn't done it when
I arrived; and so to write to you when you had
a success looked as if it would be rather mean.
I thought so, anyhow. Oh, there's one thing I
want to say—it isn't of engrossing interest, but
I should like you to know: I sent the woman in
Alfred Place her money!"

"She deserved never to get it," said Oliphant;
"but of course you did! Yes, I hoped for a
line from you; and Mrs.—er—Tubbs—oh, Mrs.
Tubbs mourned for you! You've no idea what
an impression you made on Mrs. Tubbs. She
used to talk about you daily."

"I know," said Miss King; "so she tells me.
I'm staying with her now."

Oliphant wheeled round incredulously.

"Really? Do you mean it? She's there still,
and you're staying with her?"

"I had to stay somewhere, and I thought of
her at once. In point of fact," she added meditatively, "I don't fancy Mrs. Tubbs is quite so
cheap as she was. But she's just as nice."

"How odd it seems," he said. "And is the
furniture still blue? And is she still garrulous

about the niece who was in the 'prerfession'? Did she mention *me?* She hadn't been to the Pantheon, I suppose?"

"She hadn't been yet—no; but she mentioned you the evening I arrived."

"I believe Mrs. Tubbs always took an interest in me," he said warmly. "I hope she wasn't hurt that I hadn't sent her seats? To tell you the truth, I never thought about it."

"I don't think she was; indeed, I'm sure she wasn't."

"What did she say?"

"I could tell she wasn't hurt."

"She must have said *something?*" he smiled.

"Well," replied Miss King with a glimmer of amusement in her eyes, "she said she hadn't heard of you since you left her and she hoped you were alive."

Their gaze met, and laughter broke from them both. "Thank you," exclaimed Oliphant, "I deserved it! But this is Fame! I am Mercutio in capital letters on the Pantheon bills, and my old landlady doesn't know it till you come from South Africa to tell her." It occurred to him to wonder if Miss King had heard of his marriage. "You haven't congratulated me," he said.

"Oh, I have!" she replied; "in the theatre—the first thing."

"I mean about something else. I'm married now."

"Married?" she echoed. "*Are* you? . . . I don't know why it should be astonishing, but——"

"It's perfectly true."

"Oh, I congratulate you ever so much, of course. I knew nothing about it. I don't meet many people—I'm like Mrs. Tubbs, you see. Is your wife on the stage?"

"Yes, I married Miss Blanche Ellerton. We—we've been married nearly eighteen months. I'm a husband and father; don't I look more important?"

"I attributed it to other causes," she laughed; "now it's explained!"

They had reached New Oxford Street, and she paused again, and extended her hand.

"I'm sure I've taken you miles out of your way," she said. "By the bye, what time is the call to-morrow, did you notice?"

"Twelve o'clock. Isn't it tea-time, and mightn't we go and have some tea?"

"Oh no, thanks," she said, "I want to get home."

"Or chocolate?—I can recommend the chocolate. We've only to cross the road."

"I'd rather not, thank you; Mrs. Tubbs would

be so wounded if I didn't want anything when I got in!"

"Answer me one question," he exclaimed; "do you have tea in the drawing-room, or the dining-room?"

"The drawing-room," said she gaily; "the blue drawing-room. Good-afternoon, Mr. Oliphant."

"Good-afternoon, Miss King."

He retraced his steps to the Strand, and mentally followed hers. "The drawing-room" —how vividly he saw it!—and the brown tea-pot on the dilapidated tray hidden by a soiled table-napkin; the battered cover over the toast. It had been pleasant!—after all it had been pleasant! He was happy then, only he didn't know it . . . happier than now.

CHAPTER XV

WHEN the dramatic critics say that a part is unworthy of an actor's abilities, the author may not be gratified, but it means that the actor's spurs are securely fixed. Excepting Oliphant, who gained a little kudos, it is doubtful if Mundey's drama advanced any one professionally. Oliphant wondered if it would do Miss King any good. He was glad to see that several of the papers mentioned her favourably, though her performance did not receive the notices that he considered it deserved. During the fortnight's rehearsals he had had several conversations with her on the stage, and it would have pleased him very much indeed if the little part of "Patience Banfield" had proved a stepping-stone to higher things.

He had watched her rehearsals with a curiosity that she did not divine—he was prepared to be disappointed, to find her execution fall short of her conceptions; but at least she had not fallen short of his. She was artistic to the finger-tips,

221

and her voice was delicious; he could not say
what she would do with such characters as she
aspired to play, but he was persuaded that, given
the opportunity, she would at all events get on.

Apparently no opportunity presented itself,
for when he met her in Wellington Street one
day about a month after the piece had been produced, she told him that she was "going out" with
A Lilac Chain again.

He had not known how much he had hoped
for her until he heard it; indeed, he was more
disappointed than she; in her, expectation had
long grown faint.

"I wish," he remarked to Blanche, "I could
have done something to help Miss King."

"Why?" she said.

"I like her, and she's clever. I'd have been
very glad to do her a service."

"I didn't think much of her at the Mirror.
What have you seen her play in besides Mundey's
thing?"

"Nothing else. But she was admirable in that;
you must remember there was no scope for big
effects."

"I thought you were in the provinces with her
once. How did you know her then?"

"I knew her in London," he answered; "we
stayed in the same lodgings for a week or two."

Blanche yawned, and he was relieved that she did not pursue the subject. It would hardly be fair, he thought, to explain the circumstances that had led to their being in the same lodgings. It was a story that might be misconstrued, especially by a woman like his wife.

Yes, he was sorry he had no influence to assist Miss King. He did like her. He wished, for her sake, that she were settled in town; and for his own, he wished that she and Blanche were friends. She would have been a visitor who interested him. It would have been an agreeable, a stimulating afternoon, when she called—it would have taken him out of himself for an hour; or, more precisely, he could have been himself. Then the momentary reflection caused him to perceive how improbable it was that Blanche and she would attract each other; they were so unlike—he did not think two women could be more dissimilar. Everything in Blanche that jarred upon him would jar upon Miss King. . . . Yes, that was a fact! It hadn't occurred to him before, but— but it was true.

Greatorex was about to begin his customary tour, and on his return to the Pantheon the revival of *Romeo and Juliet* would be resumed. Enormously successful as this had been, though, it could not continue much longer, and Oliphant

was again constrained to wonder if his engagement was drawing to a close. For Mercutio, as
for Faust, he had been engaged only for the "run
of the piece." If he were offered a second re-
engagement, he might reasonably expect to
obtain a second increase of terms, but as he and
Blanche were already living quite as luxuriously
as he desired, he wasn't eager for a higher salary;
he was inclined to wish that he had had a three-
years contract for a fixed sum, so that he could
have felt calmly confident of remaining at the
house until a distant date.

Blanche did not accompany her husband on
tour. Last summer she had not been well enough
to do so, and now to undertake a railway journey
every week with a baby and a nurse would have
been absurd. She had talked of taking them to
Eastbourne during his absence, for she could not
look forward to acting again until theatrical
London woke to activity in the autumn.

This year the company's "dates" included
Brighton. It was the last place they visited, and
they arrived after the August heat had subsided
and the season had begun. As the cab rattled
Oliphant past a hoarding on the way to his apartments, he caught sight of the title *A Lilac Chain*
on a poster of one of the two lesser theatres; and,
fresh from the bill-sticker's brush, the advertise-

ment was pleasant to him on entering the town.
So Miss King was here! He hoped he'd meet
her.

The hope was fulfilled on the next morning
but one. He did not admit to himself that he
was pacing the front after he was tired of it, but
he was feeling dejected when they came face to
face at last.

Naturally she was not surprised; everybody at
Brighton was aware that Greatorex was at the
Royal.

"Of course you know you're an enemy?" she
said, smiling. "The Pantheon company is ruining our business here; if I weren't a traitress to
my manager, I shouldn't talk to you."

"Oh, please *be* a traitress," he said. "I wondered if I should come across you. Are you
really doing badly?"

"Well, it's not one of the things one is supposed to confess, but I don't think we're turning
money away. Where do you go next week?
You're not against us again?"

"We go back to London. And you?"

"Oh, nothing so distinguished—we've a dreadful journey to Plymouth. How is *the* baby—and
your wife?"

"They're very well," he said, "thanks. I should
like you to meet my wife one day. She's in town

now, or I'd ask you if we might call on you. What is your part like in this? I looked to see if you had a Wednesday matinée—if you had, I should come."

"My part is very good—it always is—in the provinces or South Africa, where it doesn't advance me. When I say 'good,' please understand that I'm speaking strictly as an actress; I don't mean that it has anything in it: I mean that I've situations, and plenty to say."

"You ask for too much," he answered with a smile.

"Because I want to succeed?"

"Oh no; because you're not satisfied with situations and plenty to say."

"That's true," she said, "although you didn't mean it. I do ask for too much—perhaps that's why I get so little. It's hard, though, when you feel yourself capable of—— Oh, how terrible that sounds! I don't think I'm a vain woman, but if I'd gone on then, I should have horrified you."

He shook his head. "I don't think you would. If I were a dramatist I should want you in my cast. I don't know what you'd be like as Lady Macbeth——"

"*I* know," she said; "I should be shocking."

"But I can see you in some parts. If Mundey

had been a personage in the theatre, even 'Patience' would have proved useful to you: he thought you excellent. It was your misfortune that you were in a piece by a man who may never write another."

She did not make it easy for him to turn beside her, and after a few more seconds he took his leave. He trusted, however, that the morrow would be fine. And it was.

He chose the King's Road again, but it proved a disappointment. A board proclaiming at the entrance that the "band was now playing" suggested that she might be met on the pier, but here also he failed; and, discarding the shops as improbable, since she was only in a watering-place for a week, he sauntered next along the sea-wall.

It was on the sea-wall, on a bench with a book, that he discovered her, and now their conversation was wider, more inspiriting. This was on Wednesday; and on Thursday he reached the sea-wall earlier.

In conversation the added gravity in her demeanour that had struck him when he saw her on the Mirror stage, often fell from her. Her enthusiasm for something beautiful would brighten her face, and the man's mood. She understood so quickly—and she was so well

worth understanding.   Their ideas were not
always the same, but it was an unfamiliar joy
to him to find himself uttering his thoughts without the sharp fear of their exciting ridicule acting
as a brake.   Even when Miss King took a different view from his, they thought so much alike
essentially, that their arguments, like the sides
of a triangle, always met at the apex, and their
point was one after all.

On Friday she was not there.   But when he
tried the pier once more she was among a group
that watched the departure of the Worthing boat.

As he recognised his liking for her, it was
platonic.   If he had been told that in seeking
her he was committing an indiscretion, he would
have laughed at the statement quite honestly.
It was she who realised that for them to spend
the morning together every day was inadvisable,
though her reason was merely that his wife might
not like it.   However, now that he was here, it
would have been self-conscious to hurry away,
and he appealed to her sufficiently for her restraint to vanish ten minutes after they sat
down.

He had appealed to her always, and at the
Cape she had often looked back on their acquaintance.   No doubt it remained fresh in her memory
chiefly because it had been attributable to an

occurrence which no woman could ever forget;
but the man's personality had had something to
do with the fact as well. In retrospection, too.
she perceived much that she had ignored, or
taken for granted, at the time, and she told herself that there were few men who would have
proved so chivalrous to a girl under such condi-
tions. It was natural that these should appear
more appalling to her on every occasion that she
dwelt upon them; and the more she shuddered
at the danger that she had run, the more exaggerated was the tribute that she paid to her
companion's loyalty.

"What train do you go by on Sunday?" she
asked. "How glad you must be that you'll soon
be home."

"We go in the morning; I don't know by which
train. Oh yes, of course, it will be very nice to
be at home." He felt that his tone had had less
warmth than he had tried to throw into it, and
so did she; it was a surprise, and something of
a shock to her. He added quickly: "Fortunately,
my wife isn't playing now, or I should find the
evenings rather dull till we reopen."

"Isn't it wonderful to you sometimes," said
Miss King, "to reflect that you're Mercutio at
the Pantheon?"

"Don't think I'm ungrateful; but it isn't, any

longer. I only wonder that I *don't* find it wonderful."

"But that's pathetic," she said; "I shouldn't like that. Do you mean to say that the pleasure of success is so very fleeting, that you, who not three years ago were—may I say it?—who not three years ago were quite unknown in London, and spoke of pawning your watch, are *blasé* already?"

"I did pawn it," said Oliphant. "I don't like the word *blasé;* it always sounds a pose to me; but it's true that I haven't the thrill, the ecstasy that I always imagined I should have, presuming I ever got so far. You were stage struck before you went into the profession, of course?"

"Violently; I used to tremble at the sight of a playbill. Why?"

"Well, after you had been acting for a year, didn't you ever stand on a stage just before the curtain went up, dismayed to find yourself so cool? Didn't you ever think: 'I am an *actress; I* am standing here on a real stage, behind a real curtain, and there's a real audience on the other side of it who'll hear me speak my six lines in a minute or two'? Didn't you try to work yourself up into the state of tremor that you were astonished that you didn't feel?"

She nodded. "Often! It's just what I did do."

"Well, it's just the same when one gets further. I say, 'How rapturous it ought to be!' "

"It's not a fair comparison," she said earnestly; "that's wrong, it's wicked of you. Do you know what that will mean if you aren't careful?—it will mean that you'll lose your ambition. Don't do that. You won't—because we both love the stage, and it needs ideals—you won't be false to that dream of yours?"

"Why," he cried, "didn't we talk of it yesterday? You forget."

"I missed something yesterday," she said; "I *don't* forget. I remember how you talked that day outside the Museum, and you didn't sound quite so fervid yesterday."

Oliphant sighed. He had not married Blanche when he dreamed outside the Museum. Dulling his aspiration now was the vague consciousness that he was picturing a future which his wife would depreciate were it gained.

"I am as fervid in my heart," he said, "God knows. In my heart the stage is as dear to me, my aims are as high, as before you and I ever met—as high as when I was at the Varsity seeing visions, and worshipping a stage that doesn't live."

"I'm glad," she said. "*I'm* nobody; and when your theatre exists I shall be too old to begin to make a reputation in London, and too sad to go there only to make a living. But all for our stage, and not for myself, I should like to see you, who have the talent and the chance, keep brave enough to make your dream come true. Remember that a man is young as long as he retains his enthusiasm; you have such time in front of you—use it for all it's worth! Your opportunities are so splendid—don't waste them. Accomplish, Mr. Oliphant. Think what you've done, and strain every nerve till you've done all you meant to do."

The band had finished, and the crowd was streaming towards the turnstiles. Miss King rose, and he sauntered beside her to the Parade. Here they were about to separate, for their lodgings lay in opposite directions, but as they loitered to a standstill Oliphant was greeted by the actor who played the part of Friar Laurence. The Friar told him that a telegram for him was lying at the theatre, and having dropped the information, continued his way, which was to the Bodega. When Oliphant rejoined her, Alma saw that he had turned pale.

"Is anything the matter?"

"He says there's a wire for me at the theatre;

it can only be from home—I'm afraid the baby may be ill."

"Oh," she faltered, "why imagine such a thing?" She looked away, with a pang at her heart—she had now learned almost as much of his married life as he could have told her.

"The Royal is on your road, isn't it? Do you mind driving?" He hailed an open fly at the same moment, and she got in.

"You're very foolish to be frightened," she said, as he took his seat; "surely there may be a dozen reasons why your wife should wire you? Mightn't it be business?"

"I daresay—I don't know. I suppose it's foolish, but she has never wired me before; it was the first thing I thought of." It was only now that it occurred to him that it might be Blanche who was ill. "Of course she may be ill herself," he muttered. "Or—or it may be nothing at all."

She saw that the kindest thing she could do was to be silent; and they did not speak until the stage-door was reached.

"Don't stop inside!" she said.

The door swung to behind him, and she sat watching it.

Oliphant tore the telegram open in the passage. There was no shock, only a confirmation

of his groundless terror.   The message ran:
"Baby ill; I think you ought to come up quickly."
He put his hand over his eyes.   "Quickly?"   But
he must play Mercutio first!   And meanwhile
the child might die.

He walked back to the cab, and held the telegram out.   He did not look at her as she read
it—he was looking at nothing up the street.   The
pause in which her sympathy sought for words
seemed to the woman to last a long time.

"Is it strange for a man to care so much for
a little baby?" he asked huskily.

"What can I say to you?" she murmured, in
a voice that expressed everything.   "You can
be there to-night?   Oh, of course—Mercutio has
finished so early!   What train can you catch?"

"I don't know—I must find out.   Don't
trouble; it's awfully good of you, but——   I'm
very fond of him, you see, and of course I'm
worried.   I'll go and look at a time-table."

"It mayn't be so serious as your wife thinks.
She'd naturally be alarmed and fear the worst.
When you get home, you may find him out of
danger."   But she had noticed that the telegram
had been despatched at seven in the morning,
and she felt what this delay that he had to bear
must be to him.

"I daresay," he said; "yes—thanks.   Where

shall I tell the man to drive? No, why get out? What street did you say you were in?"

She steadied her lip between her teeth for an instant. "Dome Street," she said; "number six. Will you—Mr. Oliphant, will you let me know when you come back? Hope for the best!"

He had paid the cabman, and was turning away when she called to him eagerly.

"Get in," she cried, "get in and drive to the station! Perhaps you can get home and back before the piece begins!"

He hadn't thought of that. The suggestion, the vague chance, quickened his nerves. The cab rocked as they raced up the hill.

They learnt that the best train left at two, and was due at Victoria at 3.40. He might be at home before four; the doubt was whether he could return in time. But they had ten minutes to find out, and they saw that, allowing him an hour in the flat, it was possible; there was a train from Victoria at 5.2 which reached Brighton at seven.

"You'll soon be with him now," she said at the window of the compartment. "Don't worry more than you can help!"

Her earnest face was the last thing that impressed him vividly until he saw his wife's.

There was no need to frame the question. The

answer was in the air. He knew the child was dead.

Blanche's eyes were swollen, and the hair on her forehead was moist with eau de Cologne. Her hands hung inertly at her sides. At the sight of him she burst into tears, and he took her in his arms. Neither had spoken yet. She spoke first.

"He died at ten o'clock," she said.

Oliphant released her, and crossed the floor quite aimlessly. He stared down at the traffic for a minute, and retraced his steps.

"What time did he—die?" he asked.

"At ten o'clock," she repeated. "We thought it was only a cold—with his teeth; and then the doctor said it was pneumonia. He was a very good doctor. Mother was here, too—she's just gone out; she'll be back presently. Oh, my little angel in Heaven! I've cried myself ill!"

"Where?" said Oliphant, after another silence.

"In the nursery," she replied.

The word made him wince. He went to the room slowly, and crept forward as if the child had slept. The curtains of the cot were drawn. He parted them, and looked. He had left the door open: he went back and shut it; and sat down.

The woman wandered about the drawing-room. Her head ached badly, and she reflected that it was fortunate "Mother" was available "to see to things," for she could never have done it herself: she was too highly strung. It seemed thankless to perceive the fact—and she wouldn't for the world hurt Mother's feelings by hinting it—but to be able to attend to such matters implied a certain callousness. . . . Her little angel in Heaven! She gazed at the sky from the window where Oliphant had stared at the omnibuses. Her "precious" was with God! The possibility of a future state was a subject to which normally she never gave a thought, but now an unconscious remembrance of a Transformation Scene soothed her pain. . . .

Royce was a long while in there! He would be frightfully grieved of course—he had been so fond of Baby. What she really needed was to be with someone who hadn't loved the mite; she was so miserable that she wanted brightening up! She required to be taken away somewhere and made to forget; she ought to be compelled to gather a little amusement. . . .

Jay's! . . . Crape for an infant would be too much. In black, as she had fair hair—— How horrid it was to be obliged to think of such things! Ah, but how passionately she suffered in her heart—nobody could understand! Still people would pity her, and talk.   Even the public would speak of her loss sympathetically: "That poor Blanche Ellerton!"   If *The Era* and *The Stage* commented on it, no doubt a few of the other papers would say something too.   What day was it?   Friday.   (Oh, the unlucky day! her darling had died on a Friday!)   *The Era* came out to-morrow—they wouldn't know so soon.   Unless . . . Perhaps if the news were "expressed" to the office at once——?

Oliphant replaced the curtains gently.   He fancied it must be nearly half an hour since he entered the room; he had forgotten Blanche, and before he left he must try to comfort her.   Poor girl, how red her eyes were!

She rose and went to him quickly as he returned, and he held her close again.

"Doesn't he look sweet?" she whispered.

He found nothing to say in answer to this.

"I shall be home on Sunday, for good, you know," he said, since speech was essential.

She nodded.   "When's your train back?"

"At five."   He glanced at his watch—the time had gone more rapidly than he had supposed. "Your mother will stop with you, won't she?"

"Yes. . . . Have you had anything to eat? Will you have something now?"

"I'm not hungry; no, thanks, dear."

"You'd better have a drink," she said, turning to a syphon and a spirit-flask. "I've just had some brandy for my head. You ought to have something or other before the show!"

He sat down in the chair that she had vacated by the table. A letter, not folded yet, lay against his hand, and he drummed his fingers on it while she poured out the brandy. He pushed it to and fro. He began to read it—mechanically, with no interest in the letter. Its sense did not penetrate his stupor all at once: "I should be so grateful if you could find space to mention. . . . My little baby died this morning." What was that? "I should be so grateful if you could find space——" O God! The meaning rushed upon him and turned him sick. She could devise an advertisement from her child's death!

The soda-water spurted noisily. It was the only sound in the room for several seconds. He sat motionless, his gaze riveted on her handwriting; and Blanche, holding the glass, stood watching him. She was chagrined to find him reading the note—he might misconstrue it and think her unfeeling! Was he going to reproach her?

He was questioning what he should say. That she revolted him? He could tell her no less if he spoke of it at all. He might destroy the note, forbid its being sent. She would defend herself, perhaps have hysterics; and he was too heart-sick to remonstrate and discuss and upbraid. To what end all that? She was as she was; a painful scene wouldn't regenerate her. But was she human?

He got up, and she met him with the glass diffidently.

"You're going to have your drink, aren't you?" she asked.

"No," he said, "I don't want one, thank you. I must go, or I shall miss the train. Where's my hat? . . . Good-bye."

"Good-bye, darling," she said.

He would not, he could not, touch her face; he dropped the sound of a kiss upon her hair. She had put her arms round his neck, and he thanked Heaven when he was free of them.

To act at night was a restorative; it was the afterwards, sitting alone in his apartments, that was terrible. And more terrible still was the thought that he must so soon sit with her at home. Home? The place where she had trampled on the dead! Now that the child was gone, what did it hold? His child, even more his hopes for his child, had leavened the bitterness of his blunder; but the pictures he had seen of Hugh at three and Hugh at seven, of Hugh head boy at Harrow, could never be looked at again. They must be put away—his pictures and Baby's all together. And she could—— And she was his wife! The woman who could do this thing was his wife! Why should such women bear children? Well, she had known herself; she had done her best to prevent it!

He remembered that Miss King was waiting to hear from him—he would go in the morning. She had told him her address, and begged him to let her know. The number had escaped him, but she was staying in Dome Street. Was it six?

He went at half-past ten, before she was likely to be out. The alternative of seeking her among the crowd on the front jarred upon him to-day, and in the afternoon she would be playing at the theatre.

The landlady ushered him without inquiry into a small parlour. Alma was kneeling before a theatrical hamper, completing her packing. She lifted herself slowly, and advanced with her gaze fixed on his face.

"He is dead," said Oliphant.

She put out her hand, and he held it tightly. There was comfort in her touch.

"Sit down," she murmured, moving to the hearth. "I—I was afraid it meant that, when

no message came last night. . . . You know
what I want to ask you?"

"I was too late."

They sat opposite each other without speaking. The misery in his eyes made her heart
ache.

"You're packing early," said Oliphant at last,
with an effort.

"Yes; we've a matinée, you know, and the
lorry will be here this afternoon. We leave at
seven in the morning."

"Where do you go?—to Plymouth, isn't it?
And then? How long does the tour last?"

"I think we're booked up to the last week in
December. Don't make small talk, please. I
don't want to."

"I didn't come to depress you—perhaps it was
rather cowardly to come at all. I might have
sent you word."

"It was kinder to come. I don't like to ask
you questions, but if you could speak of him to
me, I should be glad."

"It's all *here!*" he exclaimed chokily.

"Ah, I know. But it will go—the worst. The
memory won't go, but it gets tenderer. You'll
love to think of him by and by."

"It seems so motiveless, a little child like that.
He was—if you had seen him you'd understand.

Of course everybody thinks his own child best,
but he—had ways. *Why* should he be born only
to be snatched from me again? I wanted him
so much! . . . You believe—do you believe—in
Heaven?"

"Yes. I'm so simple a woman that I've never
questioned it. When I lost my mother, my only
comfort was that I wasn't clever and full of
doubts. Are *you* so clever that you're hopeless
now?"

"No; I believe," he said. "I haven't the imagination to conceive that Heaven's a myth."

"I suppose that each of us has a different
notion of Heaven, just as all the notions are
wrong; but I only think of it as a place where
people who've loved are given back to one another and need never fear parting any more. I
don't see how mine can be *very* wrong. And I
think we shall look just the same to them,
although we may have grown old since we lost
them, as we did the day they died. I think I
shall still look a girl to my mother if I live to be
eighty." She gave a half smile. "If I am good
enough to go to Heaven!"

"And they too us?" he asked. "Should *I* find
a baby in fifty years?"

"Yes, I think you would find a little baby in
fifty years. Just the little baby you had kissed,

and remembered. But *you* should be able to give ideas to *me*—you were going to be a clergyman."

"You," said Oliphant, "are a good woman; a good woman can teach us all." He had not mentioned his wife's name, and the reservation by which he imagined that half his sorrow had been concealed was doubling Alma's compassion for him.

He was loath to take his leave, and even when he had risen, they lingered by the window.

"I'm glad I came," he said at last; "you've been very kind to me. I wish we hadn't matinées, or that you didn't start so early to-morrow. Now I'll let you finish your packing." He looked round the humble room bright with the morning sunshine. "Are those books yours? Are they to go in too?" He went to the chair where they lay, and brought them to her, and stood beside her while she put them in the hamper. "Good-bye, Miss King."

"Good-bye," she said. "And think of your art and your hopes, and make us all proud of you!"

"I wonder when I shall meet you again? You and I are always being good friends for a little while, and then losing sight of each other, aren't we?"

The firmness of her hand-clasp seemed to lend him strength, as it had given him comfort when he entered. Yes, his art remained!

Alma went back to the window, and watched him till he turned the corner of the street.

CHAPTER XVI

He did not return to town until the morning of the funeral. In the afternoon the cot and the toys, all the belongings of the dead baby, were removed from the nursery. The room was now Oliphant's; it was here that he studied and he slept.

There had been no open rupture, for Blanche had refrained from asking his reason; she knew it, and affected to attribute the expression of his wish to morbid grief. She considered that he was suffering from a temporary derangement of the intellect, and the time to show her resentment would be when he came to his senses.

But to a man of Oliphant's temperament no other course was possible if they were to remain under one roof. When he reflected that within six hours of their child's death she could do what she had done, she appeared to him a monstrosity. Every nerve in him shrank from the suggestion of contact with her. He felt that to take this abnormal creature in his arms as a wife would be a horrible action—an offence after which he would be degraded, and repulsive to himself.

Holding his cause the slightest, and yet afraid of discussing it, Blanche's disguise was at first painfully thin, her amiability was an obvious bravado. But as the weeks went by, the influence of custom softened the asperities of the anomalous relationship. Both were in engagements: Oliphant still at the Pantheon—where *Romeo and Juliet* had been succeeded by a revival of *Much Ado About Nothing*—and the woman deriving consolation from a hit at the Pall Mall. With months they acquired a manner nearly as free as that which had subsisted between them before the baby died. Oliphant could sit in a room with her without shuddering; and if a prolonged tête-à-tête distressed him still, this had its compensation to her in the fact that it made him readier to accept the invitations of "people worth knowing"—a circle which, thanks to her assiduity and his professional successes, was gradually widening to the "romantic couple."

By the time the season had well advanced, the circle had supplied a counter-irritant to her original complaint. People, otherwise well-bred, question artists about their prospects and their incomes with an effrontery that they would never dream of displaying towards those in business, and gushing matrons sometimes asked her when she and her clever, delightful husband were going to have a theatre of their own. This unconscious impertinence galled her, because if Royce had not been a noodle—that was how she mentally expressed it—they might have had their own theatre already. She craved for her own theatre and the attendant importance. When she mentioned the subject to him he was as unsatisfactory as ever, and there were moments of solitude in which she raged, and demanded of the irresponsive walls what marriage with such a visionary had given to her.

She determined to put Otho Fairbairn's friendship to the test herself; and one afternoon, when she was at home alone, he was announced. She prayed that no one else would call.

"Royce is out," she murmured; "but I daresay he'll be back soon. Put your hat down."

"You look tired," he said with concern.

She shrugged her shoulders and laughed constrainedly: "Oh no! What's the news?"

"With me? Do I ever have news? I came to hear news—to be entertained. Behold the selfishness of man and the abuse of hospitality!"

"I don't think you ever find us very entertaining, do you?" she said. "I was beginning to think you found us so dull that you weren't coming

any more. How long is it since you've been here
—three months?"

"Mrs. Royce!" He had begged leave to call
her "Mrs. Royce," saying "the other sounded
so awfully formal"; and when she had lisped
"O*tho* formal!" permission was accorded.

"Three months, isn't it?" she said; "or is it
four? We were asking each other what we had
done!"

"Mrs. Royce! It's not two! And I've been
away. You aren't offended with me really, are
you?"

Until now it had not occurred to her that she
might be offended; she had only been impatient
for his visit; but it was amusing to watch his
pink-and-white dismay. She nodded slowly.

"Oh, I say, I'm immensely sorry," he exclaimed, "if you mean it! And is Royce, too?"

"I can't answer for Royce. *I*'m offended, if
that matters!"

"Oh, please don't be unkind; I've been away,
on my honour! I left town the first week in May
—broke all my engagements and went into the
country. Impulse. But in future I am always
going to spend the season in the country. That
London should be fashionable during the months
when the country looks its loveliest is a monu-
mental instance of human perversity. I was at

Studland—I don't suppose you know it? I can't tell you how peaceful, how divine it was!"

"Has she accepted you?" asked the lady.

"Oh, now you're chaffing—that means I'm forgiven. Thank you, Mrs. Royce."

"I'm quite serious. You don't expect me to believe that you left town in May for—where was it?—somewhere peaceful and divine, unless there was an attraction?"

"There *was* an attraction," said Otho; "there was Nature! Nature and Art. I was down there with a man who was making studies for a picture. You observe I'm technical: 'making studies'! He used to paint, and I used to read poetry. I got up at eight every morning, and lived in the sunshine. When I think of all the springs I've wasted in Piccadilly I feel I've been a most awful ass, really I do."

"And you didn't read the poetry to a girl?"

"I never spoke to a girl the whole time I was there. One doesn't keep talking about some things, Mrs. Royce, but there are wounds that don't heal." He looked at her plaintively. "Did you think I was so shallow that I could forget so soon? You were very nice to me once when I stayed and bored you an unconscionable time. I thought you understood that I shouldn't forget?"

"But you *must* forget," she replied. "I remember what I said better than you do. I said you'd meet somebody before long who would make you ashamed of yourself for having railed against us poor women. All women were heartless because one girl had treated you badly. Oh, Mr. Fairbairn!"

"I know," he said. "Yes, I was very absurd—all that's past. *You* were the 'somebody' who made me ashamed of that. But I shall never love again. I could never feel more than friendship for any woman now."

"You are very faithful!" she said, regarding him with a display of eager interest. "I thought it was only my sex who could be so faithful as all that?"

"*Your* sex?" he exclaimed. "Why——"

"Ah!" she said, lifting an admonitory finger.

"*You* are always the exception, Mrs. Royce!" he laughed.

"The 'present company,'" said she. "Of course!"

"No, but I mean it honestly. I've never seen any woman so—so sympathetic, and so devoted to her husband as you are. I congratulated Royce verbally before I met you—as in duty bound; but since I've known you, I've congratulated him a hundred times in my own mind. And

how he has forged ahead since his marriage!
You've been a Mascotte to him."

She sighed.

"Don't you think you have? Why are you
looking doubtful?"

"Oh, of course he has got on," she said; "but
I wish my mascotry—what is the word?—could
take him further! I want to see Royce in a
position to choose his parts and to show people
what he can really do."

"He ought to have a theatre," said Fairbairn.

Her hands rose, and fell to her lap, in a little
impatient gesture: "Let's talk of something else,
Mr. Fairbairn, please—I didn't mean to mention
this! I know you once offered to start him in a
theatre, so it's the one subject I can't speak to
you about."

"But why?" he asked. "Why can't you?"

"Isn't it natural? You might think I——
Besides, Royce would be very angry if he knew
that I'd let you guess we were troubled."

"Do you mean that you are in trouble because
he can't take a theatre—that you are both worry-
ing about it?"

"Don't make me say any more," she begged.
"I'd rather not!"

"But"——his eyes were big and grieved. "Is
this fair to me? You know I'd like to serve

Royce. And I thought you and I were friends?
You must trust me. Between ourselves! Do
you really mean you're both worried because he
can't take a theatre?"

"Well, I'll say that *I* am. If you spoke to
Royce, he would tell you that it is too soon—
according to Royce it will always be too soon!
Royce lacks confidence. This is one of the cases
where a woman sees further than a man. Royce
is wasting his time at the Pantheon now. He
can never do any better there than he has done.
What has he to look forward to? That Greatorex
will ask him to play *his* parts? Or put on *Othello*
to give Mr. Royce Oliphant the opportunity to
make the success of the evening as Iago? Short
of management he has gone as far as he can
get. Well! one day he will go into management.
Some capitalist will come along and offer to
back him—there is no risk about it; it will be
a very good investment—but he won't be so
young then; some of his best years will have
been lost; the time between to-day and the day
when the capitalist appears will have been
wasted. I see it more clearly than the poor boy
himself, though, if he told the truth, *he* sees it
partially too. As his wife, how can I help being
distressed?"

"But, my dear Mrs. Royce," cried Otho, "why

haven't you said this to me before? You knew of my offer to him——why didn't you hint to me that it might be repeated? I've never thought about it; he seemed to me to be doing splendidly —what do *I* know of stage matters? I feel awfully guilty, really! Of course, he ought to have a theatre! Now you've put it to me, I understand. I'll have a talk to him this afternoon."

"No, no!" she said, aflame with joy; "it mustn't look as if it came from *me*—he'd never forgive me. Speak to him when you're here again; and be firm! Tell him he's a fool, and insist on having your way—I should fancy you generally get your way when your mind is made up, don't you? Say——oh, say whatever you like, but don't let him suspect that we've been exchanging confidences, or his pride will be up in arms in a moment!"

Otho promised to exercise the utmost diplomacy; the confederate was to say little, and he was to address his arguments as much to her as to Oliphant. It was arranged that he should drop in a few days later without warning. The subtlety of the well-meant scheme to deceive his friend pleased him vastly, and it was not a whit less gratifying as he took his leave to remember that "Mrs. Royce" would be benefited as well.

Blanche thought he was the most charming young man she had ever met. She had not nursed many misgivings, but the alacrity of his response warmed her heart towards him; she regretted that she had been compelled to be a trifle disingenuous.

The plan was duly executed; but, to her surprise and joy, Oliphant demurred very faintly. He proved quite willing to be persuaded that it was not premature for him to adventure management. He had been loath to take the first step, averse from asking the favour, but now that Fairbairn again came forward without solicitation, every pulse in him leapt with gladness.

"You would be backing your opinion of us very heavily, Otho," he said; "don't forget that if it proved a mistake, it would be an expensive one! If you're prepared to risk it, Heaven knows *I* can't say 'Don't'! But think the matter well over first; we'll talk of it again."

"I've nothing to think about," persisted Fairbairn; "it's for you to say 'yes' or 'no.' If I'm any judge of acting, I *shan't* lose—on the contrary, it will be a rattling good thing for me." He turned to Blanche. "You see the commercial instinct can't be silenced, Mrs. Royce; it's hereditary!"

She laughed. "A theatre is a business to

everyone.   Well, it's nothing to do with *me*—
Royce must decide."

"You know the only lines on which I'd run
a theatre," said Oliphant, speaking thickly; "I
want to produce the best available work.   There
will be no concessions to catch the crowd.   There
is no fortune, no large income, to be made from
a theatre that I control."

"It's going to be 'art for art's sake,' " returned
Otho; "I quite understand.   I haven't a con-
suming desire to drop a heap of money, but I
can't pretend that I'm only actuated by the hope
of making a pot, either.   If it does put anything
in my pocket, I shan't be angry with you; if it
only pays expenses there'll be satisfaction enough
in feeling that I've a share in an artistic undertaking.   Which theatre do you think you might
get?"

"I haven't a notion.   We shan't get a house
directly we want one, you know—I can't walk
into management next month.   And first there
are the plays to be considered—there are a great
many things to be considered!   I warn you
you'll be badgered to death before the curtain
goes up."

"Not I!   I shall come to the first night, or
the dress-rehearsal, when the bother is all over.
The work is for you, my friend!"

"Well," cried Oliphant, "we shall have to go into figures, and you shall tell me what your idea is." His excitement broke into action, and he clapped Fairbairn on the shoulder wildly. "You shall be proud of your stage, Otho! I don't swear for the actor-manager, but you shall be proud of the work, I promise you! What do you say, Blanche? We'll do him justice, won't we?"

She assented gaily, but he had not waited for her assent. Momentarily he had forgotten that their views were opposed, and his delight was boundless. It was only after an appointment had been made for the morrow, and Fairbairn had gone, that the first stir of remembrance tinged elation with regret, and he perceived anew that to his own ears the triumphal march must always have a discord.

Blanche and he paced the room. Both were shaken by the prospect, but to each the prospect was different. The wife saw the obvious—showy parts, public adulation and professional defer-ence, and a life-size portrait of herself in the foyer. How she wished that one or two women that she hated would apply for engagements! The man, to whom dramatic art was a religion, saw a theatre that should be the expression of his life. He saw on how marvellous a basis this ideal theatre would be reared—due to a friend who did not regard it as a means of money-making. As he realised the magnitude of his opportunity, Oliphant trembled, and wrung his hands in a prayer that he might be worthy of the power vested in him.

She brought him back to the practical with a jerk.

"What shall we put our salaries down at?" she asked.

"I haven't thought about it," he said. "How much do you suggest?"

"A hundred," she said promptly.

"A hundred?" he echoed. "How a hundred?"

"*I'm* getting twenty."

"But *I'm* very far from getting eighty! How a hundred? In common gratitude we must put down our salaries at less than they would be anywhere else—not more! Remember that the capital is entirely Otho's; *we* risk nothing."

" 'Less'?" she exclaimed; "when we do all the work?"

"My dear Blanche, we share the profits."

"Yes, I know. Well, if we charge the same it's fair enough—I don't see why we should charge 'less.' If it weren't for us, there wouldn't *be* any profits."

"And if it weren't for Otho's generosity, we shouldn't have a theatre. He is doing a very wonderful thing—let's show that we appreciate it! There's not one man in a million who would start another in a theatre from pure good feeling. He gives us perfect liberty—he says: 'You want a theatre; take one, and play whatever you like. If there's a loss I'll meet it.' It's an unprecedented offer. It isn't even as if he felt as—as we do. Otho is a fellow who likes literature and art everywhere excepting on the stage. If it weren't for us—and he ran a theatre at all—he'd do it for a lark and put up musical comedy. We can't treat him as if he were a speculator."

"What did you mean," she said, "by telling him there couldn't be any fortune, any large income? Why not? They say Wilkie made fifty thousand pounds out of *Only Once More* alone!"

"*Only Once More* was a farce," said Oliphant; "we don't propose to play farce, do we? You wouldn't like that yourself?"

"No, but plenty of dramas make money. Look what the Hendons made at the Mirror! That was drama. Look what Shedlock is doing at the Queen's with this last ghastly thing—I hear the people are eating it."

He shivered.

"I think you know," he said, "I'd rather be in engagements all my life than have a theatre and run it on Mr. Shedlock's lines. I'll produce

the best work, or none.   And believe me,
Blanche, you can get all you want by aiming
at the highest—you will be much more prominent
than if you content yourself with the second-
rate."

"But I *shan't* get all I want if we're going to
be poor all our lives," she answered.   "I do
hope, Royce, you aren't going to fritter this
chance away on fads?"

" 'Poor,' " he repeated; "do you think we're
poor? What more can you want? You've heaps
of frocks; we've a pretty flat; you need never
look twice at a five-pound note——"

"But all this," she interrupted impatiently,
"will be poverty when we're in management.
We aren't going to live here, and have two people
to lunch once a month, when we've our theatre.
We shall have to give garden parties, and entertain on a big scale."

He looked at her, surprised.

"Why?" he said.   "And how?   What with?"

"Yes, 'what with?'—that's just it! If we don't
make money, we can't do it.   Our salaries, especially if you're going to cut them down, won't
be enough.   One minute you say we share the
profits, and the next you say there won't be
any."

"I don't think I said that—I certainly trust

there *will* be. All I said was that they wouldn't be great, at all events at the beginning. I'm not so eccentric that I'd rather avoid a profit than make one."

"That's some comfort!" she returned. "Of course one wants to do good pieces! You don't suppose that *I*'m so eccentric that I'd prefer them bad, do you? Only no *Brand,* Royce—if you're going to open the campaign with *Brand* because you want to play the part, we shall be doomed."

"Have you read it?" he inquired.

"No, dear," she said, "but I tried to."

Oliphant converted a sigh into a laugh.

"Well," he replied, "I wasn't thinking of *Brand.* I'd like to work with you hand in hand, Blanche. Let's correct each other's mistakes— we both make them, no doubt. If you tend to one extreme, I suppose, *I* tend to the other. If we meet half-way——"

"It will be a sensible compromise!" she declared, smiling.

His heart sank at the word; he had felt it coming when he paused, and the clang of it knelled in his soul. Was he talking of "compromise" in the first hour? No, he would *not* juggle with his conscience; he would be true to his faith! Though conquest abroad would be rendered ten times harder by opposition in his home, he would stick to his colours to the last. He had yearned for this opportunity, dreamed of it, laboured and lived for it. God had sent it to him; and by God's help he would justify the boon!

CHAPTER XVII

IT was at last decided that the joint salary of the actor-manager and his wife should be fifty pounds. Otho was to be responsible for the rent, the cost of production, and all expenses "behind" and "in front," and he volunteered to spend seventy pounds a week in newspaper advertisements, though Oliphant had estimated them at less than sixty. With the work he was to have no concern. Profits were to be equally divided; and Oliphant, while stipulating that there should be no fees for cloak-rooms or programmes, undertook that the business-manager should arrange for advertisements on the programmes, the commission on the hire of opera-glasses, and the sub-letting of the bars to the best advantage. These were all details of which Otho knew nothing, and of which Oliphant knew much less than he supposed. They pertained to the seamy side of a theatrical enterprise, and could not be ignored, however; indeed, the further the project progressed, the more complicated did the seamy side become.

But before it appeared to progress at all, Oliphant was dismayed to see how time passed—how the weeks and months went by until the first night, never any nearer, seemed as elusive as a will-o'-the-wisp. The earliest idea had been to obtain a lease of the Embankment Theatre, but Otho, buoyant with champagne one night, had soared superior to the scheme just when the negotiations were assuming definite shape, and had declared that he wanted to take a bigger house and "run the whole thing on first-class lines." Oliphant, who was hankering to have a poetic play of Sylvain Lacour's done into English—a production demanding elaborate mise-en-scène—was only too ready to be convinced that the bolder course was the wiser; and the solicitor to the Embankment coming to terms tardily, found that he had come to terms too late.

A bigger house was not immediately available; nor could Sylvain Lacour be brought to believe all at once that any translation could do justice to his genius. A visit to Paris, with the offer of an increased percentage of the receipts, persuaded him that he had underrated the resources of the English language; but the English poet on whom Oliphant had set his heart was temporarily incapacitated by gout, and there were, moreover, all kinds of anxieties and disappointments relative to the modern drama by which *God and the State* was to be followed.

This *God and the State* appeared to be an admirable selection for the opening venture. Though Lacour might not be a great dramatic poet, he came as near to being one as did any writer living. The action of the play was laid on an imaginary island, and the period was described simply as "The Past," but the interest was for all lands and for all times. The central situation, too, was magnificent, and though it was a finer acting-scene for Blanche than for himself, Oliphant would have felt it a privilege merely to produce such a work. That its beauty should pass unnoticed looked to him impossible.

Blanche, who was unable to read French, had heard enough to understand that she had a very emotional part, and she therefore forgave its being in verse. Her principal objection was that her costume must be simple and poor. Oliphant had his Court apart from her, his scenes of splendour; but the heroine, like the daughter of Triboulet, lived in a world contained by four walls, and only reached the gates of the palace, in the last act, to die.

Meanwhile, she had other meditations. When they opened the theatre, they must have a larger drawing-room; she had determined that. A garden possibly she might have to waive, but a larger drawing-room was essential. It was not necessary to discuss the matter with Royce, but she utilised her morning strolls to interrogate various house-agents in the neighbourhood. On one occasion she met Otho in Victoria Street, and, as they proceeded towards the flat together, she told him where she had been.

"I'm not talking to Royce about it," she explained; "he has enough to think of; but it would be idiotic for us to remain where we are when we go into management. The more people we have home, and the more we visit, the better for all of us it will be. Did you know that?"

"It never occurred to me, Mrs. Royce; of course you're quite right, though."

"I'm so glad you agree with me," she said.

"I always do, I think."

"I think you do—it's very sweet of you! On the first night we must have a reception on the stage. I want you to bring everybody you can. Women as well! Women can be so useful. When—oh when, Mr. Fairbairn—shall we know for sure? Oh, the suspense of it all! It's simply awful."

"Royce expects to settle for the Mayfair, you know, now," he said. "I do wish we could have got ahead more quickly for your sake."

"Oh!" she turned to him with swift depreca-
tion; "please don't think me such a horrid ungrateful wretch as to grumble to you. Even
if we had got the theatre, we couldn't open
yet. Nobody can help it; and *you*—well, if I
grumbled to *you,* I should deserve a shaking."
Her eyes laughed in his for an instant. "I think
I should ask you to give it to me!"

The young man met her gaze with a touch of
embarrassment that he did not care to define.

"Well, I believe we shall have a huge triumph
when the piece *is* produced," he declared. "Don't
you? Of course I've no experience, and I only
judge as an outsider, but when I read it, I was
tremendously impressed."

"How cruel of you to remind me of my appalling ignorance! *I'm* simply dying to read it, and
I can't."

"Oh," he said, "I forgot. Tell me! Shall I
make you a rough translation? Would you like
me to?"

"Oh, no," she exclaimed; "how can you propose such a thing? Why, it would be most
frightful trouble!"

"It wouldn't be any trouble at all, done for
you. I'll start it to-night."

"Do you mean it? Really? But to-night?
Aren't you going anywhere?"

"I wasn't going anywhere particular. It will be an immense pleasure to me, I assure you. Don't expect it for a few days; you know, being verse, it will take a little time, although I shall only aim at conveying the sense. I'll send it to you directly it's finished."

"You might spare half an hour more and bring it, mightn't you?" she suggested.

"So I might," he said. "Then directly it's finished, I'll bring it to you."

"And read it!" added Blanche gaily. "Oh, you must certainly read it. The adapter always reads the play!"

His cheeks grew pinker. "My dear Mrs. Royce, I've a fair amount of self-esteem—not to call it 'vanity'—but I shouldn't have the pluck to read it aloud to *you* to save my life."

She hung her head in mock abashment.

"I shouldn't," he insisted; "honour bright!"

"Am I such a terrible person?" she inquired humbly.

"No, but you're an actress, and you'd make game of me—not openly of course, but——"

The reproach in her face shamed him.

"You can't mean that," she said; "you know better! Here we are! Come in and see Royce!"

Oliphant was in an arm-chair before the fire, with *The Stage* in his hands. Blanche asked him what he was doing with it, for it had been issued some days. She unpinned her hat, and Otho took her coat from her; he was conscious of a pleased interest as he watched her settling her hair before the glass.

"I was looking down the 'Professional Cards,'" replied Oliphant; "I want to find out where Miss King is, if I can. I'd like to offer her an engagement when the time comes."

"Miss King?" said Blanche. "Oh, yes, I know! But why—why this philanthropy?"

"Who is Miss King?" asked Otho. He found that he was still stroking Blanche's muff, and he put it aside. "I think I'll have one of your cigarettes, Royce."

"There they are, old man, behind you. Miss King is a very clever woman. 'Philanthropy'? There's no philanthropy about it. Where does 'philanthropy' come in?"

"It's a blessed word, anyhow," murmured Otho, inhaling—"like 'Mesopotamia.'"

"And just as irrelevant," said Oliphant. "I want to offer her an engagement in the piece because I don't think we could get anybody better."

Blanche laughed shortly.

"When did everyone else die?" she inquired. "How very absurd, Royce—'couldn't get anybody better'! She's a provincial actress, Mr.

Fairbairn, who fascinated my impressionable husband by the genius with which she did nothing at some matinée. Engage her, my dear boy, by all means, I'm sure *I* don't mind; but say it's because you like her, not because you couldn't get anybody better. I thought we were to have a West End company—in which case we could get a good many people better."

"Then I am going to engage her because I like her," answerd Oliphant. "But for Otho's satisfaction, perhaps you'll permit me to repeat that she has talent; I shouldn't suggest casting her for 'Astolaine' if I weren't sure of it."

Otho puffed his cigarette a shade uncomfortably.

"I daresay she'll be very good," he observed, eager to say the right thing, and failing signally. "'Astolaine' would appeal to *any* woman, I should say!"

"What do you mean?" exclaimed Blanche. "Is 'Astolaine' an important part, Royce?"

"'Astolaine' is your sister. It's not a long part—it's the most important woman's part after yours, of course; in fact, it's the only important woman's part besides yours."

She looked from one man to the other incredulously.

"And you're going to give it to a woman who

isn't known," she demanded; "to a woman who has never spoken twenty lines in town? What for? I don't think Mr. Fairbairn is so anxious to save five pounds a week on the salary list; are you, Mr. Fairbairn?"

"My dear Mrs. Royce," he stammered, "you can engage whom you like—anybody you both decide on—you know the arrangements have nothing to do with me at all."

"We shan't save *anything* on the salary list," said Oliphant. "Look here, Otho, this woman is an artist; she'll play 'Astolaine' infinitely better than many women who have big reputations. The part is worth about ten pounds a week, and I propose to pay *her* ten pounds—always presuming that she rehearses it satisfactorily. Do you object?"

"*I* don't object," said Otho; "certainly not, old chap. I don't object to anything."

"Then if I can learn where she is, I'll write to her—or she may be in South Africa, or Australia, when she's wanted."

"But there is no philanthropy about it?" cried Blanche with affected amusement. "You are going to offer her the best chance she has ever had, *and* the best salary, and there is no philanthropy about it? Why, you couldn't do any more for the woman if you were in her debt!"

"I *am* in her debt," said Oliphant; "I owe her the only comfort I received in the greatest grief of my life."

He had turned pale; and Blanche also changed colour, though she could only conjecture his meaning. Fairbairn wished he hadn't come in. It seemed to him that Royce had created a serious discussion out of a playful remonstrance. Doubtless every married couple had domestic differences; but the illusion had existed that Oliphant and his wife were the one exception.

When he went, it was with a little dismay, and the matter recurred to him during the evening while he was at work on the translation. The translation was far from being a task to be knocked off lightly by a man of taste. He put down his pen more than once, and questioned if, with the ignorance of a bachelor, he was exaggerating the suggestiveness of the incident that he had witnessed. He decided that he was, for Mrs. Royce was too charming for any man to be unhappy with her!

Oliphant had not continued his study of *The Stage* after his friend's departure, nor had Blanche revived the subject of the debate. A diversion had been effected by the entrance of Mr. and Mrs. Ellerton.

The novelist had evidently come with a purpose; and though Oliphant had always understood that he had persistently refused invitations to write for the theatre, it transpired that in the course of the last ten years he had written several very literary dramas without any invitation at all.

"It occurred to me," he said, "that *your* theatre will be conducted on my lines. Now I have *the* play for you. And I have brought it!"

"I should like to read it," answered Oliphant; "thanks. Of course you know our opening production is settled? We shall probably get the Mayfair from next September, and we open with Lacour's *God and the State*—we shall keep to the title: *God and the State!*"

"I heard something about it the last time Blanche came; I didn't know you had actually settled. Not till next September? Well, you might do this second."

"The next piece is fixed too. Still, if—if it's suitable, we might do it third or fourth."

"It's a lovely play, Royce," said Mrs. Ellerton fervently; "I'm sure you'll like it. Blanche knows it—don't you, dear?—*The Alienist.*"

"Oh yes," said Blanche, "is that it? Yes, I remember it." Her tone was not enthusiastic, and her mother repeated nervously:

"If you read it, Royce, I'm quite sure you'll like it. The hero's and heroine's parts are both beautiful. They are really!"

"The *hero* and heroine's," said the novelist. "How often have I told you that, I wonder!"

"Yes, dear," she murmured, "I'm so stupid; I must take care! They're both splendid, Royce! And the scene in the study, where he discovers the signs of insanity in his own wife, and you hear the dance-music of the children's quadrille in the next room, and the moonlight is streaming through the windows, is grand."

"It sounds so," observed Mr. Ellerton, "as you describe it; 'the moonlight streaming through the windows' has a truly literary ring! Your mother-in-law, Royce, is an estimable woman; and the Editor of *Winsome Words,* who will be one-and-twenty next birthday, has the highest opinion of her talent. His communication this week is really most flattering. But if she told you the story of a work of Tolstoy's, you might think you were listening to a synopsis of a penny novelette. It's very remarkable. She 'sees through the medium of a temperament'— to quote Emile—and her temperament is of the novelette, noveletty!"

This was one of the speeches—delivered with deliberation, and with all the points carefully

emphasised—which invariably filled Oliphant
with a desire to kick the smiling and sarcastic
gentleman; and ostentatiously ignoring him now,
he addressed himself to the poor woman who
was endeavouring to wear an easy smile.

"What was the flattering letter, Mother?" he
asked.

"Oh, nothing," she said. "Only a few lines
with the cheque, and a request for two more
stories. When are you coming to see us again?"

"If you knew how busy I am!" he exclaimed
apologetically. "How is Gertrude?"

"Yes, how is Gertrude?" said Blanche; "we
must really try to run out one afternoon this
week! I haven't seen her for an age. And you
know, Royce, we've been awfully rude to Mrs.
Le Mesurier—we've never called there since that
luncheon party. And there's Lady Liddington
—we're neglecting everyone. What Lady Fleck
will think of us I don't know. Do tell Gertie
how busy we are, Mother! Why doesn't she
come and see us? Although, as we're out so
much, she'd better not come without hearing
from me first!"

"You are becoming more fashionable every
day, I perceive," drawled Mr. Ellerton. "The
fêted favourites of Fortune."

"Don't!" she sighed languidly. "The bore it

is—if one could only be quiet! I long for a six-months holiday in a place where there are no visitors and no invitation cards. Shall I ever get it? . . . You're going to stay, aren't you?"

She liked them to stay to dinner when they came. In this building, too, there was a restaurant downstairs, and it gratified her to cavil in their presence at a cuisine which she knew they must be finding epicurean. As a rule she and Oliphant dined lightly, but when her family remained, she ordered four or five courses, and was chagrined if his refusal of chartreuse betrayed that they did not have liqueurs every evening.

Oliphant repeated his assurance that he would read *The Alienist*—which might be a good play handicapped by a bad title—and the author obviously considered that perusal implied acceptance, for his manner became quite genial before the hour arrived for the husband and wife to betake themselves to their respective stages. When the promise was fulfilled, however, Royce found that the drama possessed all the faults of Mr. Mundey's; and he was for the first time profoundly thankful that he hadn't married a devoted daughter.

Alma, whom he had not seen since they parted at Brighton, was discovered to be on tour with the Hamiltons, and having ascertained her whereabouts, he said to Blanche:

"By the way, I see Miss King is at Rochdale this week. We grew rather heated the other day about nothing. Of course I don't want her in the theatre against your wishes, but if she proves as good as anybody else, I suppose you've really nothing against the arrangement, have you?"

Blanche shrugged her shoulders.

"Why should I have?" she said, not unamiably. "If she *is* good, engage her!"

Oliphant wrote to Alma the same day, a letter, which gave him a glow of happiness. He told her that in all probability he and his wife would open the Mayfair towards the end of the following year, and that he hoped she would be free to come to them. The sentence in which he mentioned the word "salary" was a little difficult to phrase, for while he was delighted to put money in her pocket, he hated to have to talk about it. It was the first time he had written to her, and he was surprised, when he had finished, to see that he had covered six pages. But there had been so much to say about the piece, and his certainty that she would feel the part.

Her reply was briefer, but he seemed to hear her speaking. "Can I say anything more than 'Thank you with all my heart'?" she wrote. Yet she had found more to say; and almost he could divine where she had paused with the sudden fear that her pen was running away with her.

It was already close upon Christmas, and soon the Hamiltons' tour must be ending. He would have liked to ask Alma to call upon him and Blanche when she returned to town, but shrank now from speaking of her any more than he was compelled. When Christmas came, he momentarily entertained the idea of going to Burton Crescent, in the hope that she might be staying there again. But it would not be quite the thing! He dismissed the notion.

The contract for the Mayfair was signed in January; and after that the poet's progress with Lacour's play, and the models of the scenes, and a score of matters demanding attention crowded thick upon one another's heels.

With the knowledge that they would crowd more thickly still as the year advanced, Oliphant sometimes wondered what time the business cares of theatrical management would leave him to remember that he was an actor too.

CHAPTER XVIII

BLANCHE had considered that the auditorium
was shabby. She had stood between Otho and
Oliphant in the stalls one morning, and plucked
disconsolately at a loose piece of gimp on one of
the chairs. On the way back to the flat, it had
been apparent that she longed to see them newly
upholstered before the theatre was opened, and
when Otho suggested their renovation, the delighted smile that lit her face had answered him
before she spoke. There had been a cheerful
discussion about the material to be used, Oliphant
and she holding different views. Otho inclined
to the opinion that the more effective scheme
would be the one advocated by Blanche, and
thenceforward she had had further ideas on the
subject daily.

He spent eight hundred pounds in gratifying
her whims—if he had had a long lease, he would
have had the house redecorated—and behind the
curtain the services of the best scenic artists had
been sought, and the company boldly organised.

The salary list, indeed, was much higher than the figure at which it had been originally estimated, but the dress-rehearsal amply justified the selections that had been made. Every part was rendered well, and even Blanche did not deny that Alma as "Astolaine" was very good.

Otho echoed the pronouncement. He and Blanche sat in the rehabilitated stalls during the scenes in which she could escape from the stage, watching the progress of the rehearsal together. He found the evening very interesting; and although he was depressed when the thunder or lightning came at the wrong moments, the frenzy that such blunders begot, and the excited altercations that ensued, added a strong element of humour to his inexperience. There was a fascination, too, in sitting beside Blanche, swayed by the same interests, and exchanging criticisms with her. The strangeness of the woman's attire, her accentuated eyebrows, and the colour on her cheeks, all emphasised the novelty of the situation; and once, in commenting on the sleeves of her costume, when she took his hand and passed it down her arm, he felt a wave of emotion which a few months earlier would have astonished him.

Of a truth, Otho had awakened to the fact that he admired Blanche more than was desirable—

not for his own peace, but for ethics. His mental
state was so very undefined that it permitted
him to assure himself that he was supersensitive
and absurd to see anything wrong in it. Nevertheless, perceiving that he was regarding his
friend's wife somewhat differently from the way
in which he would have wished to regard her,
there had been one or two occasions on which he
had not failed to be distressed.

There was no room for distress in his mind,
however, on the following night. He was in-
fected by the fever that pervaded the ménage in
Green Street—where Blanche and Oliphant had
obtained a furnished house. As he took his seat
in his box, he was reminded of the sensations
with which he had sometimes entered a grand-
stand. Royce, who was looking tired and ill,
had been in the theatre till late in the afternoon,
and then driven home, to snatch a hasty meal,
and endeavour to rest. The curtain rose on *God
and the State* at eight o'clock, and by 8.30 a
fashionable audience had assembled in the Mayfair Theatre. The pit had ceased to cry "Ssh!"
and it was no longer necessary for people to keep
rising in order that late-comers, who showed no
consciousness of their discourtesy, might pass
them.

The actor-manager's nervousness was painfully apparent during his first lines, but Blanche had her voice under better control. After Royce, the artist whose nervousness was most visible was Alma, passionately eager to justify Oliphant's faith in her. Otho fancied he could detect through his glasses that her lips trembled.

The atmosphere seemed to gather spirit by degrees, and his craving for a strong whisky-and-soda and a cigarette grew less intense. But he remarked for the first time how cold at its best was his acquaintances' well-bred attitude towards a theatrical performance; and then with an anxiety which he had never imagined that journalists could be capable of inspiring under his shirt-front, he glanced speculatively at the rows of Press men, and at a box opposite, where one critic sat alone.

The curtain fell at twenty minutes' past eleven, and a number of the fashionable audience that had come in late, trooped through the pass-door to the stage, where Blanche was a triumphant hostess. The play, they exclaimed, was a "dream," it was "sweet," it was "quite too delightful upon their honour." Where the poetry had been spoken there was now a gush of insincere congratulation. Many of the smiling visitors thought the performance dreadfully dull, as did the majority of the pit and gallery, who had coughed and shuffled with irritating frequency during some of the scenes. But in the flow of felicitation, six months was the shortest run that anybody permitted himself to prophesy.

However, most of the notices could be called favourable to the production. Some insisted that Lacour was a lyric poet, and not a dramatist, limiting their approval to the way the work had been Englished, and the manner in which it was played; a few praised it unreservedly. There were plenty of excerpts to be made for advertising purposes, "the good quotable line" being absent only from the opinions of the novices, who were learning syntax by "criticising" for the least important periodicals. It now remained to be seen how *God and the State* would be supported by the public.

Blanche and Otho were sanguine, though the receipts were not immediately all that could be wished; they whom misgivings already oppressed were Oliphant, and the woman whom the Press had agreed to describe as "an actress of conspicuous ability, hitherto unknown to London." Every evening when he came off, in the first act, by the door at which she was waiting to make her earliest entrance, Alma looked an inquiry, and he stopped to answer it. But there was really no need for him to say that the house was bad again—she could read it in his face; nor did it need words from her to tell him that she was the only person who understood how much he had at stake.

Between these two, whom life, which has no construction and no moral, had once thrown together, and speedily separated—who had met again by chance when the weaker one was married, and been again divided by circumstances until the man's purpose brought the woman into his own theatre—there had always been a sympathy, which now grew stronger daily. Daily, Oliphant looked forward with greater eagerness to their next conversation, and remembered more vividly their preceding one. And meanwhile his home became less and less congenial. Blanche with a well-appointed house in a fashionable quarter, did not allow her opportunities to be fettered by the theatre receipts. She had removed to Green Street in order to entertain, and she was resolved to fulfil her intention. Her social functions seemed to him incessant, and from any one of them the actor-manager would joyfully have escaped to take his way to the lodgings in Bloomsbury that held Alma. He knew no more of her lodgings than their address, for she had not been asked to Green Street.

That his wife had omitted to invite her was

due to indifference, and not to any objection to Royce's conversations with Miss King. Their conversations, since he had proclaimed that they were such devoted friends, she found natural enough. Moreover, she would have been unwilling to do him the honour of evincing jealousy, unless there had been a scandal which compelled her to insist that the other woman, whoever she might be, should leave the theatre. Blanche was too much elated to be jealous. True, the business remained bad, but her passion for paragraphs was now gratified abundantly, and at the worst, *God and the State* would prove a failure. Kirtland's drama would be a hit, she supposed—his name alone was a draw—and then the failure would be retrieved. But she was sorry for Otho, because to him there hadn't been any benefit whatever from the venture. He was so "gentlemanly about the returns!" And really it was "something to be *looked* at again by a man who was in love with her! Of course there were plenty of men who tried to look as if they were—through monocles in every drawing-room. But that was only because she was on the stage, and with the ignorance of the outsider, they thought that all actresses were to be had. Otho was really in love with her. Poor fellow, how happy *he* would have been as her husband!"

A woman's reflections cannot progress so far as this without her manner altering towards the man; and it was when Blanche's manner first altered, that Otho perceived with poignant self-reproach that he could no longer apply salve to his conscience by the terms "supersensitive" and "absurd." He was at this period strong enough to leave London, if there had been no reason for his remaining, but he was weak enough to find sufficient reason in his interest in the Mayfair. Unable now to deny his sentiments, he to-day assuaged remorse by assuring himself that they didn't matter, because she would never know.

That he must sustain a heavy loss by the initial production was speedily apparent, and it was decided that Kirtland's drama should be put into rehearsal when *God and the State* had been running three weeks. Oliphant felt needlessly guilty, but he was confident that they were now about to rehearse a work which would attract all London.

Kirtland, being a dramatist with a literary reputation and an independence, had reached the point where he could afford to be courageous, and as he was a writer of brilliant ability, his courage had fascinating results. Already he had written two plays of psychological interest which had been great artistic successes, and in *The*

Average Man he had at last dared to say all he thought. Had he deliberately sat down to controvert Théophile Gautier's dictum that the theatre never becomes possessed of an idea until fiction has worn it threadbare, he could not have made a bolder experiment. To Oliphant it appeared to be one that would emancipate the English stage and make an epoch.

He had lent the manuscript to Alma, and he awaited her opinion more anxiously than he had asked for Otho's; far more anxiously than he had asked his wife's.

"It's magnificent," she said. "I don't know if his view is right, but it's a view to hear, and to think about. And the dialogue—the grip of it! Did you say I was to play 'Mrs. Ivery'?"

"I hope you like the part?" He believed that she would have played the heroine's better, but naturally Blanche must have that, though she would not be so subtle in it.

She read his thought, as she read all he had. "I like it very much," she replied quickly. "I like my part, and I admire the play—it's worthy of the Dream Theatre. Oh, please Heaven, it will be all right! I pray for it."

"Our Dream Theatre has opened badly," he said.

She nodded. "But it will come!"

"With this?"

"I think so."

"You need never go back to four or five pounds a week in the provinces anyhow!" exclaimed Oliphant, after a pause.

"Ah, don't say 'anyhow'! And I wasn't thinking of myself when I said that I prayed."

"I know. Only I'm glad, at least, that——"

"You will have much more to be glad about. But I thank you. You've done a great deal for me, Mr. Oliphant—I shall never forget it as long as I live."

"I don't want your thanks," he said; "I hate your thanks. If you've talent, thank God for it—*I* didn't give it to you. I want your friendship; and every time you 'thank' me you make me a stranger to you."

When her cue came, Oliphant went down to his dressing-room, realising, as he had realised before, that he had uttered a lie. It was not her friendship that he wanted, but her love. He loved her. He loved the timbre of her voice, and the comprehension of her silence, and inanimate things that she had hallowed by her touch. He loved her with the mind that she had dominated and the soul that was rendered greater by his love. He loved her too truly ever to tell her the truth. Again a man believed that he could love without the woman knowing it. If he had been free, and could have won her, triumphs would have been transfigured and failures robbed of their sting; if he had been free, he *would* have won her, and life could hold no more than that! Once happiness had been within his reach, and he had blundered by it. To-day he looked back, empty-handed, from a celibacy that had no rights. But though he could never touch her lips, she was his Ideal; and that he might be worthy to worship her he would always be faithful to his wife. Temptation was not avoiding him—it was in the front of his theatre often, and in his own house, and in the drawing-rooms of others; but to Oliphant it had seemed that to break his marriage-oath would make him guilty, not towards Blanche, not towards God, but towards Alma King. Lowered by an intrigue, he could not have met her eyes. Herself he would not have taken had she been willing to come to him—and he would not insult her by accepting anything less.

CHAPTER XIX

The Average Man was eulogised by those organs which embody the views of the critical for the delectation of the cultured; it was received with respect by the entire Press; it was even commented on by the public. It did not, of course, excite the interest aroused by a football match, but its thesis was mentioned; there were a great many people in London who said "Fancy!"

However, though Oliphant had continued to play it for two months, and hoped against hope, the drama was a financial failure, and this time Blanche was not a whit less anxious than he, for the rent, and the servants, and the cost of her luncheon and dinner parties, swelled the household expenses to a sum which was by no means covered by her and Royce's salary. Besides being anxious, she was incensed, for the less ardent of the newspapers had questioned whether the subject was one "calculated to attract the general playgoer, who, as we have often insisted, seeks before all things to be amused," etc., and she blamed Royce bitterly for his lack of judgment. She might have foreseen the issue, she felt: she had obtained a theatre for him, and now his idiosyncrasies were going to ruin them!

Otho had denied himself Green Street for more than a fortnight when he came one morning in response to a note from her. It was not accidental that he found her alone, for she had appointed the morning.

"I'm frightfully worried," she declared when he had lighted a cigarette. "Don't I look dreadful? Don't I? I feel a hundred. You know you must be firm! You promised me you would be. I told you six weeks ago that this thing was a frost. Now Royce is considering a play that's simply fore-doomed, and he says he has talked to you about it. You should object! You must tell him that you want your theatre to pay."

"Royce wants it to pay, you know," he said uneasily; "I—I can't very well take an attitude that looks like—— It's nobody's fault up to the present, is it? The pieces have been good enough, Heaven knows!"

"I've warned you," she sighed; "I can't do any more. But, I tell you, I feel simply miserable when I think what you've lost—if it hadn't been for me we shouldn't have had the theatre!"

"Oh, don't talk like that; we shall have a big success directly, and——"

"Never," she said emphatically. "Believe me, Mr. Fairbairn, 'never'! It's a fact. Unless Royce is checked—if you don't make a stand— we shall have one failure after another. I see it. It will mean thousands to *you,* and it will mean— well, I don't know what it will mean to *us!* The Bankruptcy Court I suppose! We can't go on like this long."

"I was afraid your affairs couldn't be alto- gether roseate; I've been thinking about it. I— if—of course if there *has* been bad judgment, it's been as much mine as Royce's, and—and it's only right that I should share the responsibility. I must have a chat with him. There needn't be any duns, Mrs. Royce."

"Do you think I'd let Royce borrow money from you?" she exclaimed. "Yes, I know, you'd lend it gladly—you'd do anything for us I be- lieve! but I wouldn't let him take it. And besides I couldn't if I wanted to."

"Why? How do you mean you 'couldn't'?"

"Because Royce doesn't quite know the state we are in. And I don't want to tell him."

"It needn't bother him if he can put things straight. It would be only a loan. When the success does come——"

"I didn't mean because he'd be bothered," she said; "at least, not only that. You see *I* insisted on this house, and asked the people here, and made the debts. I did it for the best; the policy was right enough—if the business had been decent, there wouldn't have been any trouble; but *I*'m the 'culprit'! I don't want Royce to turn round on me—as he would—and reproach me. That would be the last straw!"

"Oh," cried Otho, "how could he reproach you? He wouldn't!"

Her eyebrows rose. "Wouldn't he? But it isn't a question of money. I only want you to exert your authority, to have the theatre conducted on proper lines. There's a piece now in Paris just produced—a piece of Reybaud's; there's a notice of it in *The Era* this week. It could be bought, it could be adapted, and might make a fortune for us. But no! Royce wants a 'masterpiece' that is going to bring us to the workhouse instead. Oh, it drives me mad to think about it!"

"Why not speak to him of Reybaud's piece?" suggested Otho. "*I* couldn't urge it much because I'm no judge; but *you*—you might propose it, and use your influence with Royce."

" 'Influence'?" she echoed. "Do you really imagine that I've any influence with Royce?" She laughed. "Why, my dear boy, I've no more influence over Royce than I have over the Prime Minister!"

"Do you mean that——" He looked at her incredulously. "Do you mean that your advice —your request—would have no weight with him? Wouldn't he pay any attention to it?"

"Certainly not," she said. She met the young man's startled eyes for some seconds significantly. Then in a quiet voice, and without lowering her gaze, she added: "Royce and I have been strangers for more than two years."

In the silence that followed Otho stared dizzily at the fire. The suddenness with which she had leapt the limits of conventional parlance gave him a sensation resembling fright, and he could think of no words for answer. At last he stammered with an effort:

"Of course I'll try to do what you wish, with pleasure. I'm awfully grieved to hear that things are wrong; I always thought that you and he were so happy together."

She smiled faintly, a little to one side, her nether-lip indented by her teeth.

"I'm the loneliest woman in the world."

The compassion on his face was delicious to her, and, watching him, she was sincerely sorry for herself. Words now thronged his mind only too insistently, and he sat torn between the desire to tell her how deeply he sympathised with her, and the knowledge that if he obeyed the impulse, he would surely say something that would make it impossible for him to take Oliphant's hand any more.

"Don't look like that," she murmured. "It doesn't matter."

"What can I say?" he exclaimed. "It's so hard for a man to show a woman whom he mustn't—who is no relation to him that he's sorry for her!"

"You needn't say anything—I know you're sorry."

"It wasn't two years ago that we had our first talk about the theatre," he said after another pause.

"No," she said, "I know."

"And you were *then*——?"

She nodded. "But I was fond of him still and ambitious for him. A woman doesn't become indifferent all at once."

His eyes filled. She seemed to him all that was noble and strong to endure.

"Ah, don't! Ah, Silly Billy," she said half playfully, half tenderly, "you *mustn't!*"

Otho turned aside, and lit another cigarette with fingers that trembled a little.

"You've cut me up horribly," he muttered. "I wish to God I could do something for you!"

"You *have,* with your friendship. I don't know anybody I could have talked to like this but you."

"We *are* friends, aren't we?" he asked. "We always shall be?"

"I'm sure we shall!"

"Well, let me do what I suggested just now," he said eagerly. "I don't mean to let me speak to Royce about it, but to arrange it with *you.* It isn't much, but I shan't feel so infernally useless. If you'll only give me an idea of the sum, I'll post a cheque this afternoon. Will you? Let me put an end to your money worries, do!"

He had fulfilled a hope that had awakened in her ten minutes ago. It had then occurred to her that the loan made to herself privately would dispose of the difficulties, and spare her the unpleasantness of owning their full extent to Oliphant; but now, while her perception of the circumstances remained quite as acute, sentiment forbade her to take advantage of the young man's love for her. She would have done it ten, five, two minutes ago—but the tears had come into his eyes about her. She shook her head.

And his persuasions failed to move her outwardly, though inwardly she wavered often, and hoped he would believe her obdurate before she lost her footing on these unaccustomed heights. When he had gone, regretful, she thought of him with admiration for having raised her so much in her self-esteem.

To complete Oliphant's unhappiness, and to darken his outlook, it had needed only that he should be required to stultify the expressed pur- pose for which a theatre had been taken. By Blanche's arguments that they could not be popular socially unless the receipts enabled them to entertain, he had been uninfluenced—he did not seek social popularity; and between reaping the profit that would content her, and justifying Fairbairn's experiment, there was a wide differ- ence. He had been firm in the face of their increasing liabilities, merely praying that their expenditure might in future be reduced; he had been as resolute as he could be as an actor- manager with a backer. But when the backer joined forces with the actor-manager's wife, confidence collapsed.

Nevertheless the artist did not succumb im- mediately; he proposed Shakespeare as a com- promise. In London, if not in the provinces, he urged, Shakespeare could be made to pay, ameliorated by elaborate scenery, as a powder by a tablespoonful of jam. Shakespeare might prove successful, and Shakespeare would be art. But Blanche did not want to play Shakespeare, and she harped on Félix Reybaud's *La Curieuse,* the latest product of a playwright who was sincere in nothing but his desire to tickle the public taste; a piece which owed its success in Paris, not to its characterisation, not to any insight into life, but to a gratuitous immorality and 'le doigté du dramaturge."

Oliphant shrank from confessing this new trouble to Alma; he felt that it would be soon enough to speak of defeat when he had agreed to surrender. But for the first time Blanche suspected that she was encouraging his views. Umbrage had already been taken at several of the Press notices, which had intimated that "Miss King's acting had the rare and indefinable quality of intellectuality," the word "rare" being found an insult by implication. Originally one critic had said it; but there had poured in a multitude of cuttings from newspapers published in almost every county in the kingdom, and as some of the obscurer journals inserted the London criticisms verbatim as the opinions of imaginary Correspondents, the manageress had had the anoyance of reading the objectionable sentence more than once. The suspicion now aroused in her increased the disfavour with which she had begun to regard Miss King. And as a culminating offence, Alma chanced, on the evening of the discussion, to receive some applause at a point where hitherto there had not been any. The scene was one between her and Blanche, who stood for two or three seconds at a disadvantage. It was resentfully referred to directly they were together in the wings.

"What was the meaning of that round, Miss King? You've never had a hand there till tonight?"

"I was surprised myself," answered Alma. "But I think I felt the lines more than usual."

"Well, the next time you're going to feel them perhaps you'll let me know!" said Blanche sharply. "I don't want to be put out by your applause again!"

But here irritation was too complex to evaporate in a rebuke. To herself she said that since King's influence was supporting Royce in his folly, she shouldn't remain at the Mayfair. Momentarily she questioned if she was mistaking the nature of the influence. But no; she did not think that! Royce was deceiving her doubtless, but not with King; and the credit, she should imagine, was the woman's.

Creditable, or not, however, she did not want her in the company, and she trusted that *La*

Curieuse, if they secured it, would prove to contain no part for her.   The argument about the piece was repeated in Green Street the following afternoon.   Otho was lunching there, and Oliphant again dwelt upon his wish to revive a Shakespearian play.

"But Mrs. Royce doesn't care for the idea," said Otho.   "What is your objection to Reybaud?   I always understood that he was first-rate."

"Well, of course he is!" Blanche exclaimed. "We mayn't be able to get the thing if we try— there'll be twenty people after it.   Reybaud? If Reybaud hasn't a great reputation, I'm an amateur, Royce, I know nothing about the stage. Who in Paris has, then?"

"It depends what you mean by 'reputation,'" said Oliphant wearily.   "His name is very widely known; the crowd think him a very clever man. If that is 'reputation,' you're quite right."

"Well, I should certainly say it *was!*" she answered.   She glanced at Otho: "Wouldn't *you?*"

"I must admit, old chap," he murmured, "that I think you're inclined to be hypercritical.   I'm fairly well-read, and I flatter myself I'm not devoid of taste, but Reybaud's plays are quite good enough for *me.*"

Oliphant drummed his fingers restlessly on the cloth. "Do you ask as much from the theatre as you do from your books?" he returned. "Does Reybaud satisfy you in the library?"

"I've never read him. But I've seen two or three of his pieces, and, I'm bound to say, enjoyed them."

"And anyhow," said Blanche, "it isn't a question of reading in the library; it isn't a question whether he's good, bad, or indifferent—the question is whether he succeeds."

Otho was silent, and Oliphant looked at him inquiringly.

"Is that your view too?" he asked. "It wasn't the view you held when we took the theatre. You knew what my aim was from the beginning. Heaven knows you can't be sorrier than I am for the way things have gone so far, but it was never understood between us that if fine work spelt failure, I was to play rubbish to retrieve it. I don't *want* a theatre to play rubbish; I'd rather have none than be in management to give the lie to intentions I've expressed all my life." He turned to Blanche. "If you don't care for nine-tenths of Shakespeare, surely there's *one* character that attracts you? Is there no choice between the best modern work and Félix Reybaud?"

Otho replied for her, with affected lightness.

"Dear old man," he said, fidgeting with his coffee spoon, "aren't you taking the matter too seriously? If we—er—if we made a mistake when we opened the house—and I suppose we did make a mistake—it seems to me that we should make a bigger one still if we were ashamed to acknowledge it. When all is said, the theatre is the theatre, it's a place of entertainment; aren't you rather apt to forget that? What is it Austin Dobson says?—

> 'Parnassus' peaks still catch the sun;
> But why, O lyric brother!
> Why build a pulpit on the one,
> A platform on the other?'

I think it applies, Royce."

Oliphant had turned very pale, and the last vestige of hope sank from his heart. He nodded slowly.

"Yes," he said; "perhaps the pulpit *is* too strong in me. But circumstances are stronger, aren't they? We won't argue any more; we'll try to get *La Curieuse.*"

Now, when he was beaten, he longed for Alma's consolation, even while he winced at the thought of avowing his decision to her. If she knew all, she would be compassionate; but he could not disclose all, and he trembled lest she should find the obvious insufficient to exonerate him. She had once told him that he was weak—he had remembered that since; perhaps she would view him only as a renegade clinging to power at the price of his faith?

But her gaze was clearer than he guessed. She saw that he had mated his antithesis; and partially she understood. Her pity for him had never been so earnest, nor the love that had been born in her so deep. Only now she knew how deep it was, this love that yearned to burst from her lips and eyes—knew that if he had come to her ashamed, a coward and apostate self-condemned, she would have loved him still.

And Blanche was twice triumphant: for persistent effort obtained the English rights of *La Curieuse*, and there was no character in the piece that even Oliphant could assert would suit Miss King. As a manageress Blanche was annoyed at this period only by her father, who on hearing that the policy of the theatre was to be changed, had developed an unexpected tone, and finally appeared to have on hand a large assortment of rejected manuscripts ranging from melodrama to musical comedy. She did not read them, but he wrote urgent letters to her on the subject, and importuned her in her drawing-room, until she was so angered that she would have produced in preference the weakest of the plays that were submitted to the theatre daily by unknown men.

The adaptation of Reybaud's work had been entrusted to Campion, with the assurance that it would be put into rehearsal as speedily as the parts could be type-written. Stimulated by such startling propinquity to fees—he was still awaiting the production of a comedy that had been accepted five years ago—he completed the task in ten days, and the run of *The Average Man,* which was entailing a loss every week, drew to a conclusion.

Alma had not regretted to learn that her engagement at the Mayfair must terminate. Indeed, she had already asked herself if she could remain there even were she desired to do so. Although she honoured Royce too greatly to think he would confess his love, honoured herself too much to fear she would betray her own, the very hopelessness with which she contemplated meeting him no more showed her that their meetings should cease. After she left his theatre their lines would lie apart; she might remain in London—that was to be expected now—and yet rarely speak to him again. She would see him from the stalls sometimes, and read his notices, and pray for his success; but it was very seldom that they would meet each other in the streets.

Oliphant realised that too. He felt it as he talked to her on the last night, hungering to take her hand before the moment of adieu. From the stage, which he had just left, the dialogue of the fourth act reached them, and when the curtain fell, it would fall upon the end of more than the piece. To-night he still was playing literature, and stood beside the woman he loved—to-morrow the theatre would be void of both.

"So it is nearly over," he said. " 'For the play, I remember, pleased not the million; 'twas caviare to the general.' Are you going to wish me 'luck' before you go?" For the first time he made no effort to conceal his humiliation.

"I wish it now," she answered with the ghost of a smile. "I hope *The Modern Eve* will draw all London. You ought to feel confident: Campion writes very smartly, and I hear that Reybaud has never done anything more—more striking than *La Curieuse*."

"Then you congratulate me? . . . Hark! they're a good audience to-night, aren't they? It has never gone so well."

"It has always gone well—with the people who came," she murmured.

"With the people who came," repeated Oliphant. He turned to her passionately. "Why," he exclaimed, "why have I failed? You know I've failed. You don't say so, but you know it, and you know that I know it. Why? It wasn't to play *La Curieuse* that I dreamed of management; we didn't think of Reybaud when we talked in Brighton—and outside the Museum that day. I hate this theatre! I've lost another man's money, and my own hope. My God! I'm going to produce the worst example of the worst school, and I haven't the right to refuse!"

"Look forward!" she cried; "don't look back! No, you have *not* failed. Hark again!—that is applause for fine work. Re-read the criticisms! —there is a Press that has understood and supported you from the first. Your theatre is too big, your expenses are too large; here you must depend upon the 'million.' One day you will fight for your belief again; and with a smaller house you'll conquer yet."

He looked away from her, with haggard eyes, at the unattainable. Yes, with her he would have conquered yet; but the future that he could foresee held nothing. With her, thought would have been exalted, and purpose fortified by the grandeur of her own soul. He knew it, as—in the mightiness of his longing for her—he knew that this defeat wringing his heart to-night would have been welcome if for one moment it had yielded him the comfort of her kiss.

Now from the stage and the mouth of his wife, came the cue for his return to the scene; and when he spoke to Alma next, the last night had ended, and she wore her coat and hat. She had taken leave of Blanche and him together before she went to her dressing-room, but he had hastened from his, as she had divined he would, to clasp her hand again. It was the single weakness of which she had been guilty that her hand was bare.

They stood for a minute in the whitewashed passage, face to face.

"Are you wrapped up enough? Won't you be cold?"

"Oh, this stuff is very thick," she said, "and it's warmly lined besides."

"You ought to turn up the collar," he murmured; "you've nothing round your throat."

"No, I'm quite all right; really!"

"You'll have a cab? It's snowing hard, somebody said."

"Yes, I've sent for one—I expect it's here now."

"Well, I—I wish you all the success and happiness you can ask for yourself. But you know that, don't you?"

"Yes, I'm sure of it. And—you'll never say

you've lost your hope any more, will you? Good-night."

"Good-night," he said. . . . "I wish you'd turn your collar up."

"There! Now I'm quite safe," she answered, smiling.

And in this fashion the man and woman between whom not a word of love had yet been spoken said good-bye.

CHAPTER XX

"To speak in more favourable terms of *The Modern Eve* would be practically to discredit the enterprise and judgment of a manager who had inspired the hope that——"

Yes! Oliphant had foreseen that. He was reading a notice cut from one of the journals to which Alma had referred when she said there was a Press that had supported him. He·picked up another:

"It may not be astonishing that *The Average Man* should be followed by *The Inquisitive Woman*, but it is distressing. In Paris I was merely bored by *La Curieuse*, but at the Mayfair I was pained. I hasten to say that my pain was by no means shared by the audience, who evidently found in M. Reybaud's work, judiciously watered by Mr. Campion, a pabulum to their taste. Nevertheless——"

There was a third slip lying beside him—the tone was the same, a tone of irony and regret. From these organs he had derived gleams of consolation hitherto, and he winced this morning as if three friends had turned their faces from him in the street.

But the piece had been produced a week, and was playing to excellent business. The booking was increasing daily, and there was every promise that a great financial success would be achieved. When the box-office sheets were so agreeable to peruse, he would be held unreasonable to be depressed by three columns of type!

In a month from the date of the production Blanche's caprice had been abundantly justified. Boards announcing that the house was full were displayed outside the Mayfair every evening, and in the presence of such good fortune his attitude exasperated her. That he should comport himself as if they had had another failure, when they had the longest advertisement in *The Daily Telegraph,* and a demand for boxes, and queues at the pit and gallery-doors hours before they opened, was an annoyance which not even the additional frequency of her entertainments could assuage. He was truly an impossible person! She felt it more and more. An ordinary man would have owned that his judgment had been at fault, and thanked her; but did her husband? So far from acknowledging his error, he didn't seem to recognise that it had been demonstrated.

If it had not been for Otho, she would have been miserable; his was the only real companionship that she had. And then Royce remonstrated, and called her improvident because she gave parties! In truth—the reflection occurred to her one afternoon as she mused by the fire—in truth she was taking a very noble course in doing so; it was not every woman in her position who would have striven to interest herself in social gaieties when a young man with thousands a year was dying of love for her!

Did she care for him seriously? She pursed her lips; well, not as she had cared for Royce once, of course—that had been a headstrong passion; she would never have married Otho Fairbairn if he had been an actor in his third London engagement. Still she did like him. As he was, she would marry him like a shot if she were free. Good Lord, how happy she'd have been with him! "Happy"? What a word for the life she might have led! The jewellery he would have bought for her; and the horses and carriages!—she'd have had a Russian sable rug in the victoria, and—and she would have had a theatre too—he would have let her do anything she pleased! . . . Her foot was resting on the fender, and she admired it pensively. Royce wouldn't despair; but that would be the end of her friendship with the Flecks and—— Oh no, no, she was a virtuous woman!

She had found occasion to remind herself of it; and, though she did not realise the fact, the thought that had given her pause was that if she sinned she would lose Society.

The hundredth night of *The Modern Eve* was reached without any diminution of the receipts, and Oliphant rejoiced like a prisoner who approaches release. Now that the money that had been lost by the earlier plays would be recovered, he would be free to tell Fairbairn that he wished to withdraw from the theatre. Management on the lines he was required to travel henceforward was a prospect before which he quailed; and since the remainder of the lease could be transferred easily enough, there would be no cause for complaint on either side. That the adaptation would continue to attract the public until the middle of July—that its run in London would have made the Mayfair a profitable speculation—there could be no doubt. Therefore he would not even take the detested piece "out" in the autumn! That Otho should not suffer by his hatred of it, he would accept the best of the numerous offers for the provincial rights.

When Blanche inquired whether an autumn tour was being arranged, he told her "no."

"Well, isn't it *time* we got some dates?" she asked. "What have we got an acting-manager for? I tell you that man is no use—he looks very nice, but that's all he thinks about! I hear, when everybody was coming out the other evening, he stood at the top of the stairs saying good-night to three girls he'd passed in. That sort of thing lets the show down, you know! It's very bad—people think that half the house is paper."

Oliphant hesitated nervously. "Look here, Blanche," he said, "I don't want to go out with the piece, that's why nothing is being done. If Otho gets his money back, I want to drop *The Modern Eve,* and the Mayfair too. Let us take engagements again; I can't go on this way."

"You want to drop the Mayfair?" she stammered, paling. "Do you mean it?"

"I can't go on!" he repeated. "Oh, for Heaven's sake try to see it from my point of view for once; don't let's have another argument! I'm ashamed—that's the word; I couldn't resign myself to playing this sort of stuff; I couldn't!"

She looked at him speechlessly, her blue eyes ablaze with wrath.

"I think you're a lunatic," she said hoarsely, at last. "My God! I think you're a lunatic; I do, on my soul! You'd like to ruin yourself and everybody connected with you."

"If Otho gets his money back——"

"Oh, don't talk to me about getting his money back!" she exclaimed. "Whom has he got to thank for it, you or me? Would *you* ever have got it back for him? Never in this world! And when I proposed the piece which by your own showing has rescued you, *rescued* you from the overwhelming burden of a West End theatre, you had the insolence to sneer at me in front of him!"

"I 'sneered' at you? When?"

"You know very well when! When we were discussing the piece at lunch that day. You know you did! Your whole tone was an insult —making out that I was uneducated and had no taste. You tried to make me look as small as you could. But he didn't think any more of *you* for it, *I* could see!"

"What you say is absolutely untrue. That we shall never feel the same way about the stage as long as we live I'm quite sure, but it can't be necessary to quarrel about it. As to Otho's having to thank you for our present success, that's a fact that I've admitted often."

"You haven't!" she cried; "and *you*'ve had cause to thank me a damned sight more than Otho, if you knew it!" Her rage had mastered her.

"I don't understand you," said Oliphant sternly; "you can explain yourself when you can talk like a lady."

"I don't wish to talk at all! . . . If you'd like to know what I mean, I told him that you ought to have a theatre—I knew *you* never would! And he quite agreed with me; that's why he made you the offer."

"I see," said Oliphant; "that was it? Yes, I suppose I *have* had cause to thank you. I'd rather you hadn't done it, though it may sound ungrateful to say so. Well, we have had our theatre, and it hasn't fulfilled my hopes. Can't we recognise the fact calmly?"

"It hasn't fulfilled your hopes? We are coining money, and it hasn't fulfilled—— Oh! oh no, please don't say any more!" She clasped her head. "I am at my limit! It's quite understood —you are going to give it up. That's enough!"

She did not speak again during the day, and a perfunctory remark that he offered at dinner fell still-born. At seven o'clock they drove to the Mayfair, where the audience heard the first words that she had addressed to him for nine hours. Their love-scenes, however, "went" as well as usual, and when he led her before the curtain, and she smiled to his bow, the suggestion of connubial felicity was beautiful to behold.

But though she was resolved not to reopen the subject until the time came when it could no longer be ignored, Blanche could dwell on little else. When Otho presented himself, perturbed, for an explanation, she again rendered a mental tribute to his sympathy. Her hope that Oliphant would recant was of the slightest —his second thoughts would doubtless be as besotted as his first! Dismay engulfed her, and the ignominy of abdication poisoned her very dreams.

Her reveries were now more frequent than before. The silence between her and Oliphant had been broken, but her grievance was manifest in her accents, and their speech was very constrained. She had no heart to visit, and *he* lacked heart to sit at home viewing her resentment. Hence she was often alone in the Green Street drawing-room, and—as the reverberation of his announcement subsided—to enliven her solitude she once or twice returned with curious eyes to the edge of the abyss from which two months ago she had started back afraid. She could now look down without turning dizzy quite so soon. She repeated that there would be no more cards like these lying in a tray on her table. "Yes, she would be making a great sacrifice for him!" Of course—just for pastime imagining that she

did do such a thing—after the divorce he would
marry her; there was no doubt about that.
People did forget in time—especially when one
was an actress. And really, if they didn't plenty
of women would regard a vast fortune as ample
compensation. She could not do so herself; but
plenty of women would! Plenty of women
would consider that they were quite justified in
leaving a husband like Royce! What joy had
she in her life? If her dear little baby had been
spared to her, she would never have been
tempted. Ah, her sweet little baby, how devoted
she had been to him! When a man was indifferent to his wife, it wasn't astonishing if her craving for affection proved too great for her
strength. This tenderness that had been awakened in her was natural. As Royce had said
when he proposed to her, to be an artist a woman
must love.

Just because she had attempted to lull despair
for five minutes by the writing of a little paragraph! If he had had human instincts, he would
have pitied her the more for that pathetic effort.
And *he* was to allow himself all latitude, while
she was denied consolation? Plenty of women
would laugh at her as a fool! Of course he was
false to her—how could she question it even for

an instant? He *was* false to her with—with Alma King!

This new idea offered her comfort. In the days that followed she strove to believe it. Alma was now playing at the Pall Mall, and Oliphant had not seen her since she left their company, but Blanche wished to persuade herself that they were guilty. Vague accusations of infidelity no longer satisfied her, and to excuse her own increased temptation, she sought to point definitely to the woman.

The Modern Eve achieved its destiny, and as the business dropped and the general exodus from town commenced, it was decided that in another fortnight Oliphant's reign at the Mayfair should cease.

Blanche accepted his intimation of the fact with the fewest words possible, and rewarded herself for their sparsity by many comments to Otho. Passionately as she had exulted in the possession of a theatre, it seemed to her in this final fortnight that she had never appreciated it enough. Each time the door-keeper touched his cap to her as she entered, she suffered a pang, in picturing him saluting another manageress soon. The star-room where she dressed stung her with the reminder that where she played her next part the star-room would be another's. The respect of the vilified acting-manager with the returns was a sword-thrust, as she realised how speedily she would have declined to the insignificance of a salary.

And as the days slipped past, Otho Fairbairn suffered no less acutely. She would lose power, and he would lose pretext. With the closure of the Mayfair, the ostensible motive for his dalliance in London would be removed; and he stood face to face with the truth. Now he must either go away and resign himself to misery, or realise that he was too violently in love with his friend's wife to leave her. He decided to go away.

He determined the matter in the small hours while he lay praying for sleep, or his shaving-water; and in the afternoon when the sun shone, and he drifted to Green Street, he felt ennobled by his resolution.

Blanche, as was so often the case latterly, was sipping tea by herself. It was the half-hour he always found most charming. The shaded room was restful after the glare of the Park, and the flowers looked cooler within doors, and sweeter. Their fragrance too could be detected here; as he greeted her he felt the perfume of the roses she was wearing, roses that he saw had been chosen from the basket that he had sent.

"I wondered if you would come round," she

said. "Thanks ever so much for those—they're simply exquisite."

"Have you been out?" he asked, dropping into an arm-chair.

"No; it's too hot. Well? Tea?"

"Thanks. Well! 'Our story approaches the end'? It's extraordinary the hold a theatre takes on one; I begin to feel as if I'd been interested in the Mayfair all my life. I shall be lost when we close."

She sighed. "And *I!*"

"Well, you'll be on the stage—it won't be quite the same thing; *I* shall only be able to sit in the stalls. You can't imagine how I shall miss the pass-door and the wings. At least, *you* can, because you're an actress, but a good many people would think it affectation."

"I suppose the wings somewhere might still be possible?" she said. "But I understand what you mean, of course. You don't really think it will be a greater change for you than me, though? You can always run a theatre if you want to—that isn't difficult. To *me*—oh, my dear boy, the change will be frightful! Now that you've given me a taste for management I shall simply hate an engagement; I shall loathe it!"

He looked his commiseration, and she nodded repeatedly.

"It will be hideous. To have to go to rehearsal whether I'm in the humour or not, and be dictated to by the stage-manager, and have my pet business altered to improve somebody else's part, and—— Oh, you haven't an idea! When a woman who has once been her own manageress takes an engagement again, I can tell you she feels the difference *here*." She put her hand to her heart.

"Even now, you know," said Otho after a slight pause, "it isn't too late, if Royce is willing to go on. Nothing is settled."

"He won't; don't entertain such an idea for a moment—he won't! No, Royce is relieved—I can assure you he is *relieved*—to think that there are only four more nights before we finish."

"It's a thousand pities," he murmured; "I'm sorrier than I can say. He's been consistent, of course; one can't deny that, but—— Well, I'm bound to admit he seems to me to be playing the fool."

" 'Consistent'! Oh, let's talk about something else!"

"He explained from the beginning the course he meant to pursue. Don't fancy I'm making excuses for him, but it was understood that he'd only conduct a theatre on certain lines."

Blanche smiled.

"But it *was,* Mrs. Royce!"

"Oh, I know all that!" she said, "but do you suppose if——" She rose impatiently.

"Do I suppose if—what?"

"Never mind; it doesn't matter!"

"Tell me. What were you going to say?"

"I was going to say 'do you suppose we should be leaving the theatre if Miss King had remained in it?'" She looked round into his startled face. "That's all!"

"Miss King?" He stared up at her.

"Are you going to pretend you didn't know? You needn't be considerate—my eyes have been open a long while. As soon as he got a theatre, he brought her into it. And when a piece that meant a fortune was to be had, he opposed it because there was no part in it for *her;* and because he was furious when you took my side and he was obliged to let her go, he revenged himself on me by giving the theatre up."

"Good God! . . . Oh no?"

"I don't say that the theatre managed in an ordinary way would ever have made him happy —I know it wouldn't; but he'd never have gone to such a length as this if he thought I was blind enough to have that woman back in it. So mad as that he's not! It was plain enough surely? Everybody in the company must have talked.

In two months' time you'll see them both playing at the same house." Her arms fell impotently. "And so shall *I!*"

Unconsciously she had taken the pose that she had adopted in Oliphant's play, when as "Maud" she imagined that "Mrs. Vaughan" was "Clement's" mistress. Her expression was the same. Now, as then, her sensibilities were profoundly stirred by a situation which her judgment knew to be fictitious. She believed this thing only while she wished to believe it, and hitherto the belief had been assuasive. But impulse had carried her before an "audience"— and now she sounded the depths; the humiliation was revealed, and her voice broke.

"I can't believe it," he said huskily; "I'll swear I've never had a suspicion! You *must* be wrong."

"Heavens! Do you think I look for these things—that I'm jealous?" Her laugh was bitter. "I only care because I'm a woman and I've pride to be hurt; for Royce I care no more than I do for that chair. If I weren't a fool, I suppose I shouldn't care at all, but . . . Ah, don't worry about *me*—I'm used to it by now!"

She turned aside, and leant her elbows on the mantelpiece, her head between her closed hands.

There was a long silence, while he struggled to remain in his seat.

"I'm frightfully sorry for you," he stammered, rising.

Her face was hidden from him, but her little nods were grateful, and pathetic. He stood combating the temptation to touch her—his sympathy yearned to touch her, while his prudence warned him to resist. His hand moved towards her twice, and was twice caught back. Then he drew hers down.

"Don't—I can't bear to see you miserable," he said.

Her fingers thanked him, and now he perceived that she was crying.

"If you knew how hard my life is!" she faltered.

She raised her eyes to him; and the next moment he had kissed her.

But the words that poured from him were not the words demanded by her mood. He upbraided himself, and vowed that he would never see her again. She did not want to pity his self-reproaches—she wanted him to silence hers. He was her penitent, and she would have had him her master. She was begged to understand his remorse, and she wanted to be swept from hesitation by his love. As she listened, the outlook grew strangely dark, the gloom of it chilled her, and she felt forlorn. A sense of hopelessness overwhelmed her—and she realised that she had hoped.

He went from her abased. The kiss and his avowal had rendered him contemptible; and that she had told him she was fond of him seemed to increase his enormity. He wished she had not told him she was fond of him—the impression left by the afternoon was graver because she had said that. But if she had been anybody's wife but Oliphant's! Terrible that a woman's perfection could be patent to all the world except her husband! Her view of the retirement from the Mayfair as an act of retaliation was far-fetched, preposterous, but though she was mistaken there, the main charge might be true. What wonder that she was unhappy, poor girl? He regretted the visit passionately; he had determined to avoid her, and he was given cause to feel ashamed after all. That was cruel! And now, too, he would be ten times more wretched apart from her. It would even be wrong to take leave of her—or for them to meet in a year's time —knowing what they knew. And Oliphant! how distressing to have to meet Oliphant again!

He went from her abased, and Blanche sat motionless, with wide eyes. Never had she permitted herself to recognise her fancies as expectation, but they were buried in their real name. How their companionship had sustained her their death displayed. She knew now that she had desired to gain the existence to which Otho Fairbairn was the key; knew that, though this sudden sensation of blankness would not last, she would remember and repine as long as she lived—would think of the might-have-been when she had lost her prettiness and her figure, and the Lady Flecks of the period were oblivious of an elderly actress whose only recommendation was her virtue. Then to her despondence arose the ghost of her hope; and in sight of it she demanded why the ambition of a woman like herself should be frustrated by so weak a man. Man? He was a boy in everything but his age! Should she resign herself to being balked by his scruples?

She went to the Mayfair that evening wondering if she would see him; but Otho was not there. Nor did he appear on the next, though he had been compelled to accept a dinner invitation to support his oath. On the penultimate night he failed; but he compromised with resolution by entering the theatre only for a few minutes to mention that he was going to Trouville.

"You'll come to Green Street first?" she asked.

He had intended to make his adieux to her and

Oliphant in the office on the morrow, but now he hesitated.

"Do you think I had better go to the house?" he said.

Her face hardened, and she made no reply for a moment.

"No!" she said coldly. "Good-bye. I hope it will be a pleasant change, Mr. Fairbairn."

"For God's sake don't be cruel," he muttered. "I'm suffering enough!"

She had moved apart from him, and he followed her humbly.

"Blanche! Are you angry with me?"

" 'Angry'?" she echoed, pausing. "What right have I to be 'angry' with you? You'll do as you please, of course."

"May I come Sunday for half an hour?"

"Sunday I shall be out," she said. . . . "If you wish to, come to-morrow afternoon."

She returned to the dressing-room, her pulses quickened by suspense. To-morrow he would again tell her how miserable he was; but would he implore her to make him happy? It would be then or never! If he would but beg her to leave London with him—if he would only say the words! She would become his wife, and their elopement would be forgotten. The prospect dizzied her and swam before her gaze; she quivered in contemplating the position.

There was no sign of agitation, however, in the greeting that he was accorded; its tranquillity relieved him. Her manner had neither the resentment that he had winced at on the previous evening, nor the implication that he had vaguely dreaded. She spoke of Trouville, and asked him if it was "nice." There was a casino, she supposed? Every French watering-place had a casino, hadn't it? And one played a game called "Little Horses," which was the Monte Carlo gamble adapted for the nursery, and had ices and flirtations on a terrace overlooking the sea? How he would enjoy himself! It must be delicious, especially after dinner in the moonlight.

He felt that it would indeed be delicious were she beside him there, but merely answered that it would bore him to death. Her small talk hurt him as speedily as it was meant to do, although before he came he had perceived in the subject of Trouville some promise of safety. She was paler than usual, he noted; there were shadows beneath her eyes, and in spite of her attempt at animation, her tone, her pose itself, had a certain lassitude.

It was now for him to sustain her courageous

effort, for she was silent. In the silence her face looked wearier still.

"Where—which theatre do you think you will go to next?" he said, when the pause had grown too long.

"How can I tell?" she murmured. "Why?"

"I should have liked to know what you were going to do—I shan't be in London for a long while; I don't expect I shall remain in Europe."

"You are going to travel? Where—in impossible places? Have you made your plans?"

He shook his head.

"You mean to go just where impulse takes you? How lovely! It must be simply perfect to wander about the world like that."

" 'Perfect'?" said he. "You know that I'm going because I must! You know very well I shall be wretched!"

She did not answer, but her lips trembled. When they had trembled, she averted her face.

"*Don't* you know it?"

"Perhaps you think you will. You'll soon forget me. A man can forget so easily."

Then the scene of which she had been confident was enacted. He told her all that she had known he was going to tell her, omitting only the petition that she was eager to hear. Though his devotion dishonoured him, though his goddess was clay, this ordeal was the severest that he had been called upon to bear; to part from her tortured him; and when he cried that he "adored" her, the word was no more than the literal expression of a fact.   Her suspense began to be tinged by impatience, even by misgiving.

She tore her hands from him, and sprang to her feet.

"Why did you come into my life?" she exclaimed; "I could have borne the rest!"

As she was clasped, she was momentarily sanguine; but expectation faded, and the coldness of dismay sank through her limbs again.

"Say good-bye to me!" he urged; "for God's sake, let me say it while I can!"

Her eyes fastened on him, but he released her, and was going.   She watched him cross the room. All that she thirsted for was receding—affluence, splendour, everything that could make life worth living was in this man's hold!   In another second the darkness would have fallen, and would lift no more.   She would not, she could not, let him go!   She uttered a great cry, and threw herself sobbing on the couch.

"I've only you in the world!" she gasped, clinging to him.

Then suddenly—as she looked up into his white face—she faltered.   Morality, convention, the restraining instinct, awoke and terrified her in spite of herself. She strove to stifle it, to harden herself against it, she battled with it as a woman may battle with a physical weakness. Her mind whirled. Why did he give her time to reflect? A moment more, and horror would have conquered her! Why didn't he succumb? . . .

Fairbairn moved towards the window, and the clock ticked away a minute while he gazed fixedly at the street. A hansom was crawling along the hot road, and he observed the minutiæ of a hansom for the first time. When the hansom was out of sight he gradually became aware that he was thinking. He was conscious of a dull wonder at his own apathy. His most distinguishable feeling was regret, but neither remorse nor passion was acute; he felt dreary and sad. The clock ticked; and he stood realising the position. Well, he would make her his wife as soon as possible. . . . Oliphant would despise him—not more than he deserved. Perhaps Oliphant would marry Miss King after the divorce? If they cared for each other much, one might be sure he would—and they'd be happy. None the less, they would always condemn him, Otho Fairbairn, as a scoundrel. . . . But his worst sin was towards the angel who had sacrificed her reputation for love of him! At this point he looked round at her, furtively, ashamed.

The woman whom he had yet to understand lay back upon the sofa with her eyes closed—thinking too.